Trying NOT TO LOVE YOU

Book One in the Love Series

by

MEGAN SMITH

The following story contains mature themes, strong language and sexual situations. It is intended for adult readers.

Printed Version:
ISBN-13: 978-1484043592

ISBN-10: 1484043596

Cover Design: Wicked Designs ~ Robin Harper

Cover Art: CE Images ~ Heidi Chickerell & Emily Erdie

Models: Luke & Jada Boyles

Edited by: Katie Mac

Formatting by: Angela McLaurin, Fictional Formats

Facebook: https://www.facebook.com/pages/Author-M-Smith

Twitter: https://twitter.com/AuthorMSmith

Email: authormegansmith@gmail.com

Table of Contents

"All our dreams can come true
if we have the courage to pursue them."

- Walt Disney

Prologue

~Age 10~

"Mom, I'm home!" I called out when I opened the front door.

"Hi, baby girl. How was school?" I walked over to my mom and gave her a hug. We shuffled off to the kitchen as we did every day when I got home to make me a snack.

When we walked into the kitchen, my older brothers Mason and Cooper, who are twins and Jackson were sitting at the table doing homework with the most handsome boy I had ever seen.

"Kenzie, close your mouth." Jackson said, laughing.

I was standing there staring at him; I couldn't pry my eyes off of him. "Shut up!" I said to Jackson just as the boy looked up to see me staring at him. He smiled at me.

I quickly looked over to Mom. She had a giant smile on her face. "What would you like to eat?"

"I'm not hungry." No way could I eat in front of him. He was causing butterflies in my belly. "Is it okay if Hailey comes over?"

I heard Mason groan and mumble, "Not again."

"Of course she can," Mom said while pouring sweet tea into glasses.

I reached for the cordless phone on the kitchen island, called Hailey and asked her to come over.

She walked into the kitchen like she owned the place but stopped dead in her tracks when she noticed who was sitting at the table. I giggled and ran off to my room with Hailey close on my heels. Once she shut my bedroom door, she turned around and asked, "Umm Kenzie, who is that at the table?"

"I have no idea; he is cute though, isn't he?"

"You can say that again. We need to go ask your mom." Hailey was always brave like that. She does not hold back.

"No way." I said bashfully and sat down on the chair in front of my vanity.

"He must have just moved here." Hailey picked up a brush from my vanity to brush my hair. "I've never seen him around school."

Someone knocked on my door. "Come in."

"I thought I heard you girls up here. Here is your drink sweetie. Hello Hailey, would you like something to drink?"

"No thanks, Mrs. C. Who is that downstairs, sitting next to Mason?" Leave it to Hailey to come right out and ask.

Mom looked over at me and smiled, "That's Hunter. He just moved here with his mom and sister Jaylinn."

"How old is he?" Hailey asked while braiding my hair.

"Oh, he's thirteen, the same age as the twins."

Even at thirteen, Hunter had all the girls crazy over him at school. His dark brown hair was almost black. His bright blue eyes and the cute little dimple on his right cheek when he smiled had all the girls swooning.

From that day on, I felt drawn to Hunter, and I had a feeling I always would be.

~Age 13~

Our families took summer vacations together ever since Hunter's family moved here. We were camping this year in Virginia

Beach. There was a hurricane passing off the coast, so that meant we needed to stay inside the tents or RV because of all the rain and wind. The parents all hung out in the RV. The boys' tent was bigger than the girls' tent, so that is where the parents set us up with a bunch of different games. No one wanted to play those silly kids games. Jaylinn and Hailey voted for us to play truth or dare. Hailey chose me to go first, of course.

"Truth or Dare?" Hailey asked me.

I looked at her and smiled, knowing that trouble would find me with either answer. It did not matter which one I picked, Hunter would be involved. Hailey was the only person that knew I had a crush on Hunter. Jaylinn might have figured it out, but I had never flat out told her I liked her brother.

"Dare."

Smirking at me, she said, "Go outside with Hunter and kiss him in the rain."

All three of my brothers growled in unison. Hunter looked at me with wide eyes while both Hailey and Jaylinn started laughing and giving each other high-fives. I did not expect that from her, especially since my brothers were within striking distance.

"No way. Not happening." Mason said.

Hailey, who was still laughing, looked at Mason and said, "A dare is a dare."

Hunter reached out for my hand and helped me off the air mattress. Jaylinn open the tent flap for us so we could get out.

The rain was starting to slow down to just a drizzle. Hunter and I walked out, hands held together, and turned to face each other.

"Ready?" He asked. When I nodded my head, he said, "On the count of three. One." He took a step closer. "Two." I took the last step, our bodies just barely touching. "Three."

Our lips connected, and it felt as if someone shocked me and stole my breath. It was sweet and intoxicating, and I did not want it to end. I felt like my brothers had barely let our lips touch before they started making a giant fuss about it.

"Alright man, that's enough." Jackson said.

"Dude, that's my sister. Don't ever let me see your lips on her again." Mason said.

"Yeah or we're gonna have problems." Cooper said.

I would remember that kiss always, my first kiss. It might not have meant anything to Hunter, but it meant the world to me.

~Age 15~

My teenage hormones were in overdrive and Hunter was a massive problem, screwing with them. Only problem was, I was not on his radar, or at least I did not think I was. Hunter was going out with girls from our school, and I hated every second of it. I wanted to be the girl that he made out with at the movies. I wanted to be the girl that he took to prom this year. I wanted to be Hunter's girlfriend.

"You ready to go?" Hailey walked into my room without even knocking, disturbing me from my pity party.

"Yeah, just have to do my makeup." I grabbed the bag of make-up off my vanity that Mom and I had just bought yesterday.

"You are not wearing makeup Kenzie. You don't need that shit." Cooper said as he stood in the doorway of my room.

"Get out." I stalked over to the door and tried to shut it, but he blocked it with his foot.

"Dude, what are you doing?" I had heard Hunter's voice before I had even seen him.

I opened the door and crossed my arms. "I'm trying to shut my door, but jackass here won't move."

Cooper glared at me. "Give me the makeup Kenz and I'll leave."

"No." I yelled. "Get out."

"What the hell is all the yelling about?" Mason asked, standing behind Cooper and Hunter.

"She thinks she's going out with Hailey dressed like that, and wearing that shit on her face." Cooper answered Mason's question.

I threw my hands up in the air, walked over to my closet and grabbed my sandals. I didn't dress any differently than I was any other day. I had on a tight fitting tank top and skinny jeans, my normal every day clothes.

Hunter put his hand on Cooper's shoulder, "Just leave her alone. Come on. Let's go down to the baseball field." Hunter was once again on my side, trying to deflect the problem.

"Nah, not until she gives me that shit."

"Oh my God, would you guys knock it off? We're only going to the movies. What's the freaking deal?" Hailey asked them.

Mason eyed Hailey, then me and said, "Fine, but we are going with you." Then he walked away and Cooper followed him.

Hunter looked at the bag of makeup and then eyed me. "You don't need that shit. You're beautiful just the way you are."

My breath caught; I didn't know what to say, so I didn't say anything. Hunter tipped his head and followed Cooper and Mason. He had never called me that before. I didn't think I was beautiful, average, sure. I was shorter than most of the kids in my school, and even at fifteen, I was curvier than most of the girls. I had long, dark chocolate hair that cascaded down my back, eyes the color of the blue sky and pale skin dotted with freckles due to my Irish blood.

"Not on his radar, my ass." Hailey said, laughing at me. I am sure I was bright red.

At the end of that summer, Hunter was leaving for Old Dominion University in Norfolk, Virginia. The day Hunter left was awful; all I did was cry all day long. Hunter stopped over and said goodbye to me before he left, which only made me cry more. I was going to miss seeing him every day, and secretly, I think he was going to miss me too.

~Age 17~

When Hunter came back from school that year, I realized how smitten of him I had become. The day he came home for summer break, I was standing in the kitchen at my parents shore house, making a sandwich. Hunter walked through the door, and I nearly cut my fingers off when I caught sight of him. He was...so sexy. He seemed to have grown taller, and obviously, he worked out more. His shirt stretched tight across his broad shoulders, his sleeves pulled tight around his biceps. His hair was slightly longer than normal, and it had that sexy just rolled out of bed look.

He walked in and reached over my head, grabbing a glass out of the cabinet. I glanced over just as his shirt rode up slightly, revealing some kind of script tattoo. There was a star on his right elbow and skulls with flames covered his left arm.

After he grabbed the glass and filled it with water from the fridge, he came over and kissed the side of my head. "Hey CC."

"Those tats look good on you." I said, trying to keep my voice mild and even.

He grabbed a few chips from the bag I had left open on the counter. "I have more." He put the chips in his mouth then pulled his shirt over his head and tossed it on the counter. I almost fainted. His tan, muscular abs begged me to reach out and touch them. On his left side, starting under his arm, down his ribs and ending on his hip, in script read *Live Today As If You'll Die Tomorrow*. On his lower stomach, stretching from hip to hip, in the same script read *No Regrets*. I lifted my eyebrows and smirked at him; he smiled, shrugged his shoulders and turned around to show me a Celtic cross that took up most of his back.

"A friend of mine is working as an apprentice at a tattoo shop down by my house at school." Hunter explained.

"I like them." I padded over and grabbed my towel that was on the back of the kitchen chair. "I'll talk to you later; I'm going down to the beach." It was getting hot in here; I needed to stay away from him before I started pawing him.

Later that night, everyone was getting ready to go out to eat, but I did not want to go. I wanted to spend some alone time with Hunter. After talking to Hailey for a while, I decided I was finally going to tell him how I felt; I had to see if he had any feelings for me. I could not keep torturing myself like this.

I told my mom that I was going to stay home because I had an upset stomach. Hunter, always so quick to look out for me, told her he would stay home and would make sure I was okay. He did exactly as I thought he would do.

After everyone had left, I went upstairs into my room. I was lying on my bed when Hunter walked in, carrying a glass of ginger ale and some crackers.

"You should try to eat and drink this." He walked around my bed and put the stuff on the nightstand next to my bed.

"There's nothing wrong with me. I just didn't feel like going." I patted the bed next to me for him to come and sit. He didn't come over at first. He just stared at me, contemplating what he should do.

"It's probably not a good idea that I'm in here with you." Hunter said this as he sat down.

"Probably not, but no one is here." I sat up so my body was facing him, my knee touching his hip. He had a peevish look on his face. I reached over and slightly pushed his shoulder back to angle his body towards mine. I drifted closer to him, like a moth drawn to light and planted my lips on his.

When our lips melted together, I swear fireworks were going off somewhere in the distance. Hunter reached up with his left hand, and put it behind my neck, bringing me a little closer to him. He moved his right hand to my hip and started to lay me back on the bed. He hovered over the top half of my body. Then suddenly, it was as if someone pulled him off me. He was up pacing the room and raking his hand threw his hair.

Shocked by the sudden change, I asked, "What's the matter?"

He stopped pacing and had a sorrowful look on his face. He started pacing again, and then he finally said, "That shouldn't have happened."

"Hunter, you've known I've had feelings for you all these years. Why is it such a big deal?"

"You're brothers would freak the fuck out. Don't you remember how they acted the last time we kissed?" He made it sound as if that should answer all my questions.

I got up off the bed, straightened my shirt and walked in front of him, causing him to look at me. "Well, they'll just have to get over it." I took a deep breath--here goes nothing. "I want you Hunter."

His eyes went wide, "What! Fuck!" He was shaking his head back and forth. "No, this isn't happening. You can't. You fucking can't. You deserve someone better than me."

Well this was not going exactly as I had planned.

"I have to go." He announced and then, he was gone. When he walked away from me that day, a piece of my heart went with him. At least now, I had my answer even if it crushed me.

After that night in my room, Hunter acted as if it never happened. He was back to flirting with me but made sure we were never alone together. I was still hurt with the way things went down, but I guess I had to take what I could get from him.

When Hailey, Jaylinn and I went back to school that year, I started dating Dominic, whom I have known since kindergarten. Dominic was the exact opposite of Hunter; he was exactly what I needed, a distraction. He was shorter than Hunter, with a thin frame, shaggy blonde hair and honey brown eyes. He was always sweet, caring, and lovable, everything I wanted in a boyfriend.

Dominic was the quarterback on our football team at school. All the girls wanted him, but he only had eyes for me.

When my brothers and Hunter came home for Thanksgiving weekend, they met Dominic since I had invited him for dinner. Dominic stood up to my brothers when they threatened him about dating me. Dominic never backed down from their threats though, as most guys would have.

Hunter hated Dominic. Anytime he saw us together, he would glare at Dominic and leave the room. When Dominic was not around, Hunter would flirt like crazy with me. I loved those times, but all Hunter would give me was just flirting. That is why I chose to stay with Dominic.

Chapter One

Present

Summer was ending, and I would be heading off to college next weekend. This weekend, my best friend Hailey, Hunter's sister Jaylinn, and I were throwing a surprise 21st birthday party for my twin brothers. We were only a few days away from the party, and they knew we were up to something. My brothers were extremely protective of me since I was the baby of the family, and of course, the only girl. Dad instilled it in their heads at a young age that they were always to protect me. That made trying to plan something without them knowing near impossible, since they did not let me go anywhere without one of them or Hunter.

"Kenzie!" Mason yelled.

I jumped, dropped the shirt I was holding and my right hand flew to my heart. "Jesus, Mase you scared the shit out of me." I bent down and picked up the shirt I was trying to fold.

"What are you up to this weekend?" Mason leaned his shoulder against the laundry room door.

"Hailey, Jaylinn and I are all going out on dates together this weekend." I replied but did not look in his direction because I knew a fight was about to start. My brothers hated when I went out on dates. Hell, they hated when any of us went on a date, for that matter.

"No, you're not. It's our birthday weekend, and you guys are hanging with us. Tell Dominic he is going to have to come next weekend." I did not have to look up to know he was glaring at me.

"No, he already has plans to come this weekend since he doesn't have football practice. I'm not cancelling on him." Dominic had left a few weeks ago for college at Old Dominion University in Norfolk, Virginia, where he received a full football scholarship to play for them. Hailey and I would be joining him and Hunter there this fall. Yes, I know what you are thinking. I chose to go there because of Hunter, and yes, it was probably a mistake, but I did not care.

"Yeah, you can. Tell those assholes you have plans." With that, he turned away before I could respond. I had been dealing with this all week when Mason or Cooper would ask what my plans were. I had always tried to avoid them and to be as vague as possible.

A few minutes after Mason walked away, my phone beeped. I reach into my back pocket, grab my phone out and read the text.

Hailey – 12:22pm: Got a text from Mase telling me 2 cancel my date this weekend

Me – 12:23pm: LOL. They have no idea

Hailey – 12:23pm: I know it's going 2 be gr8

The twins had to work for the next few days with my uncle, so it was easy avoiding them. We were able to run to the store to grab things for the party without them knowing. Hunter was going to cover for us Friday night. He told my brothers that he wanted to take me to see a chic flick to repay me for when I helped him a few weeks ago. Dominic had football practice Friday, so he was not going to be here until some point on Saturday. I couldn't use Dominic as an excuse to be out of the house without one of my brothers tagging along.

Late Friday afternoon, Hunter came to pick me up before my brothers got home. We made our way to my parents shore house to start getting things set up for the party the next day.

My parents were out of town on a weekend getaway. The shore house was a lot bigger than our regular house. It was three stories with five bedrooms, two bathrooms and a full finished basement. The house also had a massive deck and the beach backed up to the yard. We had a lot more room here to accommodate everyone than we did at home. Hailey had come down earlier in the day to let the housekeeper in so they could give the house a good cleaning before everyone would arrive tomorrow.

Hunter and I walked into the house. I called out, "Hey Hails! We're here."

"Hey guys," she came over and kissed Hunter and then me on the cheek.

"I just started putting a few decorations around the house. Did you get the food and the rest of the stuff from your house?"

"Yeah we got it. It's all in my truck." Hunter yelled over his shoulder, on his way out to the truck to grab the food.

"I'm going to get started on the food. Hails, can you get Hunter to help you move the furniture around in the living room, so we have more space? Mom also said to lock all the bedroom doors so nobody can get into them. You know where the keys are, right?"

"Yes, on top of the fridge in the money jar." Hailey said, and then left to go help Hunter.

For the next couple of hours, I prepped all my brothers' favorite foods. Hailey and Hunter moved everything around so that we would have room for everyone tomorrow night.

"All done, CC. Anything else you need help with?" God, when he called me that, I just wanted to kiss him to death and punch him, all at the same time. Hunter was the only one that got away with calling me CC, short for Chubby Cheeks. There was a picture of me as a baby dressed up in an Easter dress that my parents kept on the mantle at home. I looked like a Cabbage Patch doll. Mom had put this bonnet on me that made my cheeks look super chubby and ever since Hunter saw it, he started teasing me by calling me CC.

"Nope, I think that everything is done for tonight. You ready to get out of here Hails?"

Looking as if she would drop any moment, she answered, "Yes, I'm exhausted. We should get up early to come back down here, so we better get going."

We left Hailey's car at the shore house, since it was late and she didn't want to drive the forty-five minute ride home by herself. Fifteen minutes into the ride, I looked back at Hailey, and she had passed out. I looked over at Hunter, and started picturing all the things I wanted to do with him. I knew it was wrong, because I had Dominic, but it was just something I couldn't help.

"See something you like, CC?" He had the biggest smirk on his face.

Damn, he caught me looking at him. I turned away from Hunter, and looked out the window, hoping to hide the blush creeping up my neck to my face. "You know I do." I mumbled, hoping he would not catch what I said.

"And what would Dominic think about that?" Hunter reached over and ran his fingers down my arm, causing me to shiver. Over the last year, Hunter had seriously kicked up the flirting game with me. I am sure it was because of Dominic.

I rolled my eyes at him. "You always bring him up, why?"

"Because I don't think he deserves you. Is he actually going to make it here tomorrow for the party, or is he going to blow you off again?"

"He promised he would make it this time. He didn't blow me off the last time. He got held up at practice, and it didn't make any sense for him to come all the way here, and turn right back around." He made it up to me by sending me flowers the next day. Yeah, I was still mad, but it is not as if he could drop what he was doing just to come home to see me. I knew football was his life.

"If I was him, and you were my girlfriend, I would make damn sure I was home every chance I got." I noticed when he said this, that he gripped the steering wheel a little tighter, and his knuckles were turning white.

"He's trying, Hunter."

As we were pulling into the driveway of my house, he mumbled under his breath something that sounded like, "He needs to try harder."

"What did you say?" I asked, wanting to clarify what I thought he said.

Shaking his head, he responded, "Nothing. What time do you want me back to pick you and Hailey up?"

"You don't have too; I'm going to drive my car down in the morning. I just need you to make sure my brothers are there by seven. I don't care what you have to tell them, just get them there."

I reached over the seat and shook Hailey's leg and said "Hails, wake up. We're home."

The next morning Hailey and I were up before Mason and Cooper. We quickly got ready, and made our way back down to the shore house to start getting set up for the party. Finally, after all the food was out, and everything was set up, Hailey and I went up to my room and started to get ready for the party.

"So what are you planning on wearing? I know we packed a bunch of different shit." Hailey said as she pulled out everything from the bags we had packed last night before we fell asleep.

"I'm wearing my white shorts, and that,"—I pointed to the black low cut halter-top she had in her hand—"with my black peep toe pumps." I picked this because Dominic could never keep his hands off me. He always told me that wearing white shorts made my legs look miles long.

"Your brothers are going to throw a fit. That shirt barely covers the girls."

I smiled, looking at her through the mirror in front of me, and just shrugged my shoulders. I knew she was right, but I didn't care. "You should wear those hot pink shorts on the pillow over there, with the white strapless shirt and those cute white pumps with the pink underneath them. The white shirt will bring out your tan."

Hailey picked up the outfit and held it up to herself in the mirror, "Yeah, I think you are right. I do look pretty hot in those pink shorts."

Hailey was gorgeous. She was tall with long blonde hair, dark olive skin, dark blue eyes and flawless skin. I never could understand why she felt so insecure about herself.

After Hailey and I finished getting ready, we made our way downstairs to start greeting everyone arriving for the surprise party. We had our next-door neighbor Jimmy have everyone park in his parent's driveway. Hunter and my brothers would think it was Jimmy throwing the party. Around six-thirty, I got a text from Hunter saying they would be there a little after seven.

Wondering why Dominic was not here yet, I sent him a text to find out where he was. I didn't want him ruining the surprise by showing up late.

Me – 6:36pm: Where r u?

Dominic – 6:38pm: on my way stuck in traffic

Me – 6:40pm: text me when you cross the bridge

Dominic – 6:41pm: I'll be there by 10

Me – 6:42pm: Y so late?

Dominic – 6:44pm: Traffic

Of course, he was going to be late; he would be late to his own damn wedding. I knew I should not act pissy, but he had known about this for weeks. He should have been here hours ago, but at least he was coming this time.

"Everyone, please find a hiding place. They will be here in the next few minutes." Hailey yelled over all the chatter in the house.

You would think finding hiding places for 75 people would be somewhat hard, but somehow, everyone found a place.

I heard their street bikes pulling into the driveway so I "shushed" everyone to give a warning that the boys were here.

They walked in laughing, and flipped the light switch on. Everyone screamed "Surprise!"

Cooper and Mason's eyes flew wide open. When they noticed everyone, they were in complete shock. When their eyes landed on Hailey, Jaylinn and me standing in front of the stairs, they smiled and shook their heads.

After being greeted by a few of their friends, they made their way over to us. Mason pulled me into his arms, "I knew you were up to no good." He let go of me and grabbed Hailey, while Cooper hugged me. "I can't believe you two did this. Mason said you girls were out on dates tonight."

Cooper released me, and leaned me against the wall beside Jaylinn. "Is that why you left so early this morning? I was surprised when mom said you left around ten. Your ass never gets up before noon."

Hunter walked up next to me and leaned his elbow against my shoulder; I looked up at him, then back to Cooper. "I knew you and Mason wouldn't let us leave without a fight, so we had to disappear early."

"You're damn straight we wouldn't. Oh, this," Cooper motioned behind Hunter, "is Jessica, Alexis, and Angel."

I knocked Hunter's elbow off my shoulder, and then turned towards them. I was surprised to see Alexis standing there with two other girls I did not recognize. "Hi, I'm MacKenzie, their sister, and this is my best friend Hailey, and Jaylinn over there is Hunter's sister." Alexis rolled her eyes, which she did a lot, and the other two girls just mumbled hello's.

I excused myself and walked into the kitchen to grab a drink when my older brother Jackson and his pregnant fiancé Chloe walked in. "Hey, you guys made it! How are you feeling Chloe?" I reached over to rub her baby bump.

"This morning sickness is seriously kicking my ass. I don't know how long we will be able to stay, but we wanted to show up for a little while."

"You and Hailey did an excellent job Kenzie. Mase and Coop were freaking the fuck out all day. Hunter and I had to keep them from coming to search for you girls." Jackson said.

"Well, thanks for covering for us. I am so glad they had no idea; you know how hard it is to surprise those two with anything. Hey, why don't you guys just stay in your room upstairs?" I looked over at Chloe, "That way, if you don't feel good, you can go upstairs to lie down. All the doors are locked, so no one can get into them."

Jackson looked over at Chloe, and she nodded, "Alright, I guess we can do that."

"Chloe, there are some clothes upstairs you can put on to sleep in."

Chloe stood on her tiptoes, and kissed Jackson. He placed his large hands on each side of her belly. "All right, all right, get a room already you two." Glued to each other ever since they met, it was no wonder she was pregnant.

I walked away from them to search for Hailey. Passing the stairs, I saw Alexis standing with her back to me, holding Hunter's hand. "That's just great!" I mumbled to myself. I looked past her and saw her two friends standing there, beside her. Angel was holding on to Mason's arm, and Jessica had her hands around Cooper's waist. I didn't say anything to them as I walked by. Out on the back deck, Jaylinn and Jackson were playing beer pong with Chloe's friend Sarah, and some other girl.

"Hey Kenzie, did Hailey find you?" Jackson said.

"No, that's who I was looking for." I said, looking around at all the people swimming in the pool, and sitting around the fire pit.

"Have you seen Mase, Coop and Hunter? I haven't seen them since we got here." Jackson said.

"They were over by the stairs last time I saw them." I said, watching as his ping-pong ball lands in the cup on the opposite side of the table.

"Here, take over; I'm going to go get them." As Jackson handed me the ping-pong ball, Hailey came running up the deck steps and grabbed my arm. "Fuck Kenz!"

"Hails, what the..." I spotted Hailey's ex-boyfriend Matt as he walked in with some trashy looking girl with crazy red hair. "Shit!"

"What's going on?" Jaylinn asked, looking around.

"Kenzie, what the fuck is he doing here?" Hailey was practically screaming at me. She had every right to be hysterical after the shit that asshole put her through.

"I have no idea. You know I wouldn't invite him here after what he did to you." After senior prom, about thirty of us came to party here at my parent's shore house. Alcohol flowed freely, and everyone became more and more trashed as the night passed. Matt cheated on Hailey with some skank who had come with one of our friends. They broke up that night, and Mason nearly beat the shit out of Matt.

I raised my chin in Matt's direction, "Matt is here." Jaylinn looked over at Matt, anger shooting from her eyes.

Hailey was in tears and near panic. "Why did he show up here? He knows whose house this is."

"Look, let's just hang out here, and finish the game. Try to act like he isn't even here. Chloe, can you text Jackson, and ask him to handle Matt?"

"Yeah, I sure can." She reached for her phone on the table, and I saw her tap out a text. A second later, her phone beeped. "He'll take care of it."

While Jaylinn and I finished our game, Hailey grabbed a bottle of Vodka off the outside bar, and started chugging it.

"You better slow down. I'm not being the only one responsible if this party goes to shit." I knew she would ignore me, and be plastered by the end of the night. After Matt's stunt, I seriously did not blame her.

"Just let her be Kenzie. She's a blast when she's drunk." Jaylinn said, as the ping-pong ball she threw hit the rim of one of the cups.

"Fine, but when she is puking her guts up, she is all yours." I threw my ping-pong ball in the cup and turned to look at Jaylinn with my eyebrows raised, gloating that I made my shot.

Finally, my brothers and Hunter came over, but Mason looked pissed. He was watching Hailey as she drank straight from the vodka bottle. "Kenzie, how much has she had to drink?"

I rolled my eyes at his over protective ass. "She drank the whole bottle of vodka over there,"–pointing to the empty bottle on the bar– "and just started on the second one." I scowled in Hunter's direction. "Where'd your girlfriend go, Hunter?"

Hunter had dated Alexis briefly a few summers ago, and she had dated Dominic right before he and I started dating. She still was not over either one of them, and would do anything to get their attention. She had started rumors that Dominic was going to leave me, and go back to her. She even tried to break us up by telling people that she and Dominic made out after a few of his football games that I had not attended. Dominic always denied it; I didn't think he would do something like that to me, since he was the one that broke up with her.

"She left. Where's Dominic?" Mason said, with a smug look on his face as he answered for Hunter.

"Low blow, Mase. I'm going upstairs." I threw my ping-pong ball at Mason, and turned towards Hailey, "I'm going up to my room; are you coming?"

Hailey giggled at nothing in particular, and shook her head, "No, I'm good out here. I don't think I can move at this point, since I can't feel my legs."

I glared at Mason. "You think you can keep her out of trouble, asshole?"

"Why are you going upstairs? Just stay down here with us. I'm sure Dom will be here soon, CC." Hunter spoke up, as I was getting up out of my seat.

"Kenzie, you're not going upstairs! It's my birthday, and you haven't even had a shot with me yet." Cooper said. He threw his arm over my shoulder and pulled me into a hug, trapping me.

Rolling my eyes, I said, "Fine, but if I have to stay down here, and deal with this bullshit, I'm going to need more than one shot." I got up, and stormed away from them.

In the kitchen, I was about ready to down my shot when I felt a pair of hands grip my hips. I hoped it was Dominic finally getting here, but when I turned around, I was staring at Hunter chest.

Seething through my teeth, I pushed back on him. "Hunter, don't okay, just don't. I can't believe you, of all people, would invite Alexis here."

He crossed his arms across his chest, looked down at the floor, then back up to me. "CC, let's just go out front, and talk for a sec."

"No." I was not going anywhere with him. He knew I hated the drama that bitch brought with her. I had wanted to have a good time tonight, but seeing her had ruined it for me.

"No?" He was challenging me. He knew I had a problem telling him no to pretty much anything.

God damn it!

Why did he have to be so damn hot? Even after that summer, knowing nothing could happen, I still had feelings for him. I had Dominic now, but no matter what my brain said, my heart wanted Hunter. I looked up, and he smirked at me. I rolled my eyes. "Fine, but we can't be gone long; I need to go check on Hailey."

Hunter and I made our way out to the front of the house, and I heard someone call my name. I turned around, and noticed it was Ricky, one of the football players from high school.

"Hey Ricky, what's going on? Are you down here for the night, or are you staying somewhere?"

"A couple of us from the team rented a house down the road for the summer. We got wind that you were throwing a party, so we stopped by. Is Hailey here with you, too?" For as long as I could remember, Ricky had a crush on Hailey, but Hailey was not having anything to do with him.

"Yeah, she's out on the back deck with my brothers and Jaylinn. I'll catch up with you in a little bit." I gave Ricky a hug, and walked down the front steps. Hunter and I walked down the driveway, away from the blaring music, and the people gathered on the front porch.

"What's going on with you and Ricky? You know Dominic has a problem with that asshole." Hunter asked, glaring at Ricky over my shoulder.

"Nothing is going on with me and Ricky. We are just friends. You know, I am allowed to have friends."

"Why did you have to hug him then?"

"UGH! Are we seriously doing this?" Hunter nodded his head. "Dominic only has a problem with him because he told me that he saw Dominic and Alexis together after one of the games. Look, I am not having this argument with you. Let's just go back inside. I need to go check on Hailey, and Dominic should be here soon."

I started walking away from him. "Wait!" Hunter called out, and I stopped walking, but I did not turn around. "Please don't be mad at me. I'm trying to do the right thing here."

"Yeah? And what's that?" Hunter took a few steps, pushed his body flush against my back and whispered in my ear, "Keeping you away from me, CC. You know I want you. Fuck, you can feel it." To prove his point, he shifted his hips so that I could feel his hardness. "We both know I just can't have you." Hunter backed away from me, and walked back towards the house.

Chapter Two

Hunter left me standing in the driveway, all hot and frustrated, as he walked back into the house. Yes, I knew he wanted me. That was clear. What I did not understand was why he would tell me this now. He knew I was with Dominic. Hunter would never act on his feelings; look how that turned out last time. I needed to clear my head before I could walk back into the party, so I took the little path beside the house that lead to the beach. I watched the waves crash and the moon dance on the ocean for a little while before I went back to check on Hailey. I could not imagine how trashed she would be if she had not stopped drinking yet.

I was walking between the sand dunes when I spotted Hailey sitting on the bottom step with Mason and Hunter hovering over her. I bent down to her level so I could see her. "Mase, what's wrong with her?" Hailey was sobbing.

He looked annoyed and disgusted. "I don't know. She is either crying about her ex-boyfriend, her one-night stand from last weekend or her own puke. None of those things are worth her tears, though."

Hailey had a different relationship with Mason than she did with Jackson and Cooper. I had asked her a few times if she had feelings for Mason. She had always denied it, so I left it for them to figure out.

"He...had...Slam Station...carved...into his...headboard...and he wasn't...even any good at it." Hailey was saying between the sniffling and hiccupping. She was trying to get over Matt, but was going about it the wrong way. She was going out with different guys all the time. This was the third one-night stand she had this month. Lucky for her, Mason does not know about the those. There is no telling what Mason would do to them.

Trying my hardest not to laugh at her, I reached over and put my hand on her knee. "Shut up and let's get you upstairs." I seriously hoped she was done running her mouth. I knew she was going to regret saying that tomorrow.

She tried to stand up, but nearly fell over. "I'm not sure if I should be proud of you for waiting, or disappointed in you for letting your sex life get this sad Kenzie."

"Christ, Hailey! That is enough. Come on, let's go." I grabbed Hailey by her arm to try to pull her up, but she was dead weight. Hunter grabbed her arm from me, and picked her up so we could make our way inside. When we reached my room, I dug into my pocket for the key to unlock my door. It was a pain in the ass to have the doors locked, but we really didn't want to have people hooking up in our beds.

Hailey put her arm around Hunter's neck. "You know what? I'm just so happy because I get to go to bed, and when I wake up there will be chocolate milk and Mason's penis waiting for me." I gasped, looking back at Hailey while she started to giggle.

"That is just wrong on soooo many levels Hailey." Hunter said, trying not to laugh; clearly, the situation amused him.

I just shook my head. "Like, really wrong, Hails! That is just disgusting. No one wants to hear about that shit!"

As I got the door opened, Hunter stepped in and put Hailey down on her feet. She started jumping up and down, screaming she had to pee. After she had taken off towards the bathroom, I took a few steps towards my bed. Hunter grabbed my hand, and turned me around to face him. He whispered, "CC, you look so damn sexy tonight." Then he leaned in, and kissed my forehead.

He was giving me whiplash. He wanted me, but did not want me at the same time. After a few seconds, I heard him curse under his breath. "I've got to get out of here before I do something I shouldn't. If Hailey becomes too much for you to handle, just come get me or one of your brothers." Looking puzzled, I said, "Goodnight, Hunter." Then he left.

About an hour later, there was a knock at the door. I got off my bed, went to open the door and found Dominic leaning against the wall across from my door.

I was furious. "What in hell took you so long? I thought you would have been here hours ago?"

He was standing there, looking at me as if I was crazy and being unreasonable. "Can I just come in, and we can talk?"

I walked back in my room, and he followed behind me. "Just be quiet. Hailey isn't feeling good. She had too much to drink."

"You couldn't put her in her own damn room? I haven't seen you in two weeks, MacKenzie."

I shook my head, "No, I couldn't. Hunter is in the spare room, and you know I always share this room with Hailey and Jaylinn."

Cocking his head at me, he asked, "Why are you being such a bitch? It was just a question. I drove all this way just to see you; you could have at least made sure we had our own room."

"You know what Dominic? Just leave. I don't even know why you bothered to show up this late. You didn't have practice today, so there is no excuse for why you were late."

He grabbed the bag he had left by the door. "Fine. I don't know why I bothered to drive hours just to come to this stupid ass party anyway." He walked out the door, and slammed it shut.

Hailey walked out of the bathroom, shaking her head. "I don't know why you stay with that asshat, Kenzie."

"He never used to be like that."

When I woke up the next morning, everyone was still sleeping. I decided I would make breakfast, since I bailed on them early last night. I looked around the place, and it surprised me that the house was actually fairly clean. I thought there would be a giant mess to clean up. At least now, I didn't have to tip the housekeepers any extra.

As I was making the last of the pancakes, Hunter walked into the kitchen with some girl. He walked her to the front door, and then came back to the kitchen. How did he turn his feelings for me off and on like that? Not that it mattered but still, I could not figure it out.

Hunter grabbed a bottle of water out of the fridge and asked, "Need any help, CC?"

"Nope, I'm good." *Yeah, I want you to explain to me what you were doing with her!*

"Alright." He went back towards his room, but then stopped before he opened the door. "Did Dominic ever show up last night?"

I pulled the last pancake out of the frying pan and put it on a plate. "Yeah, but not for long."

He shook his head at me, "What did he do this time?"

"I don't want to talk about it with you." He was the last person I wanted to talk to right now; let alone talk about Dominic.

"Fair enough. I'm going to pack up all my stuff." He went into his room, and I did not see him again until we were all about to leave.

Everyone else, including the girl that Cooper had hooked up with, made his or her way downstairs to have breakfast, and talk about what Hailey and I missed last night. After we ate and cleaned up, we all went to pack and get ready to head home.

As Jaylinn and I were walking out to my car to put our bags in the trunk, Cooper came up behind me and hugged me. "Thanks again for throwing us the party. We love you, lil' sis."

"Love y'all too; I'm glad y'all had fun. You know, it's not easy to surprise you and Mase."

Nodding his head, "We had a blast. Have you seen Mason or Hailey?"

"Not since breakfast." Jaylinn answered.

Shutting the door to his truck, Hunter stepped over to us. "You know, she did get her chocolate milk this morning. I wonder if she is getting Mason's...."

I punched him in the arm, and started yelling. "Stop! Just stop. I don't want to hear about that shit, jackass."

While Hunter and Cooper were laughing their asses off, Hailey and Mason walked out of the house, both with big-ass grins on their faces.

Shaking my head, I walked over to the driver's side of my car and got in, while Jaylinn got in the passenger side, and we took off for home.

When I got home Sunday afternoon, I was still pissed off at Dominic for the way he acted last night. He tried calling me all morning, but I kept sending his calls to voicemail. Around dinnertime, my mom yelled up the stairs to tell me that Dominic was here. Sighing, I got up and went downstairs to find out what he wanted.

He was standing by the front door, so I walked over and stood in front of him. "What do you want? Have you not noticed I have been avoiding your calls all day?"

He looked over my shoulder and then back at me. "Can we go out front and talk?"

I turned around to see Cooper and Hunter looking at us from the kitchen, so I turned back to Dominic and nodded.

We sat down on the porch swing. Dominic ran his hand threw his hair, and looked over at me. "Look, I know I fucked up last night Kenzie. I shouldn't have left like that. I'm sorry. I just wanted to spend some alone time with you." He let out a loud sigh. "I don't get to see you every day anymore, and I'm frustrated. We've been together for a year now. I thought you would be ready to take that next step. Now that we don't see each other as much as we did, I just miss you. I want to feel close with you."

I knew it; I knew this would happen. This is why I had told Dominic before we started dating that he would have to wait until I thought the time was right. I was not going to whore myself out. I saw what my brothers did to all the girls they messed around with and I did not want to be one of those girls.

"So, because I'm not putting out, or we aren't messing around, you're going to act like an asshole? That's fucked up Dominic. You said you would wait until I was ready, and if you can't accept that, then you need to leave."

"I'm not leaving MacKenzie. You're mine." He pulled me over to him, wrapped his arm around my shoulder and then kissed the side of my head. "I love you."

"Well then, you need to wait, and respect what I want. I told you I wanted to wait. You said you would wait."

Sighing, he said, "I've waited this long. What's a little bit longer, right?"

I looked up into his eyes. "Right."

He kissed me lightly on the lips. "Look, I have to get on the road. I have practice tomorrow morning."

We walked over to his car, and I gave him a hug and kiss, "Okay, I'll see you next weekend."

Dominic sat in his car, and slid on his sunglasses. "Love you."

I waved, and started back towards the house.

Did I love Dominic? Yes. Was I in love with him? No, I don't think so. Would I ever truly love him? Maybe, one day I would. Dominic was my first serious boyfriend. I didn't seriously date anyone because everyone in school knew my brothers; no one messed with my brothers, no one. When I was in seventh grade, I had a crush on this boy Ryan. We started going out, mostly talking on the phone and going to the movies occasionally. Right before winter break, he said he did not want to go out anymore. Ryan broke my heart, and, at thirteen, I thought my life was over. My brothers found out about what happened, and when we went back to school a week later, Ryan had a broken nose and two black eyes. To this day, when I see him, he will look the other way, or cross the street if he sees me coming. I asked my brothers what they did to him, and they always said they did not know anything about it.

Just when I was heading back upstairs to my room to take a nap, I heard Cooper talking to Hunter. "Dude, you better look out for my sister while you guys are away at school. I don't like that asshole."

"I know. I don't like him either. I'll keep her safe."

Chapter Three

Over the next few days, I was busy packing up everything I was bringing with me to Old Dominion, and doing some last minute shopping with my mom. I was both nervous and excited to start this part of my life.

Friday afternoon rolled around, and I had just finished packing my last box when Hailey came into my room. "Are you ready, Kenzie?"

"Just about." I told her, with a huge smile on my face. "Jackson, Mason and Cooper want to take us for lunch before we head out tomorrow."

She huffed at me. "They act like we're going across the country, and are never going to see them again."

"You know how they are; I'm surprised Mase and Coop haven't transferred schools just to stay close to us. Jackson is so wrapped up in Chloe that I don't think it's hit him just yet."

This certainly surprised me. It was probably because Hunter was at Old Dominion, too. They knew he would not let anything happen to us. In addition, the Harvard baseball scholarships gave them little to no choice.

"When are we going? I still have a few things I need to pack." That did not shock me. Hailey was a procrastinator.

"Around one, and I guess your ass needs help packing?" Hailey sucks at packing, always has. Every time we would go down to the shore house for the weekend, she would always forget half of her bathing suit, her toothbrush or her shoes. It was always something.

"You know it. I'll text Mason, and tell him we will just meet him there." She was tapping away on her phone. "When is Hunter coming to pick up all our stuff?"

"He asked me to dinner tonight, so I guess tomorrow morning when he picks us up."

Looking shocked, Hailey said, "Just the two of you are going to dinner?"

"Yeah, why?" We go out to dinner all the time. Why should this shock her? She quickly diverted her eyes back to her phone, "Oh, um, just wondering."

"What the hell, Hailey? It's not the first time I have been to dinner with Hunter."

Still not meeting my eyes, she said, "Nothing. Let's go."

Huh? What the hell is going on? "Hailey," I turned around, so I was staring at her. "I'm not leaving this room until you tell me what the fuck is going on."

"Nothing. Just forget I said anything." She grabbed her purse, and started towards to door.

"Whatever, but I'm not forgetting it."

We left and headed to Hailey's house. Just as we were getting out of the car in her driveway, Hailey's head whipped around, and she cursed under her breath.

"What's the matter?" I asked in a panic, thinking I had done something wrong.

She looked straight ahead. "Nothing. Can you just pull into the garage?"

Looking at her skeptically, I said, "Yeah. Your parents aren't going to block me in though, right?"

"Umm, no, we'll be OK. I can always have them move if they do come home," she said quickly.

I turned the car back on, and moved it into to garage. She was acting strange all day, but I thought maybe it was just the fact that we were leaving tomorrow morning.

"Kenzie, I need to tell you something, and I don't want you to get upset."

"How can you say something like that, and expect me not to get upset? What's going on?"

"Have you talked to Dominic?"

"Yeah, this morning."

"What did he say to you?"

What the hell is up with the 20 questions? "Just the usual. We talked about football, and how excited he is that I'll be there with him."

"He's home."

No kidding! "Yeah, I know. He has practice tomorrow morning."

"No, he's home. Like at his house, home."

Whipping my head around to look at her, I asked, "How do you know?"

"He is next door, at Alexis' house. I saw him pulling up when my mom and I were leaving to go to your house. I asked him what he was doing there. He said he had something to take care of, and then he was heading back to school."

There is no way he is here, is there? "You're sure it was him?"

"Kenzie, I talked to him. Of course, I'm sure."

"Is he still over there now? Is that why you had me pull into the garage?"

Nodding, she turned to get out of the car. "I told him I was going to tell you. He said he did not have anything to hide, so that is why I am telling you. I don't believe him."

"Well, if he didn't have anything to hide, why didn't he tell me he was coming home? Why the fuck is he with that bitch? He knows I hate her for starting all that shit last year."

"That's what I was wondering."

I got out of the car, walked out of the garage door and looked over at Alexis' house. Dominic's car was not there. I quickly sent him a text message.

Me – 10:58am: Hey, where u @

Dominic – 10:59am: Home

Me – 11:01am: @ ur house or school

Dominic – 11:03am: House, was on my way to surprise you

Me – 11:04am: Nice surprise it was 2 see u leave Alexis'

Dominic – 11:06am: She said she needed 2 talk 2 me, she caught me on my way out

Me – 11:08am: Y didn't u tell me u were coming home

Dominic – 11:10am: Where r u

Me 11:11am: Hails

Dominic – 11:13am: On my way

I looked up at Hailey and said, "He's on his way here; he said she caught him on his way to surprise me."

"You believe him?"

I just nodded at her. "I don't exactly have a reason not to."

Shaking her head, she huffed and said, "I'll be in my room."

I sat on her front steps for about ten minutes before he pulled up. I walked over to his car. He motioned me to over to his window.

"Hey, baby." He leaned out of the window and kissed me.

"So, why didn't you tell me you were coming home?"

"I told you, I wanted to surprise you. I thought maybe you needed some help packing."

Did I believe that was the reason he was here? No, not really, because I knew he was up to something. He had changed so much for having only being gone a few weeks. "Oh, well, I wish you would have told me last weekend that you were coming home. I could have used some help this morning." I tapped my finger on the door of his car. "So, what did Alexis want?"

"Sorry, I guess maybe I should have told you. She just wanted to talk about the party last weekend. She asked if I had been there cause she hadn't seen me."

What the hell! "Why would she care if you were at the party? She's trying to start shit again." The more I thought about her, the more pissed I got.

"I said the same thing to her." He turned his head to stare out the front windshield. "She was going on about seeing Hunter with his hands all over you, and you guys walking out of the party by yourselves." Then he turned back to me. "I don't care if you did. I told her I trusted you."

"That's good, because you should trust me."

"I know. That's why I'm not worried about it." He did not sound very sure of himself. Dominic knew I had feelings for Hunter. He knew what happened between us last summer.

"Good. Look, I have to go help Hailey pack, and then we are going to lunch with my brothers. I wish you had told me you were going to come home. Let me see if they would mind you coming to lunch too. Or, if you want, I can hang out with you when I'm done."

"No, don't worry about it. It's my fault. I'm just going to head back. I'll see you tomorrow at school." He leaned out of the window again to kiss me, "Love you."

After he left, I went inside to help Hailey pack the things that she was taking with her. After convincing her she did not need to pack her whole room, we headed to the restaurant for lunch with my brothers.

It was neat to get together with them one last time before not seeing them for the next few months. Mason and Cooper could not wait for baseball to start up again. They were looking forward to the parties that would start back up too. Jackson and Chloe were having a tough time coming up with a baby's name; they kept tossing ideas back and forth but could not both agree on any one name.

After we finished lunch, I dropped Hailey off at her house. I needed to get home to pack the last minute things I had thought of during lunch. Once I was finished, I still had a few hours until dinner with Hunter, so I decided to finish the book I was reading to kill some time.

Around six, Hunter picked me up, and we went for pizza at my favorite place. It was just a little hole in the wall, but I loved it.

I put my pizza down and wiped my face with my napkin, "I'm going to miss this pizza. Thanks for bringing me here."

"You're welcome. So, Dominic is home, huh?" He asked, watching me take a bite of my pizza.

"Christ! How did you know?" How did everyone know this, and I didn't?

"I saw him and Alexis together, walking into her house last night?"

What! I snapped my head up to look at him, hoping he was joking. "What? He didn't come home until this morning." *At least that is what he told me.*

Glaring down at his pizza, he said, "No, he was home last night, and he was with her."

"You must have seen wrong. He wasn't home then." My cheeks were beginning to burn from embarrassment.

He looked at me for a minute before he asked, "CC, can I ask you something?" I nodded at him. "Why are you with him?"

"Why does it matter to you?" *I wish I was with you* is what I honestly wanted to tell him.

He let out a sigh. "He doesn't treat you right. Why would he not tell you he was home? Why is he even talking to Alexis after all that shit that went down last year?"

I need this conversation to end; I don't want to talk to him about this. "I asked him about that. He said that she told him you and I fooled around with each other at the party last week. I guess he wanted to see what she had to say."

"And what did she say?"

"Hunter." I said with a warning tone. "I can't do this. I can't have everyone questioning my relationship with Dominic. It's my relationship, not anyone else's. I'm finished eating, so can you take me home now?" I stood up from the booth, and headed towards the bathroom. I needed a few minutes to calm down.

When I walked out of the bathroom, Hunter was at the counter paying for our food. I kept right on walking out of the restaurant, and waited by his street bike.

He came walking over to me, but did not say anything at first. He put his helmet on, and then gently put mine on. He lifted my chin to snap the strap, and looked into my eyes. "I'm not sorry for caring about you, CC."

I did not respond. I did not think he wanted me to. He threw his leg on the bike, kicked the kickstand up and then steadied the bike so I could get on. As we took off back to my house, with the wind in my face and hair, I started to feel bad for blowing up on him the way I did, but I am tired of everyone worrying about my relationship. I was not worried about it, why should they be.

We pulled up in front of my house, and I got off the bike. I reached for the snap on the helmet, but Hunter grabbed my hand and did it himself. I took it off, and started running my fingers through my hair to get the knots out. I looked over at him and was about to apologize when he grabbed the front pocket of my jeans and pulled me to him, "Don't apologize."

I rested my hand on his toned chest, and nodded, "I'll be here around noon to pack up all your shit, then we will grab Hailey, and get the hell out of here."

"Okay, see you then." I turn to head inside as he started his bike and left.

I strolled into the house and went straight to my room. I tossed and turned all night long. Was it just me or did he have a hard time fighting his feelings for me? He tells me nothing can happen between us, but he flirts and acts as if he wants something to happen. Was it because I was with Dominic? Hunter knew he kept pushing me away by trying to keep his distance from me.

The next morning, when I finally got my ass out of bed, I went downstairs to eat breakfast with mom and dad.

I walked over to the kitchen table to sit down. Mom started in on me first thing. "Are you sure you want to go to the ODU, Kenzie? There are plenty of schools here in New Jersey."

Rolling my eyes behind her back, I patiently answered, "Yes Mom, I'm more than sure." She must have asked me this same question at least 100 times this week.

I looked over at Mom, and she had tears in her eyes, "It's not going to be the same without you here; we're all going to miss you." My mom had a lot of time on her hands. With my leaving, she was going to have even more. She became a stay-at-home mom after she had the twins. Dad, being a stockbroker for the New York Stock Exchange, made more than enough money for her to stay home.

Dad came sauntering in with his coffee cup, and added his two cents. "We are baby girl, and it's going be different without you around."

"Don't worry mom and dad; I'll make sure she is taken care of." My eyebrows shot up when Hailey walked into the kitchen, with Mason right behind her. What in the hell is she doing here?

"That's what I'm worried about," my mom said under her breath. Looking at Hailey, I wondered if she had heard mom. If she did, she wasn't letting on about it. I know my mom and dad love

Hailey, but my mom always thought she was a little wild. This is what I loved about Hailey.

"I'll come home whenever I can. I need to do this, and we've talked about this." We did talk about this for almost a year, as I was trying to convince my parents to let me go to ODU for school. I think it helped that Hailey and Hunter were going to be there with me; well mostly that Hunter would be there.

"What the hell are you doing here?" I asked Hailey, as she stole a piece of bacon off my plate. She just shrugged her shoulders at me.

Shaking my head at her, I picked up my plate, put it in the dishwasher and then went back up to my room to take a shower.

Hunter showed up right on time to help load all of my stuff in his truck. My brothers were also there helping him. My mom was crying because she did not want me to go. I promised her I would be home for Thanksgiving, and I would call her every chance I got. I think that helped ease her mind, maybe just a little.

My dad pulled me aside, and handed me a check. "What's this for? I don't need your money dad; I saved up all my money from babysitting, and working over the summer."

"I know, but I'm not going to be there to spoil you like I would if you were here. If you don't spend the money, at least deposit it in the bank for emergencies." Dad grabbed me, pulled me into a tight hug and kissed the top of my head. "We're really going to miss you, baby girl."

I wiped the tears away that were running down my cheeks. "I'm going to miss you too dad. I love you." I was going to miss him and mom; this was the first time I was seriously going to be on my own.

"Alright, go say good-bye to your Mom, and then I'll get her out of here so you can leave." He said with a chuckle.

I walked over to my mom and hugged her. I told her I would call her as soon as I settled into my dorm. Mom was still clinging on to me, crying when Dad wrapped his arm around her, and walked her to the car to go out to lunch.

Jackson hugged and kissed my cheek, told me he would miss me like crazy, and that he and Chloe would call me during the week to check up on me.

Cooper was next to say goodbye. "Don't let anyone mess with you Kenzie. If you have any problems, call me. I don't care what time it is."

"I will, I promise. Love you; take care of Mom for me." Cooper was my mom's favorite; I knew he would look out for her.

Finally, it was Mason's turn. Even though we fought all the time, I was going to miss him the most. "Give your sister a hug." I told him, with tears rolling down my cheeks again.

Hugging me, he whispered, "I really wish you weren't going away Kenzie. We need you here." Then he pulled back and wiped the tears from my cheeks.

"You're not going to be here in a few weeks Mase. You guys will be ok without me. Y'all are going to come visit us in a few weeks anyway."

"I know we'll be gone, but I can't keep an eye on you Kenzie. I have to rely on Hunter to protect you now that I can't." Always the over protective one, I loved him, but this was another reason I chose this college.

"I have Dominic too, you know. No one is going to mess with me with him and Hunter around. Go to school, have fun and stay out of trouble." I winked at him, trying to lighten the situation. He was always getting into trouble until baseball season started up.

"Love ya; call me when you get there. If you don't, I'll be there by tomorrow morning." I knew he was not kidding.

Chuckling, I said, "Yes *Dad*. Love you too."

I walked over to Hunter's truck, and looked over to him. "Finally, let's get the hell out of here before they handcuff me here."

Chapter Four

After we stopped at Hailey's and picked up all her stuff, we started on our five-hour drive. We played Hot Seat to kill some of the time. Since Hunter was driving, he was in the Hot Seat first. Hailey and I had to ask five questions each, and he could veto only one question.

I started, "Who was the first person you ever kissed?"

He glanced over at me. "You." That surprised me. I am shocked he even remembered it. He was sixteen and the girls flocked to him. I would have thought he would have kissed someone before me.

Hailey piped up from the back seat, "Who was the first person you had sex with?" Of course, she would jump into that.

Hunter looked in the rear view mirror at Hailey. "Lilly."

"How old were you?" I asked curiously.

He honestly did not want to answer, but did anyway, "16."

Hailey laughed, "When was the last time you had sex?"

He looked straight out the window, "Two months ago."

Hold on...what? "You walked that girl out of your room last weekend."

"That's not a question."

I rolled my eyes, "You didn't sleep with that girl you spent the night with last weekend?"

"No," was all he said.

Hailey was bouncing in her seat, "My turn, would you have sex with Kenzie?"

"Really, Hails?" I looked at Hunter, "You don't have to..."

"Yes." he said, before I could even finish what I was saying.

I needed to change the subject quickly. "What's your favorite color?"

He looked over, and winked at me, "Blue, like the color of your eyes." Ugh, this is not going the way I wanted it to. I did not want this to become awkward.

Hailey was laughing hysterically, "How big is your dick?" *Now it was awkward.*

Turning around in my seat, I glowered at Hailey, and she shrugged her shoulders at me.

Hunter started laughing, "No one has ever complained."

I wanted to change the subject completely. It was becoming extremely hot in here, thinking about his size, "What did you have for breakfast?"

He was still laughing, "Coffee."

I braced myself for what was about to come next out of Hailey's mouth. "Would you date Kenzie if you weren't friends with her brothers?"

He looked at me, smiled and then checked both ways before entering the intersection, "Hell yeah." *Damn brothers!*

"Alright Hailey, you're next." Hunter looked in the rearview mirror once we were safely through the intersection.

Hailey started whining. "Let's play something else; I don't want to play this anymore."

I had a pretty good feeling it was because she knew we were going to ask questions about her and Mason. Since Hunter is an easygoing guy, we dropped the game and started playing Name that Song. Hunter had the radio buttons on his steering wheel, so he would hit the seek button, and the three of us would try to guess the song. This kept us entertained for a little bit until Hailey and I busted out dancing and singing *Call Me Maybe* at the top of our lungs, while Hunter laughed at us. After a while, my throat started hurting from yelling, so I gave up. I laid down along the seat, stuck my feet out the window and read for a while.

It was late when we finally made it to campus, but because it was check-in weekend, it really did not matter. When we pulled up to the dorms, I texted Dominic to let him know we were here, and to ask if he could come help me unload my stuff.

My parents wanted me to experience college life, but did not want me sharing a room with three strange people, or sharing a common bathroom with an entire dorm floor of strangers. They paid extra money for a two-room suite. It was perfect for Hailey and me. We had two oversized single beds, individual desks, chairs and bookshelves. There were also two closets and chests of drawers. We even had our own private bathroom. We would miss having a laundry room right at hand. There was one on the first floor of our building, so at least we would not have to lug our dirty clothes all over campus.

Dominic thought we would be spending as much time together as possible, because Housing had assigned us to the same co-ed building. The school would not allow a male and a female together in the same room, and I think my parents and brothers were very happy about that. They would never allow me to room with Dominic.

Dominic walked over to where we parked, and wrapped his arms around me. "Hey baby, you finally made it. I was starting to get worried Hunter kidnapped you." Dominic glared over at Hunter.

I kissed his cheek, walked to the tailgate of the truck and handed him a bag. "I told you we weren't leaving until early afternoon."

He grabbed a few more bags from the back. "Well, let's get you unpacked. I'm sure Hunter has stuff he needs to do, maybe a party to go to or something."

Hunter just shrugged and said, "I'm good. Just going to my place and getting settled in."

Hailey walked over to Hunter, and put her hand on his arm. "Since Dominic has Kenzie covered, can you help me with my stuff?"

He nodded his head, and started grabbing some of Hailey's stuff. After everything was in our room, Hunter said goodbye to Hailey. Then he walked over to me, hugged me and whispered in my ear that if I needed anything at all to call him. I told him I would, and then he left.

Dominic seemed antsy, "Look baby, I'm going to head out and let you and Hailey get some sleep."

"Okay, I'll text you in the morning."

He kissed me, said he loved me and left. Hailey and I just looked at each other, confusion plain on our faces. *What just happened here?*

"It sure was nice of him to show us around. He said he was so happy about you staying in the same building, but it seemed like he couldn't wait to get out of here." Hailey said after Dominic left.

"Maybe he doesn't want to crowd me since we just got here. Besides, we were in the car for the last five hours."

"If you say so." She turned around, and started to unpack some of the boxes; I grabbed one, and started doing the same thing.

We stayed up until three in the morning, and then finally passed out. I had plans of getting up early and finishing up, but I did not wake up until I heard my phone ringing.

"Kenzie, what the fuck? I told you to call me when you got there." Mason yelled frantically into the phone.

I let out a huge groan. "Good God, Mason, calm down. I'm fine; we got in late, started unpacking and then fell asleep."

"It's one in the fucking afternoon Kenzie. Where is Hailey? Is she with you?"

"Yeah, she's sleeping; we were up till three this morning. Would you relax? If you were so worried, you could have called Hunter. He would have told you we made it."

"I did talk to him, but I told you to call me. Hunter isn't living with you. He doesn't know what you are doing, any more than I do."

"Seriously, if you don't knock it off, I'm hanging up on you. You are worse than Mom and Dad. Dominic is in the same building, so if anything happens to me, he is right here to help."

"Fine, whatever." Then he hung up on me. I dropped my head back on my pillow. A few seconds later, I heard Hailey's phone beep. I figured it was Mason chewing her ass out for not calling too.

I sent a text to Dominic, and asked if he would take me out to breakfast and show me around campus. He texted back, saying he was busy helping his roommate this afternoon, but he would take me out for dinner.

I did not know what to do with myself since Dominic had made other plans. I got up and headed to the bathroom to take a long hot shower. I stood, letting the water pour over my head, hoping that my coming here was not going to be a mistake. I was only here one day, and Dominic was already blowing me off. I would not have cared as much if I knew my way around campus. I was not expecting Dominic to be by my side twenty-four hours a day. He had football practice, and that took up a lot of his time, but it would have been nice if he could have set aside my first day here to spend with me.

A knock on the door interrupted me from my thoughts. "Door is unlocked, Hails." I pulled back the shower curtain and peeked my head out.

I let out a squeak, surprised to see that it was Hunter, not Hailey, who had come in.

"Hey, what are you doing in here?" I jerked the curtain closed, feeling slightly uncomfortable that the only thing keeping Hunter from seeing me naked, was a shower curtain.

I heard the toilet seat shut. "I came to see if you wanted to go grab some lunch. I could show you around campus a little bit." He cleared his throat. "Hailey said that Dominic split right after I left. If I would have known that, I would have come back over."

I rinsed the soap out of my hair. "Yeah, he left, but it's okay. Hails and I unpacked some of our stuff and then we slept in. Dominic is busy right now, but he's going to take me out to dinner." Shutting off the water, I reached my hand out and grabbed my towel. "Can you give me ten minutes, and I'll be ready?"

"You don't have to hide from me CC; it's not like I've never seen you." I blushed, remembering the time at home when I had just opened the shower curtain to step out at the exact same time that Hunter came barging into the bathroom. I had tried to cover myself the best I could, but it was too late. He had already seen me.

I wrapped myself in the towel, pulled the shower curtain back and glared at him.

Hunter stood, and put both of his hands up. "Okay, okay, I'm going." He turned, and strolled out of the room, laughing.

After Hailey and I were ready, Hunter took us out to lunch, and showed us around town before my dinner date with Dominic. Hunter had just dropped us off when Dominic came to collect me for dinner, and then a movie back in his room.

Dominic took me to The Raven. He said they had great food, and he was right. We both ate until we were stuffed. The Raven was across the street from the beach, so after eating, we decided to walk off a little of our dinner.

We went back to his room, and Dominic walked over to the bookstand where he kept his movies. "So, what movie do you want to watch?"

"Whatever, it doesn't matter to me." I knew we were not going to be watching it anyway; he could barely keep his hands off me all night.

As we were lying on Dominic's bed, making out, someone knocked on his door.

He rolled off me with a groan. "Be right back." He grabbed a pair of sweat pants off the floor, put them on and then went over to answer the door.

I sat up on his bed, and pulled the covers up over me, in case it was his roommate coming back. Dom had told me they had a room rule. If there was a sock on the doorknob, you had to knock before you walked in. I hoped that rule was for his roommate and not Dominic, since I had just gotten here last night. From where I was sitting on the bed, I could not see Dominic, but I could hear a girl's voice.

"I told you, I was busy tonight." I heard Dominic say to whoever was standing there.

"Who is in there with you?" the girl asked.

"It doesn't matter. Look, I've got to go." Dominic shut and locked the door before he came back over to the bed. I was reaching for my shirt to put back on. The mood for our make out session was completely ruined.

Dominic frowned. "Where are you going baby? We were just getting started."

Looking around for my pants, I said, "Who was that at the door?"

Dominic sat on the bed and tried to reach for me, but I moved before he could touch me. "She's no one. She was looking for Tommy."

"You said *I told you I was busy*. Why would you say that?" Something was not adding up here.

"Because I am busy, and I wanted her to get lost." He grabbed my hand and pulled me towards him. "Baby, stay here with me."

I shook my head. "I shouldn't. I don't want to leave Hailey alone all night. She doesn't know anyone yet."

He dropped my hand and huffed. "Fine, I forgot everything is always about Hailey."

Now he was acting like a two year old, and pissing me off. "Really? Are you going to act like that? I texted you today, and asked you to lunch, and you blew me off for your roommate."

He walked over to the door, and opened it. "Whatever. I'll see you tomorrow."

The asshat couldn't even walk me to my room.

When I got back to the room, Hailey was sitting on her bed, Hunter was sitting in the chair next to her bed and they were playing cards.

"Hey, you're back early. I didn't expect to see you until tomorrow." Hailey looked up from the cards in her hand. By the look on his face, Hunter was surprised to see me too.

I tried to make it sound as if it was not a huge deal that some girl just ruined our night, so I told them what I told Dominic. "I didn't want to leave you by yourself already. We just got here. Besides, I'll have plenty of time with Dominic."

"CC...," Hunter said, in that *we know you too well for your bullshit* voice. "I know you better than that. What did he do?"

I crossed my arms over my chest and defiantly said, "Nothing."

Hailey shook her head, knowing I was not going to say anymore. "Alright then, you want to play?"

I felt Hunter's eyes on me and looked over at him. "What?"

"Nothing." Then he studied his cards, ending the conversation.

After playing cards for a few hours, we called it a night. Our first classes were in the morning, and we needed to get some sleep.

Chapter Five

I barely slept last night, worrying about how Dominic and I had left things and worrying about my first day of classes. Hailey and I had our first class together, and we were lucky it did not start until 10 a.m. Dominic had to be up at 5 a.m. to run with the football team, and then they had practice and meetings until noon. He was not going to be around much to walk me to class, but I wish he could have today so we could talk about what happened last night.

I gathered up my books and purse, getting ready to head out to class when there was a knock at the door. When I opened it, I was shocked to see Dominic. He had his arm up against the doorframe, and his hair was still damp from his shower. He was wearing my favorite jeans and a Yankee's t-shirt. "Are you ready to leave Kenzie? We have a little bit of a walk."

Still feeling a bit puzzled that he was here, I asked, "What are you doing here? I thought you had practice."

"They let us go after our workout, since it's the first day of classes." He closed the distance between us and moved his hand to cup my face. "I'm sorry about last night. That wasn't how I saw the night going."

I just shrugged. "It's okay. We will talk about it later." I did not want to be late on my first day. I yelled over my shoulder, "Hails, let's go."

She came out, looking all disorganized. "Ok, ok I'm ready."

It was about a fifteen-minute walk to class, and when we arrived, there was already a bunch of people there. We all walked in, and Dominic spotted Logan, a football teammate of his, so we walked over to him so Dominic could introduce us. As we were approaching, Hailey nudged me in the ribs and wiggled her eyebrows at me.

"Geez, Hails, you haven't even talked to him yet." I said in a loud whisper.

With a dreamy look on her face, she said, "Who needs to talk when he looks like that?"

Laughing, I cannot help but think she truly is something else. "You're impossible, you know that right?"

Logan was a handsome guy. He was tall and skinny and his t-shirt stretched across his toned chest. He had hair that was sticking up all over the place, but it looked good on him. I also noticed a tattoo on his upper arm that was peeking out from his t-shirt. He was just Hailey's type.

After introducing everyone, Logan asked Dominic, "Are you going to the party on Friday night?"

"Of course I'm going; I haven't missed a party yet."

I snapped my head towards Hailey, and gave her a *what the hell* look. I now know what he has been doing every weekend since he got here.

Logan looked over in Hailey's direction, with a twinkle in his eye. "Hailey, are you going to come to the party with MacKenzie?"

I looked over at Dominic, and answered Logan for Hailey, "No, Hailey isn't coming with me because I wasn't invited."

Dominic slung his arm around my shoulder, "Babe, of course your invited."

"How do you know I don't already have plans? It would have been nice of you to invite me first."

"Well, do you have plans?" he asked.

"No. What plans could I possibly have already? I don't know anyone here."

He squeezed my shoulder a little. "Good, then it is settled. You and Hailey are coming to the party. I'll pick you girls up tonight at 9."

I looked at Hailey to see if she was ok with that. She nodded and I said, "All right, we'll go."

He kissed the side of my head. "Sorry, I just assumed you would want to go. You never had a problem going to parties with me when we were at home."

"Yeah well, I knew about those."

Class was about to start, so Dominic and Logan said their goodbyes and left. After class was over, I said goodbye to Hailey. On the way to my second class, I heard someone call my name. I turned around and saw Hunter jogging towards me. A few girls did a double take as he passed them. He was wearing his favorite black Yankee's hat, a tight fitting black and white Yankee's t-shirt and dark blue jeans.

"Hey CC, how was your first class? Did you find it okay?" Hunter asked.

"Yeah, Dominic walked Hailey and me to class." I looked at the door, and then back to Hunter, "Do you have a class in this building?"

"Yeah," He looked down at his watch, and then up to me, "in about ten minutes."

My stomach grumbled. "Nice, want to grab lunch after this?"

He held the door open for me. "Yeah sure, I'll meet you here after class." He gave me a hug, and then said goodbye.

My class seemed to drag on forever. I was hungry, but I was also looking forward to spending some time with Hunter too. I walked out when class was over, and Hunter was leaning against the railing with his foot propped up, waiting for me.

As the rest of the week went by, Hailey and I had a little routine going. She and I would walk to class in the mornings. Afterwards, Hunter and I would go grab some lunch. The middle of the second week, Hailey and I met Gracie and Zoey. Since they also lived on our floor, they started walking with us in the mornings.

Friday, after I had lunch with Hunter, I came home and there was a black box with a pink bow sitting on my bed.

"What's this?" I asked Hailey, who was lying on her bed reading, a magazine.

She put the magazine down on her stomach. "It was sitting against the door when I got here; the card has your name on it."

I put my purse and books down on my desk and grabbed the box. I slipped off the pink bow, lifted the top up and removed the tissue paper. There was a pair of pink studded earrings, a pair of pink peep toe heels and a little black dress.

As I laid it all out on my bed, Hailey came over to see what it was. "Damn Kenzie, that's hot." She picked up the card that Dominic had put on the box, and read it. "Dominic is doing some serious ass-kissing. He needs to, after the way he has been treating you."

"Yeah, I guess he is." Grinning like a fool, I sent a quick text to Dominic, thanking him for the gift.

"Well, let's get ready. I want to curl my hair, so I'm going to need your help." I took my curling iron into the bathroom and plugged it in the outlet.

Hailey walked in behind me with a huge-ass grin on her face. "You have got to find me something just as hot to wear tonight. I'm hoping that a certain football player will pay attention to me." Then she winked at me, and went to the closet to go through my clothes.

I could not figure out why she was not the crazy, happy girl she normally was. Ever since we came here, she had been just a little different. Then, it dawned on me. I wondered if she missed Mason. "So Hails, are you going to tell me what's going on with Mase?"

Groaning, she said, "I told you and everyone else, there is nothing going on with us. We're just friends. Besides, I don't think he wants anything more than that anyway."

I smiled. "If you say so. One day Hails, you are going to spill it, and tell me everything. It's just a matter of time. So until then, I will just have to wait until you are ready to talk about your feelings for him, and admit to yourself and everyone else that you have them."

"Whatever, now shut up and help me pick something out already." Just like that, the conversation ended, as we started to get ready for our first college party.

I texted Dominic, asked for the address and told him we were just going to grab a cab. We were going to be a little late and did not want to hold him up.

We were about an hour late to the party, since it took us twice as long to curl our hair. We pulled up to a gorgeous contemporary house that was a cheery yellow color. There was no way a college student could afford a place like this. The property was right on the beach, and I knew from my parent's house that it cost a pretty penny. When we walked in, the party was already in full swing. There were people everywhere, dancing, playing poker, guys doing body shots off girls in the kitchen and people playing beer pong on the kitchen table. I knew there was no way I would find Dominic, so I texted him, told him we were in the kitchen and to come get us.

We made our way around the crowd surrounding the girls on the table. We found the guy that was manning the keg; he asked us if we wanted a beer. We both took the beer he offered to us, and he introduced himself as Bentley and told us that this was his house.

"You live in this big ass house all by yourself?" Hailey asked, looking around. Everything was stainless steel and modern. The kitchen even had one of those flat surface stoves, very similar to the one my mom had.

Bentley looked Hailey up and down, and gave her a sly smile. "No, I have a roommate, but he's working tonight. There's an extra bedroom, if you want to move in, too." Bentley was definitely not Hailey's type. He was a scrawny tall kid with bright red hair and brown eyes. Hailey liked a guy with meat on his bones.

Hailey laughed a nervous laugh. "Oh no, I'm good back at the dorms, but thanks."

"So Bentley, do you know Logan and Dominic? They play on the football team here." I asked.

"Oh yeah, Logan is actually right over there." He pointed to Logan, who was in the corner near the DJ, talking to a couple of the other guys dressed in their football jerseys. "I saw Dominic a few minutes ago out on the back deck."

Hailey and I talked to Bentley for a little while, and then Dominic finally made his way into the kitchen. I was standing near the back door but he had not seen me yet.

"Psst." I said, trying to get his attention.

When he noticed me, his face broke out in a grin. Then he gave me the once over, examining my outfit. He came over to me, let out a low whistle and said, "Damn baby, I knew you were going to look hot, but damn, I'm speechless."

Dominic pulled me tight to his body, started kissing me lightly, at first and then deepened the kiss as his tongue met mine. I almost forgot we were at a party with a bunch of people all around us.

I ran my hands slowly up Dominic's chest, under his shirt; I looked up at him and gave him a sly smile. He grabbed my hand and quickly took us out the sliding glass doors, down the stairs and to the side of the house.

Dominic placed both hands on either side of my face, caging me in. "Kenzie, you look fucking amazing in this." He kissed me hard, teeth to teeth. "I can't wait to strip you out of this later."

I reached down between us and started rubbing him through his jeans. He groaned at the contact. "Baby, stop."

I started to unbutton his jeans. "But you're so worked up." I looked around to make sure no one was in sight, and slid his zipper down. I would never have done this, but we had worked ourselves into a frenzy.

"Kenzie stop, really, I don't want..."

I interrupted him. "Dominic, just shut up, okay?" I dropped to my knees in front of him, looked up with a sexy smirk on my face, then pulled him inside my mouth and proceeded to twist my hand up and down, as I moved him in and out of my mouth.

Dominic's hands wrapped tightly in my hair, holding my head in place. He groaned his approval of what I was doing. I continually sucked and swirled my tongue along his length. I knew he was not going to last long, not with the way he was moving his hips back a forth.

"Ahh, baby that feels amazing...I'm not going to last long." Moaning my name repeatedly, his breath hitched and I felt his legs go stiff.

"Baby..." He gripped my hair a little tighter, pumped into my mouth once, twice and then he let go.

A few seconds later Dominic pulled me back up and wrapped his arms around me. He started placing kisses on me while he whispered, "Damn, baby that was hot. Now let me take care of you."

I cupped his face with both of my hands. "No, that was a thank you for the outfit. I love it."

"I love you so damn much, Kenzie. I am so glad that you are finally here with me." We stood there together for a few more minutes, just holding each other before we headed back into the party to find our friends.

Dominic straightened his clothes out, and made sure my hair was back in place before we made our way back into the house to find Hailey, and get some beer. I looked around for her but did not see her. I texted her but she did not answer.

I was getting worried and Dominic sensed it. "Hey Bentley, can you watch Kenzie for a minute? I'm going to go see if I can find Hailey."

"Yeah, sure man." Bentley said. Dominic gave me a kiss and then went to search for Hailey.

Bentley grinned at me and handed me another beer. I told myself this was going to be my last one. I needed to get Hailey and me home in one piece.

"Have you been here since he came down a few weeks ago?" Bentley asked, while peering at me as if he was trying to put a puzzle together.

I shook my head. "Oh no, we just got here.." I looked out into the crowded living room, trying to figure out what was taking Dominic so long. "So do you live here all the time, or is this just where you stay for school?"

"This is my parent's vacation house so I live here all the time. Like I said, during school, I have a roommate." He shrugged. "It helps pay for the bills and shit."

I looked back out in the crowd, trying to spot Dominic again, but I still could not find him or Hailey anywhere. I know Hailey would not just leave me at the party without at least texting me first. I was starting to get worried that neither one of them had come back.

I turned on the stool I was sitting on to face Bentley, "I'm going to go look for Dominic. He should have been back by now." Bentley put both his hands on the tops of my thighs, and I froze.

"No, uh...," he looked over my shoulder, and then back at me, "You'll never find him with all the people in there. Plus, you don't know your way around. I'll go get him. You stay here, just in case Hailey shows up looking for you."

He released my thighs and walked past me. I let out the breath I did not realize I was holding. That was strange. I followed Bentley with my eye, and that was when I saw what exactly was holding Dominic up. Some girl was grinding herself all up on him, and kissing his neck. Being nearly tipsy from all the refills Bentley gave me, I stormed over to where Dominic was.

I shoved his shoulder. "What the fuck was that Dominic?"

He tried to grab my hand, but I yanked it back. "Baby what are you talking about; I was just telling her I had to go find you."

"Kenzie, what's wrong?" Hailey asked from behind me. *Now she shows up.*

"Stop the bullshit Dominic. I saw you dancing with her, and she was kissing your neck. You just left me in the fucking kitchen, waiting for you to come back." I looked back at Hailey, "I think I have had enough fun for one night. I'm leaving."

"Baby...," he started to say something, but I cut him off by grabbing Hailey's arm, and pulling her towards the front door. After what we just did outside, how he was doing this to me? What happened to the Dominic that made me feel as if I was his whole world?

Hailey pulled her arm, causing me to stop walking and turn around to look at her. "Kenzie, wait a second. I was just coming to find you to tell you I was going to stay with Logan for the night."

"Shit! Hailey, you just met him and you are already going to spend the night with him? Do you think that is such a good idea after you have been drinking?"

Looking past me over to where Logan was standing, she gave him an *I'm sorry* look, and then she nodded her head at me. "Okay let's get out of here."

I knew we both had not made many friends here at school since we had only been here a week. It was not fair to Hailey for me to guilt her into coming home with me tonight.

"No, no it's okay Hailey. You stay here and have some fun. I'm going to go out front and call a cab to come pick me up. Send me a text in the morning when you wake up, and please, be careful."

She gave me a hug, "Are you sure? I know he'll understand. We both have been drinking pretty heavy, so we were just going to stay here anyway. Logan knows Bentley, and he said we could take the extra bedroom for the night."

I gave Hailey a kiss on the cheek. "Yeah I'm sure. I'll see you tomorrow."

I was upset, and on the verge of breaking down in tears. I needed to get out of here. I opened the front door, and ran right into a hard chest. Groaning to myself for not paying attention, I mumbled, "I'm sorry," and tried to move around him. He kept blocking my path so I could not move past him. I looked up, wondering what the hell this guy's problem was. I started to tell him to get the fuck out of my way, but was shocked to see that it was Hunter.

I was frozen in place by his piercing blue eyes. "W-what are you doing here? You're a little late for the party."

He broke eye contact, and looked me up and down, "I live here CC. Where you off to by yourself, and where the hell is Hailey?"

The beer was starting to catch up to me. My words were slurring. "Dominic and I got into a fight, Hailey is going to stay here with Logan and I'm going home. If you could move out of my way now, I need to go out front and call a cab to come get my ass."

Hunter put his hands on my shoulders to steady me. "First, you're not calling a fucking cab. Second, you aren't going anywhere. You can stay here tonight, in my room. I'd take you home, but I'm too damn tired, and I don't want you to stay by yourself like this."

Hiccupping, I said, "I can call a cab. You don't need to take me home. I'm a big girl." Damn Bentley, and the way he kept refilling my cup!

Hunter did not respond, and I did not have the energy to fight anymore. I knew I was going to lose this battle. Hunter guided me up the stairs to what I assumed was his bedroom. Once he unlocked the door, he flipped the light on, pulled me inside and then locked the door behind him. He walked to his dresser, put his keys down, took out his wallet from his back pocket and placed that on the dresser as well.

"I have my own bathroom over there." He pointed to another door. He opened his drawer, pulled out a pair of boxers and a t-shirt and handed them to me. "Here, you can sleep in this, because you sure as hell can't sleep in that."

I grabbed the clothes he handed me and made my way to the bathroom to change and wash my face. As I walked out of the bathroom, I saw Hunter grab a pillow, and a blanket from the bed and place them both on the couch that was up against the wall.

"What are you doing?" I asked.

He turned to look at me as if I asked a stupid question, "I'm sleeping on the couch. You can take my bed."

I shook my head, "No, I'll take the couch. I'm smaller than you."

"CC, no, just take the bed. I'm fine on the couch."

"Fine, I'll take the bed, but only if you sleep with me. I can't have you giving up your bed for me."

He looked at me for a minute before he grabbed the pillow and blanket off the couch, and put them back on his bed. I climbed in while Hunter stripped down to his boxers, and then he climbed in too. After laying there for a few minutes staring at the ceiling, I looked over at Hunter, who was also looking at the ceiling.

"Thanks for letting me crash here. I hope this isn't going to be weird for you. I can go sleep on the couch. I really don't mind."

Turning his head, he looked at me with a painful expression. "This isn't weird CC. It's not like we've never fallen asleep together before." He grabbed an extra pillow that he had thrown at the foot of the bed and positioned it between us. "There, just like we used to have it."

Sighing, I said, "It's too loud out there; I'll never be able to fall asleep like this."

Hunter reached over, careful not to touch me, and grabbed the remote to turn the radio on. The radio stared playing *Trying Not To Love You.*

When he laid back down, I looked over at him and whispered, "Thanks." Then I flipped to my other side to try to get some sleep. I was thoroughly exhausted from the events of the night, and just wanted to shut my brain off for a while. I would deal with all the other problems tomorrow.

I heard Hunter mumble, "Nice fucking song," to himself and that was the last thing I remember.

Chapter Six

When I woke up the next morning, Hunter was still sound asleep on his stomach, turned in my direction, with his right hand tucked under his face. He looked so at ease. Despite having a hangover, I had one of the best nights of sleep in a long time. I laid there for a little while watching his back rise and fall with every breath he took, but nature called. I got up as quietly as I could and went into the bathroom. While I was in there, I looked in his cabinets for some pain reliever to help with my slight hangover from the night before. After I took some, I made my way down to the kitchen to get something to drink.

I walked down the stairs, and I could not believe my eyes when I reached the bottom. The house was a mess, and there were people passed out everywhere. I looked across the living room to the couch, and just about died at what I saw. Two girls were duct taped to it. I shook my head and mumbled to myself, "Looks like they aren't getting up anytime soon." I made my way toward what I was hoping was the kitchen. As I approached, I saw a guy duct taped to the bathroom door. I mumbled to myself again, "What is it with people being duct taped to shit?" Walking back down the hallway, I passed a guy asleep on the floor. Someone had taken black marker and had drawn all over his face, arms and legs. In the kitchen, there were still a few people playing poker. I grabbed a water bottle out of the fridge, and headed back upstairs. I walked past a huge window at the top of the stairs, and looked outside. I noticed the picnic table had been set on fire at some point during the night, and there was a guy and a girl sleeping on an air mattress in the pool.

Shaking my head at the mess left behind, I opened the door quietly to Hunter's room, hoping that I wouldn't wake him up. I was surprised to find Hunter sitting up and running his hand through his hair.

"Damn it CC, I thought you left." He was pissed.

As calmly as I could, I said, "Relax Hunter, I just went to find something to drink."

"Fuck! I'm sorry. I thought you had left me." He pointed towards the fridge that was in the corner of his room. Somehow, I had missed that earlier. "There's water and orange juice in there."

I sat on his bed and pulled the covers over my legs. "Sorry, didn't see that over there. I wish I had though," I started giggling. "You don't want to go out there. Your house is trashed."

He looked up to the ceiling. "I'm not surprised. Every time Bentley throws a party at the beginning of the year, this shit happens. He hires a cleaning company to come clean all that."

"Thank God, because it's going to take forever to get that shit cleaned up. You should see the people duct taped downstairs."

Groaning, he looks over at me. "Are you serious?"

I shook my head at him. "There is some guy that was colored with a Sharpie all over. That shit is going to take forever to clean off."

"At least the police weren't called this time." Hunter got up and adjusted his boxers. "I'm going to jump in the shower, and then I'll take you home."

"Ok, sounds good. I'm going to go back to sleep; wake me up when you're ready." I laid down, pulled the covers up to my neck and watched Hunter walk across the room to the bathroom. God, he was a sight to look at. He has one of the nicest asses I have ever seen. One of my favorite tattoos was on his upper right arm, praying hands holding Rosary beads and above that, it said *Only God Can Judge Me* in old English lettering.

He must have sensed me staring, because he turned around and winked. I pulled the blankets up to my nose, trying to cover that fact that I was blushing because he caught me, but I could not tear my eyes away. When he closed the bathroom, I kicked my feet and squealed like a little girl. I could not believe I actually spent the night with him, *alone,* and in his clothes.

A while later, the sound of my phone buzzing woke me up. Rolling over on my side, I picked it up off the bed. There was a text message from Hailey asking me where I was. I checked the time. Christ, I was asleep for two hours.

I could not help but wonder where the hell Hunter was, and why he didn't wake me up. I sat up and jumped in surprise. He was sitting at the foot of the bed watching me. "Damn you scared me. Why didn't you wake me up?"

He shrugged. "I like you sleeping in my bed. You looked so relaxed."

"Have you been watching me sleep the whole time?" *God I hope I did not talk in my sleep.*

"No, after my shower I tried to wake you up, but you weren't having it. I went for a run, and just came back and took another shower."

"Well, thanks for letting me sleep in."

He went over to his dresser. "Do you want a pair of sweat pants to put on for the ride home? I don't think it's a good idea for you put that dress back on."

I did not answer him. There was no way I could go back to campus wearing his clothes. Dominic would flip his shit. I took off the t-shirt I was wearing, threw it in the corner with the rest of his dirty clothes and stood in only my bra, and his boxers. I heard him gasp. Since I now had his attention, I decided to throw a little flirting back at him. I picked my dress up off the floor and slid it on. Then, I reached under my dress and slowly started pulling the boxers down; I glanced back and saw him watching me intently.

Smirking at him, I winked and asked, "See something you like?"

He shook his head at me. "You have no idea." He mumbled just loud enough for me to make out what he said. "We have to get the hell out of here." He grabbed his keys, hat and wallet and opened the door, saying over his shoulder, "I'll meet you downstairs, so hurry up."

After running into the bathroom and throwing my hair up in a ponytail, I met Hunter downstairs. I was still laughing at the chaos that was all around when I asked him, "So, how did you become roommates with Bentley?"

Hunter ushered me out the front door, "I uh, helped his sister out last year."

I did not like that answer and was content to drop the conversation, but he continued as he opened the truck door for me. "It's not what you think CC. Bentley had a party here last year. Things got a little out of hand with a football player. He wasn't taking no for an answer from her, so I taught him a lesson."

"Where is his sister now?" I certainly hoped she did not live there with him.

"She dropped out of school and moved back home."

Thank God!

"She was ok though, right?" I asked, wondering what he meant by the football player not taking no for an answer.

"No, not at first, but she is getting better."

Hunter shut the door, got in the driver's side and we drove back to campus. He dropped me off and said he would call me later on to check up on me. I walked into my room and Hailey was lying on her bed watching TV.

"Where have you been? You never texted me back last night."

"I ran into Hunter as I was leaving. He wouldn't let me go by myself so I stayed with him last night." I sat down on my bed and kicked my shoes off. "When did you get back?"

"Last night. I felt bad about you coming home alone after what happened at the party. Now I wish I hadn't."

"Sorry, I should have texted you." I really did not want to know but asked anyway. "What happened after I left last night?"

"I don't think you want to know Kenzie." She looked over at me then continued, "You really need to open your eyes, and see what is going on. He's not the same guy he was when you first started dating."

"Just tell me what happened? I feel him changing too, but I need him. I know you don't understand."

"That girl he was dancing with..." When I nodded at her, she continued. "He stormed off with her after you left. A little while later, they came back."

I gazed over at the picture of Dominic and me on my desk, remembering all the fun times I had with him. "Do you think he cheated on me?"

"Kenzie look at me." I turned towards her, tears on the verge of spilling. God, I hope he did not. "No, not that I saw anyway, and don't you dare cry. He isn't worth the tears. I mean it."

After talking with Hailey, I took a long hot bath. As I was relaxing in the bath, I checked my phone since I had not checked it since this morning. I had two text messages. One from my mom, making sure I was coming home for Thanksgiving. She wanted to plan Chloe's baby shower for that weekend, since that was when we would all be home together before she had the baby. The other one was from Dominic this morning, asking if we could talk.

A few hours later, I was getting hungry. I decided to text Dominic to see if he wanted to grab some pizza, and come over to talk. He responded back saying yes, and that he would see me soon.

About an hour later, he knocked before he came in. "Baby?"

I sat up in bed and pulled my ponytail tighter. "I'm here."

He put the pizza down on my desk, and came to sit next to me, "I don't know exactly what happened last night, but we need to figure it out. I can't lose you because of a misunderstanding."

I scowled at him. "You sure didn't seem too concerned about it last night; you and that bitch were fucking dry humping each other. How could you do that Dominic, ten minutes after I gave you a blow job?"

"She's my roommate's girlfriend babe." He reached over and put his hand on the back of my neck. I pushed his hand off. "Remember the girl that came over the other night?" I nodded, remembering exactly whom he was talking about. "That was Brittany; she's no one, no reason to get upset."

"She sure didn't seem like she is a no one. Not to mention, you made me look like a complete fool in front of your friends. You didn't even come after me when I tried to leave. I ran into Hunter, and he made me crash in his room because I was a little too drunk to go home by myself."

"No one thinks you're a fool. He made you crash in his room? Where the fuck did he sleep?" He stood up and started pacing in front of me.

I knew I was being spiteful. I could not help but gloat at my payback for his acting like an asshole, so I told him the truth. "Where else would he sleep, but in his room, with me."

"You have got to be fucking kidding me." He yelled.

"Maybe you should have been the one to make sure I was ok to get home, instead of worrying about that skank."

"I'm sorry Kenzie. I acted like a fucking idiot. I drank too much. I love you, and only you." He came over and cupped my face.

Sighing, I said, "I'm scared Dominic. I feel like you are changing, and I'm going to end up getting hurt."

"I'm not going to hurt you, I promise. Come on; let's eat before it gets any colder." He kissed my head, then put a slice of pizza on a plate and handed it me.

While we were eating, Dominic mentioned that he was not going to have a lot of time to spend with me, now that football was picking up. I told him I was going to look for a part time job to keep me busy. He agreed that would be a good idea, and offered to let me borrow his car to go job hunting. Times like this, I wished I had brought my own car. Dad had suggested I leave it home, since I really would not be using it. He figured that Dominic and Hunter would be here to help me out if I was stuck. Dominic stayed and watched a movie with me, and then he went back to his room to sleep since he had to be up so early in the morning.

Later that night, when Hailey came back, I asked if she wanted to go out with me tomorrow and look for a job. She agreed, saying she could use some money with the holidays coming up. She could not rely on her mom to help her out, since she was already helping her so much with school.

The next afternoon, Hailey and I got all dressed up and went out looking for jobs. Dominic had slid his key under the door as he said he would. We applied at a few local coffee shops that were within walking distance, and they all said they would get back to us. We stopped at a few places at the mall too, which were not too far from the dorm.

By the time we were done, Hailey and I were both hungry, so we decided to stop at the little café near campus. We ran into Gracie while we were there.

"Why don't you try the library? They are always looking for people. All the good shifts are probably taken, but it's worth a try." Gracie said.

Hailey looked over at me and knew that I would not last at a job like that. I always needed some kind of noise. This was something outside of what I would normally do and I needed to give it a shot. "Thanks. I think I'll stop over there tomorrow on my way home from class."

"Kenzie, you will never last at that job." Hailey said, shaking her head.

"I will be fine, plus if they hire the both of us, I won't have to worry about the quiet with your mouth always running." I said, smiling at her, because she knew I was right.

"With it being a Sunday, it's pretty quiet over there; you could try and see if anyone could talk to you now." Gracie smirked at Hailey. "I think Logan is working, actually." As I said, Hailey's mouth was always running, so I was not surprised Gracie knew about Logan.

Hailey practically jumped from her seat. "Running into Logan sounds good to me, so let's go."

When we walked up to the building, she turned to me. "Let me do the talking and we'll both have jobs." She winked, and then walked in.

There was a nerdy looking girl with pigtails and glasses sitting behind the desk. We walked up to her, and Hailey asked if she knew where we could find Logan. The nerdy girl looked from Hailey to me, then back again to Hailey. Then she pointed to a row of shelves to the right of where we were standing.

Hailey grabbed my arm and practically dragged me in the direction the girl pointed. We looked down the first couple of rows and did not see him. Finally, we found him in the last row; he was standing there with his back to us. We walked down the aisle towards him, but Hailey stopped dead in her tracks.

I nearly ran into her, but she turned to look at a book. She shushed me, and shifted her eyes to Logan and then back at me.

"Leave her the fuck alone Britt. She doesn't know anything about you." Logan said this just loud enough for us to hear. Hailey looked at me with wide eyes.

"He needs to tell her. I should have done it the night I showed up and she was in his room." Brittany said.

I raised my eyes brows at Hailey and she did the same to me.

Logan turned around, right as Hailey turned to look at him. "Oh, hey Hailey, what are you doing here?" He leaned back a little so that I was in his view. He cursed under his breath, and looked back at Brittany before acknowledging me. "Hey Kenzie."

"Hey Logan." I glared over his shoulder towards Brittany. She looked like she was caught doing something she was not supposed to be doing.

"We were looking for a book on..." Hailey grabbed a book off the shelf. "Ah, here it is, *The Big Book of Lesbian Horse Stories*."

Way to go Hailey. She was making this even more awkward. I snorted, and turned to walk away. I heard Hailey say something to Logan in a hushed voice, and then heard her groaning as she came up behind me.

"Let's never come into the library again, unless it's absolutely necessary." Hailey said.

I stopped and looked at her. "We came here to get a job, Hails. I'm at least trying. What did Logan say?"

She squeezed her eyes shut. "Nothing. Just go fill out the application with nerdy girl so we can get the hell out of here. I need a drink."

I asked the girl for an application, which she provided, and I filled it out while Hailey walked off to hide from Logan. I finished and handed in the application, found Hailey and went to the dorms. We stopped at Dominic's first, so I could drop off his keys. When we walked in, I went over to his desk to write him a thank you note.

"Um, Kenzie, what the hell is that?" Hailey said, pointing to a pair of panties on the floor by Dominic's bed.

I was dumbfounded. What the hell were those panties doing by his bed? They sure as shit were not mine. Dominic would not be stupid enough to bring someone here, would he? Was he cheating on me? I know everyone thought he was up to something, but I always brushed it off because he was so different when we were together.

After staring at them for what felt like forever, I looked at Hailey and said, "Come on. I think we both need that drink."

"Already taken care of. I texted Hunter; he's on his way." Hailey grabbed my hand to lead me away from the panties.

"Have I ever told you I love it when you take care of me?"

She nodded at me, but stopped suddenly. "Now what?" I asked.

She dropped my hand and walked back to the desk; she grabbed the pen, bent down to pick up the panties with it and then dropped them on the keys. She grabbed my hand again, and then said, "Now we can go."

Chapter Seven

When Hailey and I made it downstairs, I noticed in the corner of my eye that Dominic was walking towards us. I yanked on Hailey's hand and practically ran to Hunter's truck.

"In a hurry?" Hunter asked, with a sly grin on his face.

"Yeah, hurry up, Dominic's on his way over." I told him, still making a point not to look out the window in Dominic's direction.

Hunter looked in his rear view mirror at Hailey. "Where are we headed?"

"Anywhere away from the asshat." Hailey told him, pointing her thumb in Dominic's direction. I tensed a little, thinking about what Dominic would see when he made it to his room.

Hunter put the truck in drive and pulled away from the curb. "Then we're going back to my place. I don't really feel like going out anywhere."

The rest of the drive was fairly quiet, with just the sound of Hailey humming to the songs from the back seat. I heard my phone buzzing from my purse on the floor, and I knew it was Dominic. I sat there pondering what he would say when I finally did talk to him. They belonged to his roommate's girlfriend. That was not going to fly this time. Why would they be on his side of the room?

Hunter pulled me from my thoughts by placing his hand on my bare leg. This caused an electric shock to run through my body and I could not hold back the shiver. "You ok?"

I looked around, and noticed we were in his driveway. I gave him a tight smile, and climbed out of the truck.

"Movie and popcorn?" Hunter asked. He walked beside me into the house.

"And ice cream," I whispered back.

"And shots, lots of shots," Hailey said from behind me.

When we walked into his kitchen, Hunter went over to the cabinet and grabbed a bag of popcorn. Hailey went over to the bar in the living room to grab shot glasses and vodka. I went to the freezer to get the ice cream. When I opened the freezer door, a small smile formed when I noticed he had my favorite kind, Ben and Jerry's Chunky Monkey.

I put the ice cream down on the counter, and noticed Hunter staring at me. I smiled at him and mouthed, "Thank you." He winked at me.

"So, I say a shot every 10 minutes for the next hour, and then we should be good to go home, right Kenzie?" Hailey asked, while pouring the vodka in our shot glasses.

"Um, I don't think you two are going anywhere tonight." Hunter said, taking the popcorn out of the microwave.

"I don't have any clothes here, and we have class in the morning." I said to Hunter and then to Hailey. "Remind me again, whose idea it was to have a Monday morning class?"

"You picked the classes, not me, sweetheart." She picked up her shot glass, downed it, poured another one and then said, "Well come on, let's get this party started."

Hunter and I picked up our shots and downed them with her. After wiping my mouth with the back on my hand, I dished my ice cream into the bowl. Hailey grabbed the bottle of vodka, Hunter grabbed the popcorn and we went to the living room to watch Super Troopers. We needed a good laugh after the last hour.

Halfway through the movie, Hailey had fallen asleep in the recliner, cuddled up with the bottle of vodka. Hunter was on one end of the couch, and I was comfortably lying across the rest of the couch with my head on Hunters lap. He had grabbed a blanket from his bed for me, and I wrapped up tightly in it. I was starting to doze in and out when his phone started vibrating in his pocket.

Hunter shifted slightly, and reached into his pocket to get his phone. I started to sit up so he could reach it, but he held my head lightly in place, and pulled his phone out. Groaning, he hit the reject call button and put it on the arm of the couch.

He was just about to say something, when his phone started going off again. He exhaled loudly, and showed me that it was Dominic who had called. I shook my head, and he rejected the call again. I laid my head back down on his lap, and snuggled a little tighter in the blanket.

About ten minutes later, his phone buzzed again. He picked it up, and answered it this time. "What's up, Coop?"

I lifted my head from his lap, and sat up. I mouthed, "I'll be right back." He nodded his head.

I went into the kitchen, grabbed my purse from the counter and searched for my phone. I saw that I had 26 missed calls, 2 voicemails and 6 text messages, all of them from Dominic.

I read through a couple of the texts where he was saying they weren't his, it's not what it looked like, he was sorry and just to call him, he could explain everything.

I dialed Dominic's number, ready to get this over with.

He answered right away. "Baby, it's not what it looked like. Those were Brittany's. You can talk to her. I told her she can't do shit like this." He was rambling. He rambled a lot when he was hiding something.

"Dominic, I need a break. This isn't working. I feel like you're hiding shit from me."

"Ok, a break. I can do a break. I just can't lose you." He sounded defeated.

"No calling, no texting, no nothing. I need time." Then I hung up, and turned off my phone. I put it back in my purse, and started walking back to the living room when Hunter came around the corner, still on the phone.

"Mase wants to talk to you." He handed me the phone.

"Hey Mase, what's up?" I tried to sound cheery. I did not want him to think that I was upset about my fight with Dominic.

"I'm coming down there in a few weeks. Make sure you don't have any plans," he told me.

"You know, it wouldn't hurt to ask me nicely." I huffed.

"Kenzie, you're lucky I'm not down there now." He said through his teeth.

"What the hell is that supposed to mean?" I asked, and looked up at Hunter, who was leaning against the fridge.

"You think he wouldn't tell me what that asshat is putting your through?" Mase was pissed. He never did like Dominic, and this was just enforcing the reasons behind his hatred.

"I'm a big girl Mase. I can handle myself. Look, I have to go. Hunter's phone is about to die. Love you." I hung up before he could even respond.

"Nice." Hunter said, catching his phone as I threw it at him.

I opened the sliding glass doors, and walked down the stairs towards the beach. I needed to clear my head.

Could I believe what Dominic was saying? Maybe. Maybe not. I knew he was busy with football, and that it took up a lot of his time. If he had no time to hang out with me, did he have time for someone else? Maybe. Maybe not.

I realized that he was not the same guy that I started dating a year ago. He was changing a lot. I was changing. We were growing apart.

"Hey." Hunter said, putting his hands on my shoulders from behind me.

"Hey." I tilted my head to look up at him.

"You ok? You know, I didn't have a choice in telling Mason. I was avoiding his calls. He knew something was up, that's why he got Coop to call." He was trying to defend himself but there was no need. This was my family, and nothing was ever going to change.

"I know." I looked out over the ocean. "I told Dominic I needed a break."

"I kind of heard. I was coming to give you the phone, but figured you needed a minute." He started massaging my shoulders. God that felt good. "You're so tense CC. Relax."

I tried to relax, and enjoy the feel of his hands on me. As soon as I did, I felt the tears in my eyes. Trying hard not to think about either him or Dominic, I put my hands on his hands and brushed them off. He did not know that he was making this harder on me. I wanted to run into his arms. I wanted him take all the shit Dominic was causing away, but he could not, because he would not.

I walked down to the ocean. The waves crashed around my legs. It was freezing, but I did not care. I was already numb. I kept walking until I could not reach the bottom anymore. Hunter came up behind me and grabbed me, pulling me to him. I wanted this, and I just did not have the energy to push him away anymore tonight. I let him hold me, as the current pushed us around. After a while, I started shivering, and we made our way back to the house.

Hailey was still sound asleep in the recliner when we walked into the living room.

"I think we should leave her here. I'll grab a blanket from my room," Hunter said, and walked off towards the stairs.

I decided to follow him up so I could borrow some of his clothes, and get out of these wet ones.

I pushed his door open and walked in. "Can I borrow some of your clothes again?"

"Yeah, help yourself. T-shirts are in the second drawer, boxers are in the first." He said from inside his walk in closet. "I'll be back, so you can change in here." He walked out with a blanket for Hailey.

I grabbed one of his t-shirts and a pair of boxers and quickly changed. I walked over to his closet, and grabbed another pillow and blanket for myself. When I opened the closet door, there were pictures of the two of us together from a few summers taped to the door. As I was standing there staring at them, he walked in.

"Um," He took a deep breath, and then continued, "Do you want to sleep in here, or downstairs with Hailey?"

I turned to look at him, but did not say anything for a long moment. "Why do you have these in here?"

"It's just pictures CC." He said, as walked back towards his dresser.

I did not say anything else. I just shut the closet door.

He reached in one of the drawers, grabbed a pair of boxers and walked into the bathroom. A second later, he came out wearing just boxers and walked to his bed.

"You staying here, or downstairs?" He asked me again.

I didn't answer him. I just walked over to the bed, pulled the covers down and climbed in. Hunter reached over to the side table and turned off the lamp, then climbed into bed. I knew he was uncomfortable because he could not stop moving.

"Am I making you uncomfortable?" I asked him, after he started shaking his foot, making the whole bed move.

"No, why?" He asked.

"Because, you are shaking the whole bed with your foot. I don't mind sleeping down stairs."

"No, you are fine." He turned on his side facing me.

I was never going to be able to sleep with him watching me. I turned away from him, but that was not making me any more comfortable. I knew what I wanted, but I only wished he would do it. He must have read my mind because he reached for my hip, and pulled me towards him.

"Is this ok?" He whispered in my ear.

I nodded, and snuggled a little closer. That was exactly what I needed, and within minutes, I was fast asleep.

Chapter Eight

The next morning, I woke up to something tickling my feet. Trying to kick it away so I could go back to sleep, I heard someone say "Shit."

I sat straight up. "Sorry Hails." Looking around, I was very confused for a minute, and then I realized where I was. "What time is it?"

"Six-thirty. I thought I should wake you up so we can get back to the dorm and get ready for class." She said, rubbing her wrist that I kicked.

Groaning, I flopped back down in bed, threw the pillow that was next to me and hit Hunter with it. "Hunter, get up."

"I am up." He said, as he started to sit up against the headboard. He took the pillow I threw at him and put it over his lap.

Hailey started laughing hysterically. I sat up and glared at her. "What the hell is so funny?"

Wiping the tears from her eyes, she pointed to the pillow on Hunter's lap. "That is." Then she turned, and walked away, still laughing.

Hunter moved the pillow to get out of bed, and I saw what Hailey had laughed at. I started laughing. "You know, I can help you with that."

"Laugh it up." Hunter said, as he walked to his dresser to put on a pair of jeans.

I finally calmed down enough to get out of bed. I went into the bathroom to relieve myself and throw some water on my face. Remembering my clothes were soaked and there was no way I could wear them home, I went back into the bedroom and found Hunter leaning up against his dresser.

"My clothes are still soaked. Can I borrow a pair of sweats?"

He shook his head and started laughing, "No. It looks like you are wearing that back."

I just shrugged my shoulders. "Fine by me." Then I walked away, swaying my hips.

I heard Hunter groan, and a minute later, his drawer slammed shut. I sat down at the kitchen island where Hailey was eating cereal.

"So, did you talk to Dominic last night?" She asked, putting a spoonful of cereal in her mouth.

"Yeah, I told him I needed a break. I need time to think."

"Humph," was her response.

I turned to look at the clock on the stove, and then looked back at Hailey. "We need to get going; I need a shower before class starts."

I got up out of my chair to grab my cell phone from my purse. She got up as well, placed her bowl in the sink and went into the living room. Hunter came into the kitchen, threw a bag and a pair of sweat pants at me.

"That's what I thought." I said, laughing at him.

He glared at me. "I'll be in the car."

Hunter dropped us off, and said he would call us later. Hailey and I got ready and headed off to class. I did not see Dominic all day; I guess he was giving me the break that I asked for. During the week, football took up a lot of his time, but a small piece of me was hoping he would at least try to talk to me.

The rest of the week went by, and I did not hear from or see Dominic. Hailey was trying to keep me busy, but his lack of trying stung a little. I had hoped I would have heard back from the library by now, but nothing yet. By the end of the week, I needed to go out and have a little fun.

Hunter called Friday afternoon and asked what we had planned for the weekend. We made plans to hang at his house since he did not have to work. I hung up and told Hailey to pack a bag. Hunter would be here in a half hour. As we were on our way out, we ran into Dominic in the hallway. I looked up at him, but he looked down at the ground and walked away.

When we got into Hunter's truck, I was immediately hit with the scent of his cologne. I was not the only one that noticed. Hailey said, "Damn Hunter, you have a hot date or something?"

"Ha-ha, smartass, no, but we are going out tonight." Hunter said, casting a glance over to me.

"What? Where?" I asked.

"The bar where I work."

"I didn't know that is where you worked. We didn't pack anything to wear." I looked behind me at Hailey. "Let's run back in."

We ran back in. I grabbed my black mini, lime green and black tank top and my black pumps. I also grabbed the white dress that Hailey loved, and my white heels, and threw everything in a bag. Hailey had a bag with our makeup, hairspray, straightener and everything else we would need to get ready. Five minutes later, we were walking back out to the truck just as Brittany opened the door to our dorm, crying. Hailey mumbled, "Bitch," under her breath as she pushed me past her.

When we arrived at Hunter's, we took over his room so we could start getting ready. I jumped in the shower while Hailey started pre-gaming. I loved Hunter's bathroom; it was huge. There were three showerheads that sprayed your entire body and the shower itself was big enough to have five people stand in it.

When I finally pulled myself out of the shower, I walked out into the bedroom in just a towel. Hunter stopped mid-sentence when he noticed me. Smiling to myself, I walked over to the bag by his leg, grabbed my black thong, black bra, mini and tank top and walked back into the bathroom to change.

When I came back out, Hailey went in to take a shower. I started blow drying my hair so it would be ready to straighten when she got out. Hunter was watching me intently the whole time.

"Does it always take you guys this long to get ready?" He asked from where he was perched on the bed.

"Perfection takes time." I answered and winked at him.

An hour later, we were ready to hit the bar with Hunter. When we pulled up, the parking lot was packed. There was a line at the door, but Hunter went right past it. He walked up to the bouncer and did the guy handshake he did with my brothers all the time.

"CC, Hailey, this is my boy Zeke. He does my tattoos."

Zeke was your typical bad boy: tall, dark hair, brown eyes, covered in tattoos and piercings.

"So this is CC, huh?" Zeke asked Hunter.

"Yeah, this is her." He looked at me and winked.

Zeke grabbed my hand, lifted it to his mouth, placed a kiss on it and then did the same to Hailey. That is all it took and I knew Hailey was done for.

I was right. She looked at me with a dreamy look in her eyes. Shaking my head, I looked over at Hunter. He nodded his head for me to walk in first.

We made it to the bar and Hailey asked Hunter, "Does he do piercings too?"

"Yeah, he does it all." Hunter answered.

Hailey looked at me and before she could even ask, I said to Hunter "Can you take us to go see him this weekend?"

"Yeah, I can get him to hook you up." He looked at the door and then back at me.

When he noticed me smiling innocently, his eyes widened. "What?" I asked.

He squeezed his eyes shut and then opened them. I could see the battle he was having with himself. "Nothing."

Hunter smiled his pantie-dropping smile at the bartender, and she came over. "Hey hot stuff, what can I get ya?"

"I'll take my normal." He looked at me and winked, then looked back at the bartender. "And a Sex on the Beach and a Cosmo."

"You got it." She turned away to make our drinks.

I started to blush thinking about actually having sex with Hunter on the beach. I should not be thinking that way with all the shit I was dealing with Dominic about, but I could not help it. I glanced over at Hailey, and she just smiled at me.

After a few drinks, Hailey said, "Come dance with me." I grabbed her hand, and we walked out onto the dance floor.

We danced for a couple of songs and this ugly guy started trying to move in on us. He could not dance to save his life. I was not in the mood for this shit tonight. I looked over at Hunter, begging him with my eyes to come save us, and he just winked at me. The jackass winked! I shook my head and continued dancing with Hailey again, as the ugly ass guy tried to dance between us.

I had my back to Hunter. Someone grabbed my hips and pulled me to them. I tried to turn and punch this guy in the face, hoping that he would get the picture but then the hands on my hips gripped tighter into my skin. "You're driving me fucking crazy." I immediately relaxed when I realized it was Hunter.

I looked over my shoulder at Hunter. "Yeah, well you deserve it. Why didn't you come out here earlier?"

Hunter started grinding his hips into my ass. "That's why."

Thank God I was already flushed from dancing, because if not, it would be downright embarrassing. I looked to the side and saw that Hailey was dancing with Zeke. He was whispering something in her ear, and she threw her head back laughing.

"This is dangerous, you know." Hunter said just loudly enough for me to hear.

I froze for a second, and then spun around so I was facing him. I was waiting for him to pull away, but he put one arm around my waist, put his knee between my legs and he started to move to the beat again.

We danced like this for what seemed like forever. I was so lost in him that nothing else mattered to me. I forgot all about my problems with Dominic. I forgot about him caring what my brothers thought. This right here was what I wanted more than anything; I just wished he was mine forever.

Hunter moved the hand that was on my hip to my lower back, and then ever so slowly, started to move it down to my ass. I moved closer to him, if that was even possible, and buried my face in his neck. As I placed a kiss on Hunter's neck, I heard him suck in a breath. I pulled my face back and looked at him, but he was not looking at me. He was looking past me. I turned my head to see what he was looking at, and that was when I saw Dominic glaring at me.

"Shit!" I said as I let go of Hunter, and spun around to face Dominic.

Dominic walked over to me and grabbed my arm tightly. I knew I would have a bruise by morning. "Ow! Dominic you're hurting me. Let go." I tried to yank my arm free.

"What the fuck do you call that MacKenzie?" He seethed through his teeth while still glaring at Hunter.

"We were just dancing. Relax and let go of my damn arm." I said, trying to pry his fingers off me.

"Let her go Dom." Hunter demanded.

Dominic let go of my arm, then said, "You said you needed a break. I give you your space, and this is what you fucking do?"

"I wasn't doing anything." I said.

"Bullshit. We're leaving." Dominic stated, and reached for my hand.

"I'm not leaving with you like this. Calm the hell down. You have no right to be pissed off. I found fucking panties in your room. You didn't find boxers in mine." I yelled back at him.

He did not respond. He just pulled me towards the front door. I looked back to Hunter who was following me, and shook my head no. I did not want them to fight, and I knew that was where this was leading. When we made it outside and around the corner into an alleyway, Dominic pushed me up against the wall hard and crushed his lips to mine.

He groaned as he tried to deepen the kiss, and once his tongue swept into my mouth, I knew he had been drinking. I could taste the alcohol in his mouth. He fisted his left hand in my hair while his right hand reached down to the hem of my skirt. I squeezed my legs closed and pushed back on his chest, trying to get him to stop. Finally breaking the kissing, I yelled, "Damn it Dominic, what the fuck?"

Dominic dropped the hand that was on my upper thigh, and took a few calming breathes before he spoke. "You have no idea what you do to me. We need to get the fuck out of here."

"Hailey is in there. I'm not leaving without telling her first." Did he really think I was just going to leave with him?

"Fine, we'll go in and tell her we are leaving. And you're going to tell that prick to stay the hell away from you." He said.

"I'm not telling him to stay away from me. He didn't do anything wrong. We were just dancing." I said following behind him back into the bar.

He stopped right before he got to the door. "He wasn't doing anything? You're kidding right? He had his hands all over you, Kenzie." He ran his hands through his hair and pulled on it. "I know he has feelings for you. I've known for a long time. He will never pick you over your brothers. He's just using you."

I did not respond to him. I just walked past him, and opened the door to go tell Hailey I was leaving. I knew Dominic was right. Hunter would never be disloyal to my brothers. I was pissed at Dominic for bringing that up; I was pissed at myself for even thinking that tonight would mean anything to Hunter. I was only asking for more heartache.

Finally making it to Hailey, I told her I was leaving, and asked if she could grab my things from Hunter's, and bring them back with her. She told me she would, and that she would see me in the morning. As I was heading back to Dominic, Hunter stepped in my way.

"Where are you going?" He asked with a slight panicked look on his face.

"I'm leaving with Dominic. Tonight shouldn't have happened. You know that Hunter." I tried to step around him, but he stopped me.

He just stared at me as if he wanted to argue with me, but he did not say anything. That just pissed me off even more. I wanted him to tell me I was wrong, but he did not, he never would.

"You need to stay the hell away from me Hunter. You can't keep playing these head games with me. One minute, you are flirting and acting like you want me, then the next you are pushing me away. I'm tired of the back and forth." This time when I moved around him, he let me.

As Dominic and I made our way back to campus, neither one of us said anything to each other. I was pissed at myself for letting Hunter get to me. I was pissed off at Dominic for not being the boyfriend he used to be. When we pulled up to the dorms, I got out of Dominic's car, slammed the door shut and ran right to my room, locking the door behind me. Dominic tried knocking, but I did not answer and eventually, he left.

Chapter Nine

The next morning when Hailey came home, she was pretty quiet; I did not have much to say either. What would I have said? I freaked out because I was losing Dominic, and he pointed out the fact that Hunter would never want me. I wanted to know what happened after I left, but what would it have changed? Nothing. I just needed to get over Hunter, concentrate on Dominic and hope things would work out.

Hailey had made plans to meet up with Zeke from the bar last night, and she asked if I wanted to go along. I told her was not in the mood to go out, and that I was going to spend a quite night in bed reading. She told me I had until Monday to sulk, and that would be it. If I was not over my shit by then, she was calling my brothers. I promised her things would be ok. I just needed a little time by myself.

On Monday afternoon, I received a phone call from the library offering me a job. The only down fall was that it was from 6 p.m. until midnight, Monday through Thursday. I accepted the job because I needed time to myself and the distraction would be good for me. I was starting the following Monday, and Logan, of all people, would be training me.

When Hailey came back after her last class, I told her about the library job, and that Logan would be the person training me. She just shook her head and told me to watch my back. She had not talked to him since that day in the library and I was actually surprised by that, especially since she kept going on about him from the first time they met.

As the rest of the week went by, I would go to class, and come straight back to the dorms. Hailey wasn't around much since she seemed to be hanging out at Hunter's lately. When I saw her, I would act like I was fine and that nothing was bothering me. I think she bought my act. If she did not, she was not calling me out on it.

Saturday night, I got my first text from Dominic. I guess our taking a break was not bothering him as much as it was me. I finally caved, and texted him that we needed to talk. I did not trust him one hundred percent, but I still missed him. I missed him holding me. I missed him being sweet and caring. I even missed all the football talk. I finally gave up on him texting me back, so I plugged my phone into the charger and fell asleep.

The new text message alert on my phone woke me from a deep sleep. Sitting up, I rub the sleep from my eyes only to see that I actually had two new messages. The first was from Mason, letting me know that he would be staying at Hunter's in two weeks. The second one was from Dominic. It came in around four this morning, and made no sense whatsoever.

I quickly sent Mason a text back letting him know that I had a new job, and that I would have to let him know what my schedule was like. I also let him know that I would make time to have dinner with him, Cooper and Jackson when they came. I did not want to tell him I was not speaking to Hunter. I then sent a text to Dominic to come over whenever he woke up.

I was drying my hair when I heard someone knocking; I turned the dryer off, and went to see who was at the door.

"Hey, I didn't think I would see you till later." I said to Dominic, opening the door wider so he could walk in.

"I'm actually surprised I'm up this early too. So, you wanted to talk?" He walked over to my bed and sat down.

"Yeah, I think it's about time. What do you think?" I said, taking a seat next to him.

"I don't really want to talk right now." He looked up at me with regret in his eyes. "Can I just hold you for a little while?"

I moved to lean against my headboard, and he did the same. He pulled me so I was cuddled into him, with my head resting on his chest.

"I miss this Kenzie. I miss you. Being here at school is so different from being at home," he said, as he kissed the top of my head.

I nodded my agreement, and he continued, "What you found in my room was Brittany's. I told my roommate he needed to keep his shit on his side of the room. I explained to him what you found, and he asked me to apologize to you." He grabbed my chin, and made me look up at him. "I can't lose you Kenzie."

"I miss us too; we worked when we were at home. Things are so different here, and I am trying to trust you, but it's hard. When I walked in, and saw those panties sitting on your side of the room, I didn't know what to think. I knew you couldn't be that stupid to leave them there in plain sight."

"I know that I wouldn't have known how to react if I found some guy's boxers in here either. Can we just put it behind us and move on?" He whispered the last part to me.

I watched, as his eyes grew heavy. "I'm trying Dominic, but you can't keep screwing up all the time. I've cut Hunter out, so you don't have to worry about him anymore."

"I love you baby." He blinked once, twice and then he was asleep. I put my head back down on his chest, and listened to his breathing. I laid there, thinking for a long time, before I finally fell asleep.

When I woke up, I lifted my head and looked at Dominic. He was still sound asleep. I must have slept for a few hours because now it was dark outside. I tried to get up without waking Dominic, but when I sat up, he grabbed my arm.

I turned to look at him and he smiled at me. "You're so beautiful."

Blushing, I shook my head, and turned away from him. "I'm not."

"You have no idea the feelings I get when I look into your pretty blue eyes."

This is the Dominic that I loved, the one who knew what to say to make me feel beautiful. This is the relationship with him that I wanted, not the one we seemed to be having lately.

"I love you. I'm sorry things have been so messed up for us lately."

I smiled at him and said, "Me too."

"I'm starving. You want to head out to grab something to eat?" He asked, stretching out on my bed.

"Yeah, I haven't been eating too well lately," I admitted to him. I never could eat right when something was bothering me.

"Baby we talked about this. You are too skinny now as it is. You need to eat."

"You know how I get. I'm starving now, so let's go."

We drove down to The Raven. This was becoming a favorite place of mine. The burgers there were to die for. When we arrived, Dominic asked to be seated by the windows. This was my favorite place to sit, and I loved watching all the people passing by. When we followed behind the waitress, I was surprised to see Hunter, Hailey and Zeke sitting at one of the booths.

Dominic stopped walking when he noticed them too. He turned his head to look at me. "You want to go somewhere else?"

"No, we're already here. I'm starving and I can't avoid him forever. He's practically family." I knew that with my brothers coming into town, I would not be able to avoid him while they were here.

"Alright, I guess you're right, I still don't like it though."

I leaned in, placed a kiss on his lips and said, "You don't have anything to worry about, I promise."

"I know. That still doesn't mean I have to like it." I knew it would be a while for him to get over what he saw and I knew I would be hearing about it again.

We continued to walk to the booth that the waitress sat us at, which happened to be right behind where they were sitting. Dominic kept walking but I stopped to say hi.

"Hey sweetie." Zeke said.

"What's going on?"

Hailey looked at me, trying to gauge my mood. "I'm fine," I said.

"Well since you're here and Zeke has to get back to work, let's go get our nose pierced." Hailey said practically bouncing out of her seat.

I looked over her head to Dominic who just shrugged his shoulder at me. I guess that was my answer.

"Alright, but we have to eat first. We're starving."

"Of course, we were just heading out. Zeke has to get back to work so Hunter and I will go take a walk. Text me when you're done." She stood up from the booth, gave me a hug and whispered in my ear. "He's a mess."

I nodded, and looked over at Hunter, sitting at the table with his head down. I think this was the longest we had ever gone without talking.

I took a few steps towards him and placed my hand on his shoulder, "Hey."

He looked up at me and my heart broke. He looked like shit and I could not fix it. We both knew nothing would ever come of our relationship, which is why I needed to stay with Dominic.

I started to move my hand from his shoulder, but he reached up to grab it. "I'm sorry." He said it just loud enough for me hear him.

"I know. Everything will be fine. We just need time." I winked at him and walked to my booth. I hated to see him like this but he chose them over me and now I am choosing Dominic over him.

Hailey, Zeke and Hunter left as I sat down to eat with Dominic. I ordered my favorite burger while he ordered wings. "So, you're going to get your nose pierced?" He asked while taking a drink of his soda.

"Yeah, Zeke is a friend of Hunter's. He's the same guy that has done all of Hunter's tattoos."

Staring at me for a minute, he picked up another wing and started to eat it. We really did not talk much after that. When the check came, he paid it while I sent a text to Hailey letting her know that we were ready.

We met Hailey and Hunter outside, and walked the few blocks down to Ocean Mystique where Zeke worked. The walk was insanely quiet and it was uncomfortable, to say the least. There was so much tension in the air.

When we walked in, Hailey and I went to the back of the shop were Zeke was setting everything up for us. Since the room was small, Hunter and Dominic waited out front. Hailey was very nervous after she saw all the stuff lying on the tray, and made me go first.

I hopped up on the table. Zeke walked over to me and asked which side. I pointed to my right. He took his marker, and made a dot where the stud would go. He handed me the mirror. I smiled, and said, "Perfect."

He went back over to his tray, grabbed the needle and the clamp and then turned around back to me. "Now the only thing that is going to happen is your eyes will water, and you will feel some pressure."

I nodded, understanding what he was telling me. He placed the clamp on my nose, and then said, "Now take a deep breath in." I did, and I felt the pressure of the needle going through my nose. "Now let it out."

He turned back around to his tray, grabbed the stud and then said, "You're going to feel a little more pressure." He was slowly sliding the needle out and putting the stud in.

"You're done, quick and painless." He handed me the mirror so I could check it out. I loved it.

"I want my tongue done, too."

His eyes shot up to mine as if I said something crazy.

"What?" I asked, shrugging my shoulder

"You sure? That one will hurt, and your tongue will be swollen for a few days."

"I'm sure."

Zeke walked out of the room to grab the bar bell, and when he came back, we did the same basic procedure all over again. When I was all done, I hopped off the table.

"You're turn." I said, smirking at Hailey.

She jumped up on the table. Zeke did the exact thing he did to me. When he finished, we walked out to the front of the store so we could pay.

I grabbed my wallet from my purse, and looked at Zeke, waiting for him to tell me how much I owed him. He shook his head, and looked over my shoulder. I turned around, and Hunter winked at me. Not wanting to piss Dominic off about Hunter paying, I turned back to Zeke and handed him money for a tip. That way, it looked like I paid.

I walked over to Dominic, put my arms around him and asked him what he thought.

"Looks cute. I like it." Then he leaned in to kiss me.

I pulled back a second later and said, "No getting carried away." Then I stuck my tongue out at him, and took off running and laughing, out of the store.

I heard Dominic groaning as he came up behind me. He put his hands on my hips, pulled me back to him and then he said, "Baby that is fucking sexy."

We said our goodbyes to Hunter and Hailey, who had come down on Hunter's street bike. How the hell did he get that down here? I got a little jealous of the fact that he was riding with her; he never let anyone ride with him but me.

On the way home with Dominic, I decided to tell him about my brothers' visit. Because everything seemed to be going better for us again, I did not want to start of hiding stuff from him.

"Babe, you know that I don't care about you hanging out with your brothers, but I have a problem with you being with Hunter."

"And I have told you a hundred times, you have nothing to worry about." I said, squeezing his hand as we were walking back to his car.

"It's not you, it's him. Just don't go anywhere alone with him, alright?" He said, squeezing my hand back.

"Promise." I was making a lot of promises lately; I just prayed that I could keep them all.

Chapter Ten

Everything was finally feeling back to normal with Dominic and me. We were spending a lot of time with each other. Cooper and Mason kept postponing their trip because of Jackson. Chloe was having some blood pressure issues with her pregnancy, and he did not want to leave her until he knew she was ok. Finally, after the third time rescheduling, Jackson just told Cooper and Mason to go without him. My brothers were arriving today. We had a whole weekend of shit to do while they were here. They were going to call me when they finally made it to Hunter's, and then we were all going to meet at Raven's to get something to eat.

I needed to do some studying since I would not have time this weekend. Hailey had been spending more and more time with Hunter and Zeke lately, but she was here today. I guess she was excited to see Mason, even though she would not admit it. She jumped in the shower since we still had a little while before we would meet up with everyone.

When she walked out of bathroom, I heard her sniffle. I looked up at her, and her eyes were all red and swollen.

"Hails, what's going on? Why are you crying?"

She just shook her, and walked over to her dresser, her back turned towards me. I got up and went over to her. I place my hand on her shoulder, and she just broke down.

"Please sweetie, tell me what is wrong."

She just shook her head again. I pulled her over to the bed and sat down; she curled up in a ball on the bed, and put her head on my lap. We stayed like this for a while. She cried and I ran my fingers through her hair. I knew she would talk to me when she was ready.

Finally, she started to calm down. I reached over and handed her a tissue. She wiped the remaining tears, sat up and played with the tissue in her hand.

Then she said so low I barely heard her, "I love Mason."

I knew it! "OH Hails, I already knew this." I reached over and hugged her. "You think I didn't notice all the sneaking around you were doing back home?"

She shrugged her shoulders.

"Why didn't you tell me before?"

Sighing, she looked up at me and said, "I didn't want you to get upset with me and freak out that I had a crush on your brother. I know you hated all the fussing the girls did at school over them."

"You are my best friend, and you are nothing like those girls were. I am glad you finally told me, but what about Zeke? You guys have been seeing each other a lot."

"We are just friends, and most of the time Hunter is with us. Zeke is fun to hang around with, and he helps keep my mind off Mason."

"So, I guess you're excited Mason is coming?"

"Hell yeah, I can't wait to see his sexy ass." I cringed and she started laughing.

Groaning, I said, "Ok here's the deal; if you're talking to me about my brother, I only want the PG version. I don't want nightmares."

She got serious, "So you are seriously ok with me and Mason? He seems to think you're going to have a problem with it."

"He may think I have issues, but I don't. I love you Hailey. I know you'll take care of him and that's all I can ask."

"I love you Kenzie." She hugged me again, and then asked, "How are things with Dominic?"

"Surprisingly, we haven't had any drama lately, and things are good. He's a little worried about me spending time with Hunter when he's not around." Dominic and I talked about it a lot last night, and I just kept telling him over and over again that he had nothing to worry about. I was not going anywhere.

"Well that's good." She looked down at her lap again and then back up at me. "Hunter misses you like crazy. I don't think I've ever seen him like this, not even after last summer."

I sighed. "I miss him too, but to keep Dominic happy, and my heart intact, I can't hang around him like I did anymore. He made it perfectly clear there could never be a him and me. Things are going good with Dominic. I don't want to rock the boat. Time will tell if Dominic and I will last, but for now, I want to be with him. He stood up to my brothers when he wanted to date me Hails. Hunter would never do that."

"I get it, I do. I just wish he would pull his head out of his ass, and figure his shit out. He looks like someone has kicked his puppy."

"He'll figure it out. He'll meet someone that will take over the feelings that he has for me."

Hailey fell back on her pillow and said, "I hope it's soon. He is such a downer. I thought I was bad. He's got it way worse than I do."

My phone pinged, so I got up and went to get see who it was. Cooper had texted me that they just got to Hunter's. They were going to swing by and pick us up, instead of us taking a cab.

Hailey and I got ready to spend the night with my brothers and Hunter; I made sure Hailey looked extra hot for Mason. We straightened her long blonde hair and did her eye makeup dark to bring out her eyes. She dressed in a pair of black shorts that were tight and really short, along with a hot pink halter top that made her boobs look great.

After we got her dressed, she helped me straighten my hair. I picked out something a little less sexy, but still super cute. I wore a short spaghetti strap sundress and a pair of peep toe wedges. It was the end of October but thankfully, it was still warm enough to wear my summer clothes.

I stopped by Dominic's room before I headed out for dinner. He told me to have a fun, and that he would see me at the party at Hunter's later on tonight. I stood on my tiptoes, gave him a kiss and told him I loved him and would see him later.

As soon as we walked out of the doors to our dorm, Hunter's head shot up, he nudged Mason and lifted his chin in our direction.

"Damn, he's hot," I heard Hailey say to herself. I shook my head and laughed at her.

"What?" She asked, with a smirk on her face.

"Not a thing. Now go get your lover boy," I told her.

"Don't have to tell me twice." She took off running to Mason and leaped on him. He caught her and swung her around.

Cooper and Hunter both looked at me. I assumed they were waiting for me to have some kind of reaction. What was the big deal? They are adults. He is my brother and she is my best friend. Even if things did not work out for them, I would still have them both in my life. Yeah, it may get weird but it is what it is.

Cooper wrapped me up in his arms and asked, "You're ok with that?" He looked over at them and grimaced. "Because I don't know if I am. She's like a sister to me."

"What's the big deal?" I said.

He shuddered after thinking about it. "I still don't like it. It's just weird."

I kissed his cheek and said "Well, get over it."

I walked over to Hunter and gave him a hug too. He clung to me as if I was going to disappear. He took a deep breath, like he had been holding it forever. "I'm sorry."

I pulled my face back, and looked into his bright blue eyes, the same eyes I dreamed about every night, even if he was the wrong person to dream about. I sighed, "It's ok. Why do you keep saying that? I get it; there will never be a me and you."

"I have a lot to be sorry for." He hugged me tighter, and then let go.

I turned around and went over to Mason and Hailey. They were still wrapped around each other. I cleared my throat. "Um, hello?"

Mason turned his head to me, and then lowered Hailey to the ground. "Hey sis."

I grabbed him and hugged him tight. "Love you, Mase." I lowered my voice so only he could hear me. "Don't hurt her, ok?"

"So you're ok with this?" He dropped his arms from around my waist, and took a step back. "It's not going to be weird or anything?"

"I don't understand why everyone thinks I'm going to have a problem with this. If you ask me, I think it's awesome. I may actually get my best friend as my sister in law." I winked over his shoulder to Hailey, and she smiled back at me.

"Whoa." Mason put his hands up, and had a frightened look on his face. "Who said anything about getting married? Let's not get carried away."

We all started laughing, and walked towards Mason's car. When I opened the door to climb in, Hunter grabbed my elbow, lifted his chin towards his bike and raised his eyebrow. I looked over at it and was surprised to see my helmet sitting on the seat.

I looked in the car at Hailey. "Go get it girl," she said, smiling at me.

How could I say no? I loved riding with him, loved the adrenaline rush from feeling free. I walked over and grabbed my helmet, then looked down at what I was wearing. Damn it, I wish I had worn shorts now. Oh well I was not going to back out now.

Hunter sat on the bike and balanced it, so I could climb on behind him; I did it as gracefully as I could. Once I sat down and had Hunter between my thighs, I tucked my dress under my legs so it would not fly up. I squeezed my legs around his hips, and wrapped my arms around his stomach. Hunter's stomach muscles tensed. I loosened up my hold, thinking he did not want my hands around him, but he grabbed my hands and held them there for a second.

What was I thinking? This was not a good idea.

I felt him take a deep breath, then let it out, then he dropped his hand from mine and started up the bike. We took off, leading the way to Raven's with Mason following behind us.

Dinner went great. Everyone was having a good time laughing and joking with each other, just like old times. Hunter and I even got along great, as if nothing had happened.

"Why didn't Jaylinn come?" I asked the boys.

"She had a soccer game this weekend." Cooper answered me, but stared at Hunter. Huh?

Trying to pry some details from Cooper, I asked him, "Are you spending a lot of time with her?"

"Yeah he is. He goes to every one of her home games, and tries to go to the away ones too," Mason piped up. I glanced over at Hunter who was glaring at Cooper, while Cooper was glaring at Mason. I found this entertaining.

"So, how are the parties down here Kenzie?" Cooper asked, trying to break the weirdness going on.

"Oh, you know normal college parties." I laughed, remembering the aftermath of the last party at Hunter's house. "The last party at Hunter's was a little crazy though. The house was trashed; there were people duct taped to couches and doors, and people colored with sharpie marker."

"No shit!"

"Yeah, you'll see the craziness tonight. Speaking of craziness, we should get over there and lock up the rooms," Hunter said while getting up from the booth.

Cooper paid the bill and we all walked out. I went over to Hunter's bike. I was putting my helmet on when he looked over at me. "Glad you got on with me. I didn't think you would."

What the hell did I just see?

"Stick your tongue out." I told him.

He wiggled his eyebrows at me and smirked.

I put my hands on my hips. "Stick your tongue out or I'm not getting back on."

"Why?" Then he ever so slowly stuck his tongue out, and licked his bottom lip.

I whimpered. Dear God, he got his tongue pierced.

Hunter looked over to Mason's car, where everyone was in and ready to go, then he smiled at me. "Now, get on so we can go for a ride."

Fuck me! I wanted to ride more than just his bike. Shit I should not be thinking of him like this.

I shook my head and climbed back on his bike; we made the ten-minute ride back to his place. When we pulled into the driveway, he had to maneuver his bike between the cars, so he could park in the garage. I climbed off, handed him my helmet and walked out before I found myself cornered with him alone. There was no telling what I might do to him at this point.

Everyone but Hunter walked down to the beach where the fire pit was going. "So, everything ok with you guys? It seems like everything is finally getting back to normal." Hailey said, as Mason and Cooper were talking about baseball to some guy sitting near us.

"It seems that way, but we'll have to wait and see. Oh, by the way, when in the hell did he get his tongue pierced?"

She snapped her head in my direction, "Did you kiss him?"

"Hailey!" I yelled. "Christ no. I saw it when he was talking to me."

Hailey took a drink of the beer Mason had handed her a few minutes ago. "Oh, okay, he got it that night we got ours done."

All of a sudden, Hailey, Cooper and Mason's phones chirped. What the hell? Hailey read hers, squeezed her eyes shut then turned to look at Mason. Mason looked livid. Cooper, my laid-back brother, looked as if he wanted to murder someone.

I stood up, and so did everyone else. "What the hell is going on?"

Mason spoke up first. "Nothing, we'll go handle it. Stay here with Hailey." Cooper and Mason walked off towards the house, leaving me standing there with Hailey.

"Hails, what's happened?" If someone did not tell me what was going on, I might really lose it.

"Just let Mase and Coop handle it. They'll come back in a few minutes and everything will be okay," she said, with a haunted look on her face.

She would not look me in the eyes, so something had to be wrong. We had only been here for all of twenty minutes. What could have happened that fast?

Then I remembered that Dominic was here. Oh God, he must have seen me on Hunter's bike. I looked at Hailey, then back at the house, and took off running towards the house after Mason and Cooper.

I made it inside and searched for them, but I could not see anything with all these people in here. I finally caught sight of the back of Cooper's shirt heading up the stairs.

I pushed my way through the crowd, and tried to make my way up the stairs when I heard the yelling. Shit, this was not good.

Mason saw me first, and held up a finger telling me to hold on. I stopped and waited for a second, and then I heard a girl crying. I went up a few more stairs so I could hear what was going on.

"FUCK!" I heard and instantly realized it was Dominic's voice.

I froze in place. Mason looked down at me again, and shook his head at me, telling me to not coming up any more.

"What did you think would happen Dominic?" I heard the girl's voice again.

"Not this. We were fucking careful. This isn't happening." Dominic shouted. There was a loud bang as if he punched something.

"Watch it Dom." Hunter said. He must have been the one that texted everyone.

"Yeah, I'm about to watch my girl walk out of my life for fucking good this time." Oh God, what did he do?

"You should have thought about that before you knocked me up, asshat," the girl said.

Wait, what did she just say? She is knocked up? I am about to walk out of Dominic's life? Then it all hit my like a ton of bricks. I quickly grabbed the back of Cooper's shirt as I started to sway. He turned around, grabbed me and pulled me up in front of him.

Standing there in the hallway were Dominic, Brittany, Hunter, Mason and Cooper. I took a deep breath and looked from Brittany to Dominic to Hunter and back to Dominic.

"Baby, oh God baby," Dominic said, walking towards me.

I put my hand up. "Stop, don't you dare come near me." I looked past him to Brittany, who was sitting on the floor with mascara and tears running down her face. "Your roommates girlfriend huh?"

Brittany laughed bitterly. "So that's what he told you."

"Shut up!" Dominic screamed at her. "Baby I can explain..."

I cut him off. "There's nothing to explain Dominic." I stood there for a second staring at him. Everybody else had their eyes on me. I had to get out of here.

"Mase, give me your keys," he reached in his front pocket and handed them to me.

"NO! Baby wait..."

"Let her go Dom." Cooper said.

I ran down the steps, pushed my way back through the crowd to the front door and right to Mason's car at the end of the driveway where Hailey was waiting for me.

I unlocked the door and got in. Hailey knocked on the window for me to unlock the door, but I did not pay her any attention. I started the car and left. I had to get out of here.

Chapter Eleven

I did not go home right away. I could not; they would be looking for me there. Normally I would have run to Hunter to vent, but not this time. I drove down Atlantic Ave to the parking lot for the beach. I locked up the car, walked down to the ocean and sat down in the sand, trying to process everything that had just happened.

Dominic cheated on me. He got Brittany pregnant. Brittany, his roommate's girlfriend, or at least that was what he had told me. He said he loved me and would never hurt me. Ha! I was stupid for believing him. I knew better. All the signs were there, but I choose to ignore them.

I was hurting, but I think what surprised me the most was the fact that he was stupid enough to get her pregnant. He came here on a full scholarship to play football. He barely had time for me. How would he have time to help raise a baby? Idiot!

He was not my problem anymore. He had made his bed and now he could lay in it.

Just when I thought things were going great with us, this had to happen. I had not seen Brittany since the day I had run out of the dorms, she had been outside crying. I bet she was on her way up to see Dominic. I thought back to that first night when I was with him. SHE had knocked on the door and he had told her that he was busy; I had known then that something was up, but I ignored it.

Fool me once, shame on you. Fool me twice, shame on me.

I bet he cheated on me with Alexis too, after he told me there was nothing going on with her.

I sat there for a while, throwing myself a pity party. I knew I needed to pull my big girl panties up and face the music. I just hoped I have the strength to keep up my brave face for everyone. Times like this, I wish I were home, in my own room, where I could block out the rest of the world.

When I got back into Mason's car, I lost it. Who did I think I was kidding? I felt tremendously crushed. I had thought things would work out with Dominic in the long run. I had really wanted things to work out between us.

I took a few deep breaths, wiped the tears from my face and drove back to my dorm. Everyone was there; I knew they would be. Hailey had curled up with Mason on her bed. Cooper was sitting on the end of my bed with his head in his hands. Hunter was pacing back and forth.

"I'm fine." That is all I said, all I could say as I tried to hold back the tears. I would let myself cry again, when I was in the shower.

Hunter stopped where he was and looked at me; I nodded my head at him. He was waiting for me to give him permission to comfort me. He came over, wrapped me in his arms and rocked me slightly back and forth, just as he had done all those times before when I needed him.

"You ok?" He whispered in my ear.

"I will be. It'll just take some time to get over the hurt."

I dropped my arms from around him, and I went to sit on my bed next to Cooper. He slung his arm over me, and kissed me on my head.

We all sat there for a little while, no one talking, everybody in their own world. This was not helping me; I needed to do something to keep myself busy.

I needed a shower; I needed to wash this whole night away. I got up from the bed, grabbed my things from my dresser but stopped instantly when I looked in the mirror, and saw Cooper's face. He had a gash by his eyebrow that was bleeding.

He looked at me when I asked, "What happened?"

He shook his head. "Nothing."

His answer did not surprise me. He had been protecting me. I just stood there, staring at him. "Tell me, please." I finally say, breaking the eye contact in the mirror.

"Nothing happened Kenzie." Mason spoke up for the first time since I walked in the door.

I looked over at him. I noticed that he had a tear in his shirt and there was blood on it. "Whose blood is that?"

Hailey untangled herself from Mason, came over to me and wrapped her arms around me. I did not move to hug her back. I was pissed off that she did not try to warn me about what was happening. She may not have known exactly what was going on, but she knew it involved me.

"I'm sorry." She told me, and then let go of me as she walked back over to Mason.

"You could have warned me that something was going down with Dominic, Hails."

"I know and I'm sorry. I was trying to look out for you. You would have gone after them if you knew."

She was right, but still, it hurt.

I walked into the bathroom to take a shower, and I hoped when I was finished, everyone would have left.

I turned the shower on as hot as I could stand it and got in. I stood there, letting the water run over my body. I finally cried all the tears that I had tried so hard to hold inside me. I curled up into the fetal position on the shower floor and stayed that way until the water ran cold. I got up, quickly washed myself, got out of the shower and threw on my sweat pants and hoodie.

When I finally worked up the courage to walk out of the bathroom and face everybody, I was surprised that no one was in the room but Hunter. I did not say anything to him as I walked over to my bed and climbed in. I pulled the hood of my sweatshirt over my head, and snuggled into my pillow. I just wanted to go to sleep and forget today even happened.

Hunter walked over and turned the lights off. I waited to hear the door open but it did not. He pulled my desk chair over to my bed and started to rub my back, trying to comfort me.

The tears came back and slowly fell down my cheeks and onto my pillow. I tried to wipe them away so that Hunter would not know that I was crying again.

I heard Hunter's phone beep with an incoming text. He stopped rubbing my back and pulled his phone out. He cursed under his breath and said, "Dominic is on his way over."

I did not answer him right away. I just sat up. "I need to talk to him." I looked at Hunter. "Alone."

"No." He deadpans.

I did not respond back to him. I was not in the mood for another fight. Maybe it would be good if Hunter stayed here with me. I do not want to be alone with Dominic.

I gathered all of Dominic's stuff that was here, his jersey that I loved to wear every Saturday, and a couple of his t-shirts that I slept in. I walked over to the mirror on my dresser and took off the pictures that had Dominic in them. I took off the ring that he bought me for my birthday. I needed to remove everything that tied me to him.

I heard a knock on the door and then yelling in the hallway that startled me. I thought everyone had left but they had not. They must have been waiting in the lounge, watching TV.

I looked at the door as it opened and Dominic walked in. He had a black eye, split lip and a gash across the bridge of his nose. I felt certain that his nose was also broken. Blood covered his shirt.

"Baby..."

I cut him off. "Don't baby me!" I seethed through my teeth.

"I can expl..."

"No, no you fucking can't." I cut him off again. "There is nothing to explain. What's done is done Dominic."

"She's lying, Kenz. She can't be pregnant. We used protection every time. It's not possible. Even if she is pregnant, it isn't mine."

I crossed my arms across my chest and looked to the floor. "It doesn't matter if she is or isn't. We are finished. You told me she was your roommate's girlfriend. Now you are telling me that you used protection every time. Was she really your roommate's girlfriend?"

He ignored my question.

"So I guess you're leaving me for this asshat now?" He asked, looking over at Hunter who still sat in the chair next to my bed.

"No, I told you that you could trust me. I kept my promises."

"Give me a break. Just give it time. Your piece of shit brothers can't stop you from doing everything. You'll run to him. It's just a matter of time."

"Watch it Dominic, you can talk all the shit you want to about me, but don't bring my brothers into this. We have had our own fucked up problems all along." I growled.

He walked over to me and I could see the defeated look in his eyes but I did not look away from him. I stood my ground; he hurt me in the worst way.

He looked down to the ground, then back up to me and then back down to the ground. He reached in his pocket, pulled a little black box out and then dropped to one knee.

Are you kidding me? Please do not let this happen. This cannot be happening.

He looked up at me, a single tear running down his cheek. Hunter cursed behind me. The chair scraped across the floor, the door opened and then slammed shut.

I scrubbed my face with my hands. "Please don't do this." I begged Dominic.

"Baby, I love you. I fucked up, but that will never happen again. I want to spend the rest of my life with you; I want to take care of you. I want to start a family with you, and grow old with you. You keep me grounded when I am with you; I feel like everything in the world is right. I don't have that feeling when I'm not with you; everything spirals out of control. MacKenzie, will you marry me?"

I started crying, so hard that I could not even make out what the ring looked like. I shook my head no, and I heard him whisper, "Please Kenzie?"

"I can't Dominic. You broke me. You broke us. You don't want to marry me."

I wiped my cheeks with the sleeves of my sweatshirt and knelt down in front of him, so that we were eye to eye. "You're not in love with me..." He started to argue but I placed my index finger to his lips to keep him quiet. "Yes, you love me but we're not in love with each other. I don't think we ever were."

I dropped my finger from his lips and his head followed my hand down to my side where my hands now rested. I stared down and saw tears hit the floor. I almost feel bad for him, almost.

I gave him a few minutes before I stood up and went over to my dresser where the bag of all his stuff was. I walked over to him. He stood up and I handed him the bag.

"I'm so sorry I fucked this all up."

"I'm sorry you did too."

He walked over to the door but turned back to look at me one more time before he walked out for good this time.

Chapter Twelve

After Dominic left, I turned the lights off and crawled back in bed just as I was before he came over. I just laid there and stared into the dark room when I heard the door open.

"Kenzie?" I heard a thump. Hunter must have walked into Hailey's bed. I picked up my phone from my bed and turned it on so he could see where he was walking.

"You ok?"

"I don't want to talk about it right now. I just want to go to sleep and forget this shit ever happened." I turned on my side and faced away from him.

I heard the chair as it scrapped against the floor. He sat down and started running his fingers up and down my back. I slowly drifted off to sleep.

My sleep did not last, and I woke up crying. I wiped the tears away and turned to see if anyone was still here. Hunter sat in the chair, gazing over at me.

He reached over to the nightstand and handed me some pain reliever and water. "Here take these." He knew me so well. He knew after a night like I was having, I would wake up with a pounding headache.

"Thanks. You don't have to sit there all night. I will be fine." I tell him.

"Yeah I do. Just try and get some more sleep." He was pissed. I could sense it. What was I supposed to do? This was not in my control.

I laid there for a while and eventually fell back asleep, but again, it was not for very long. At least this time when I woke up, I was not crying.

I looked over at Hunter and he still sat in the same place he had been since he walked in but now, his head rested on his hand and he was asleep.

I sat up and looked over at Hailey's empty bed; I got up and pulled her covers down. I walked over to Hunter and woke him.

"Hey, wake up." He stirred slightly and opened his eyes. "Come on. If you are going to stay here, sleep in Hailey's bed."

He got up, crawled into Hailey's bed and faced the direction of my bed. I got back into my bed and faced him. I knew he was not going to fall back asleep until I did, so I closed my eyes and pretended to fall back asleep. I laid there for what seemed like forever but then I heard Hunter's heavy breathing. I concentrated on breathing in and out and I eventually fell back asleep too.

When I woke up again, the sun was shining in my room. I got up and took another shower; my brothers did not come here to help nurse my broken heart. I had to pull myself together because we had plans to go to Busch Gardens today and I was going. I would have felt guilty for backing out on them. I knew they would understand, but I needed to get out of here anyway.

When I got out of the shower and got myself ready to go I opened the door and saw that Hunter was still asleep. I did not want to wake him but we had to get going.

I ran my fingers through his hair and ruffled it. "Hunter, come on get up; we have to go."

He stretched and yawned then looked at me and said, "We don't have to go; they'll understand."

Just the thought of sitting here and rehashing everything that had happened makes me want to cry again. "And what are we going to do? Sit here and stare at the walls? I can't do that; I can't sit here and cry."

We need to go.

"You sure you're up for it?" He asked still skeptical.

"I'm fine." I will be, at least for a little while. "Plus dad gave me money for an emergency and today is an emergency, so I'm using it."

"Alright, let's go back to my house so I can grab a quick shower."

When we got there, Mason, Hailey and Cooper were all upstairs still getting ready. It actually shocked me that party last night had not left the place trashed. There were still a few people asleep on the couch and a couple of pizza boxes and cups all over the kitchen, but nothing like the last party.

"That was a shitty thing that happened to you." Bentley said from the kitchen table.

"Yeah." Don't people understand that you normally don't want to talk about a break up? I did not want to be rude to him but I did not want to get into the details of what happened either, so I got up and walked out on the deck to get some fresh air.

I heard the sliding glass door open a few minutes after I walked out. "You ok?" Hunter asked, coming up next to me to lean on the banister.

"I'm fine."

"So I assume you told Dom no last night?"

Really? Did he think for a second I would tell him yes? "Definitely no."

Hunter reached out and tucked a piece of my hair behind my ear. He moved closer so that we were shoulder to shoulder. He grabbed my hand and we stayed like that until Mason came out and said, "What the fuck Hunter?"

I quickly swung around, wondering what I missed.

"What?" Hunter asked, looking around, trying to figure out what was going on.

"You know what. Stay the fuck away from her; she doesn't need to deal with anymore bullshit."

What the hell?

"Mase, what the hell is going on?"

"Nothing, come on let's go." He turned around and stormed off into the house.

I looked over at Hunter and he just shook his head and walked in behind Mason. What the hell was going on? I did not feel like dealing with anything else, so if this was how today was going to be, I would just go home.

"Hey, you ready?" Hailey asked me, peaking out the door.

"I guess, but what the hell happened last night? Mase damn near bit off Hunter's head."

"Don't worry about it. It's nothing they can't work out themselves."

I shook my head and followed Hailey out to Mason's car. During most of the drive to the park, Hunter and Cooper talked about the upcoming baseball season, but Mason and Hunter said nothing to each other. There was so much tension that I could not stand it; it was doing nothing to help my mood. I only felt slightly calmer when Hunter would brush my knee when he saw me glaring at the back of Mason's head, or when Cooper would make stupid jokes and we would all laugh. The only person Mason was talking to was Hailey.

We finally made it to the park, but when I tried to pay for the tickets using my emergency money, Hunter stopped me. "I got it." He took my card and put it in his back pocket.

"No, I got it. Give me my card back." I held my hand out.

"Just let him pay Kenzie." Cooper said from behind us.

I gave Cooper a dirty look but followed behind Hunter and walked into the park. I will find a way to get the money back to him whether he likes it or not.

We all had a great time at the park; that was exactly what I needed. I did not think about anything but the next roller coaster or the person who was going to jump out and scare me since we went on Halloween weekend.

There was still tension between Mason and Hunter but I just ignored it. I did not want our time here to end, I did not want to go back to the dorms to remember Dominic and I definitely did not want to run into him either.

Hailey must have read my mind, because she suggested we go back to Hunter's house, sleep over and watch movies until we pass out like we used to at home.

"Sounds good, Hailey, your bed is like sleeping on a cinder block. My shoulders are stiff as hell." Hunter complained.

"My bed is not. I love it. I sleep like a princess." Hailey said beaming.

"Maybe it had to do with the fact that you slept half the night in the chair." I added.

"Dude, I told you I would have stayed with her." Cooper commented.

"And I told you that it wasn't a good idea to stay with her Hunter." Mason said, walking up to us from the bathroom.

No one said anything after that; Hailey pulled Mason in front of us to make our way back to the car. I followed behind with Cooper and Hunter.

"Will someone please tell me what happened between you two?" I asked Hunter and Cooper.

Cooper looked down at the ground, but spoke up first. "Mason doesn't want you with Hunter."

I stopped walking but Cooper kept walking until he realized I had stopped. Hunter just kept on walking. Either he did not realize I had stopped, or he did not want to hear anymore.

"Wait a second, what are you even talking about? Hunter doesn't want me." I really must have missed something last night.

Cooper nodded his head. "Yeah he does. He told us last night." Coop glanced over to see my reaction.

Taken back by this, I said, "It doesn't matter if he does or not. There will never be a Hunter and me. He would not do that to you guys."

He told them he wanted me after he told me last summer there could not ever be an us? Why now, after Dominic broke my heart?

"You're right, it doesn't if he does or not. Mason still hates the idea. I don't have a problem with it as much as he does, but I still don't like it. I know he has always been there for you when we couldn't but you are our sister and it's just not right."

"Yeah well, you guys have nothing to worry about." I said as I stormed past Cooper.

When I caught up to Mason I nudged his shoulder and whispered, "You don't have anything to worry about," then glanced in Hunter's direction. Mason just nodded. I don't even want to think about being in a relationship with anyone at this point, even if the one person I wanted the most finally wanted me.

Arriving back at Hunter's house, Bentley was there with a few of his friends. They were going out for the night so he told us to make ourselves at home. Hailey pulled out the vodka that she had the last time we were here and poured me a shot. I looked over at her and gave her a small smile. She knew I was still a little upset and when I needed her, she was always there.

I went into the freezer and much to my surprise; Hunter had replenished my ice cream supply. I shut the freezer door and Hunter was standing there.

"Damn it, you scared me."

He smirked at me; they all loved it when they snuck up on me.

"You hanging in there?" He asked.

"Yeah. No tears today right?" I was trying my damnedest all day not to think of what I would have to deal with when I got back home.

He grabbed the ice cream from me and scooped some out for us. Cooper came in and wanted popcorn, so Hunter threw him the box to make while I went into the living room.

After everyone settled, we started the movie, but I didn't last long. I was exhausted from not getting much sleep and being at the park all day. I was awakened by someone running a finger from my temple down my neck and back again.

When I opened my eyes, Hunter was looking at me. I glanced around the room. Everyone was gone except Cooper who was asleep on the couch across from us.

I snuggled into his touch and asked, "Can you tell me what happened with you and Mason?"

He stared at me for a few minutes; it was as if he had to decide if he wanted to tell me or not. Then he finally said, "I told him I loved you and that I have for a long time."

My eyes went wide with surprise. "Why did you do that?"

"It just came out." He stared off into the other direction and then back at me. "I was pissed at Dominic for proposing to you. I lost it when I left your room."

I sat up; I could not believe this was happening now. God, I wanted him, but why now? This was too much, too soon. "You shouldn't have told them that."

"I know, I didn't mean to just blurt it out like that. Mason was pissed." He looked down to the ground. "I know you don't need to deal with any more shit right now."

"You're right. I don't, not now." I laid back down but turned away from him.

He sat on the floor next to where I was sleeping for a while, before I heard him say, "I'm sorry CC," then he got up to go back to his room.

Chapter Thirteen

The next morning when everyone got up, things seemed to be less intense between everyone. Mason seemed to be in a much better mood, and I am sure Hailey was to thank for that. We all hung around Hunter's until lunchtime when Mason and Cooper had to leave to go back to school.

We were all saying our goodbyes when Mason pulled me aside. I knew this was coming. "I don't like it, Kenz." He ran his hand through his hair. "I know you don't understand. You might be pissed off but I'm just protecting you. You just had your heartbroken; I don't want to see you go through that again."

"Mase..." he cut me off before I could finish telling him I agreed.

"I know what happened last summer. I heard all of it. I was there that night you thought everyone was gone."

Shit. How embarrassing that he heard me tell Hunter that I wanted him.

"I told Hunter to stay away from you. I know he broke your heart that night because he didn't have the balls to tell you back then that he loved you. I'm just protecting you."

This is why Mason and I had a love/hate relationship; sometimes he was too over protective. "Mase I love you, but sometimes you need to let me learn my own lessons. You can't always be here to protect me."

"Well, while I am here, I am going to protect you. Please, for me, just stay away from him, and give yourself some time. I know he told me he loves you but he hasn't told you."

He was right. Hunter did not tell me directly that he loved me. I understood where Mason was coming from. I was not ready to think about loving someone else right now. I needed to concentrate on me, no one else but me.

"Get over here and hug me goodbye."

I hugged Mason, then walked over and said my goodbyes to Cooper, and then they left to head back to Boston. Hailey and I went back inside to help clean up our mess and then had Hunter take us back to the dorms.

God, I did not want to go back there.

Before we left Hunter asked me to take a walk out on the beach with him for a few minutes. Hailey just smiled at me and nodded her head at me.

I walked down the steps to the beach, slipped off my flip-flops and stepped into the sand. I loved the feel of sand on my feet; it had a way of massaging my feet. Hunter came up behind me, wrapped his arms around me and just held me for a while.

Hunter rested his chin on my shoulder and said, "I know you need space, so I'm going to give it to you but I just want you to know I'll be here waiting for you when you're ready. There is no one else CC that has ever had my heart like you. I'm sorry I never told you how I felt back then."

I did not answer him right away; I just stared out over the ocean. "Why now?" I asked.

He took a few minutes before he answered me. "After what I saw that asshat put you through, I can't have you going through that again. It is killing me seeing you like this. I know I fucked up last summer when I bailed on you like that, but you caught me off guard." He took a deep breath and then let it out. "I didn't know what to do."

"I get it, I do, but you hurt me too. I cannot go through that again. I need time."

"Your right, I did and it's been killing me ever since that night. I thought leaving you alone was the right thing to do. You met Dominic when I left for school, so I thought you were over me and I stayed away." He kissed the side of my head then continued. "I'll be here when you are ready to talk, but I didn't just say what I said because I was pissed that Dominic was asking you to marry him. I mean it CC."

"What did you tell Mason? I want to hear it from you." I needed him to tell me those three words more than I needed anything right now.

"You're not ready to hear them again." He let go of me, reached for my hand and walked us back to the house. I was slipping my flip-flops back on when he said, "When you're ready to hear those words I'll tell you. I'll tell you a million times, but I need you to know I mean them when I say them.

That was the problem; I needed to hear them now. He would not tell me and I could not handle that. I was already broken. I could not let him break me anymore then I already am. I need time to figure out things. "Ok let's go; I want to go home."

Over the next few weeks, I concentrated on me, school, work and nothing else. I was lucky enough that I had not run into

Dominic at all since that night. I did see him a few times around campus, but I always turned and went the other way. Hunter, on the other hand, I still saw. We would still go to lunch after class, but that was it. I never went over to his house when Hailey hung out with him and Zeke. I was not trying to be a bitch but I just needed time, time to deal with all my shit.

Tuesday after class Hunter, Hailey and I were going home for Thanksgiving break. I could not wait. I missed being home. I had been talking to my mom a lot lately, trying to plan different things for Chloe's baby shower that weekend. That was a huge distraction for me. I knew once I was home, I would be busy. We were having everyone over for dinner Thursday, going shopping Black Friday and then Saturday was Chloe's baby shower. Mom planned it that weekend since we would all be home. Chloe was due in just three weeks; I was excited about becoming an aunt. I know Jackson was extremely nervous about becoming a father, but regardless, he was going to be a great dad.

Hunter called to make sure we were packed and ready to go on Tuesday. He wanted to get on the road before rush hour traffic started. "Yeah, I just put the last of my things in my bag."

"Alright I'm on my way over now; see you in a few CC."

"Alright, bye." I hung up the phone and asked, "Hails, are you ready? Hunter is on his way over."

"Yes, let's get the hell out of here. I miss my bed back home."

I raised my eyebrows at her. "Is that all you miss?"

"What else would I miss?" She asked, sitting on her bed, twirling her hair around her finger.

"Oh I don't know, maybe my brother?"

She started to blush and I knew that she was missing him like crazy. "No, why would you think that?" Then she started giggling.

"Yeah, sure" I answered, rolling my eyes at her.

There was a knock at the door and I yelled, "It's open." I was expecting it to be Hunter but it was not. It was Dominic.

Hailey jumped off her bed, stood next to me and said, "What the hell are you doing here?"

"I came by to say Happy Thanksgiving to Kenzie and to make sure she had a ride home."

"Yes, Hunter is giving us a ride home. Now please leave." Just as I finished my sentence, the door flew open and Hunter walked in with a murderous look on his face.

"What the fuck are you doing here? I thought I made it pretty clear to stay the fuck away from her." Hunter walked over and shoved Dominic towards the door.

"Chill out Hunter. I was just checking to make sure she had a ride home. I know Chloe's baby shower is this weekend, and she is looking forward to it. I would have called but she changed her number."

The day after all the shit went down, Cooper called and had my number changed, so there would be no way for him to get in contact with me.

"Yeah well, she did that for a reason Dom. Now get the fuck out."

Dominic looked over to me before he turned and walked out the door. I did not understand why he was trying to hang onto me. He did this to us, not me. He was expecting a baby in a few months for Christ sakes.

"You okay CC?" Hunter asked.

"Yes. Ready to go, Hailey?"

"Yes please, before any more bullshit goes down."

The ride home was fairly quiet. I sat up front with Hunter while Hailey curled up in the back and fell asleep. I was not in the best of moods since Dominic made his impromptu visit. Hunter could sense it, so he let me be. I was trying to get comfortable enough to take a nap but I just could not find the right position. Finally settling in, Hunter reached over and grabbed my hand, linking our fingers together. I fell asleep within minutes.

Hunter squeezed my hand, and I slowly started to wake up to him saying, "CC, we're home."

I stretched and asked, "You coming in to say hi to everyone, or are you going to head home?"

"I'm going to drop Hailey off then head home. Mom and Jaylinn are waiting for me. I'll see you tomorrow."

"Ok." I put my hand on the door handle and dropped his hand that was still holding onto mine, but stopped before I got out. "Thanks again for everything Hunter."

He smiled that smile that I loved so much and said, "Anytime."

I got out of the truck and made my way around to the bed where Hunter met me to hand me my bags. Before I could grab it, he reached over, pulled me into a hug and he kissed the top of my head.

I hugged him back and said, "Bye Hunter. When you wake Hailey up, tell her I will call her tomorrow."

"Sure."

I walked towards the house, so happy to be home and away from school for a few days. When I walked in, my mom sat on the couch reading and my dad sat next to her, watching TV.

"There's our baby girl." Mom said when I came into her view.

"Hey mom, hey dad, I'm exhausted. I'm going to head on up to bed. We'll talk more in the morning." I said while yawning.

"Ok, you need me to make you anything to eat?" Mom asked.

"No, we stopped before we got here. I just need some sleep."

I went up to my room, loving the comfortable feeling being home already gave me. As soon as I opened my door, I dropped my bags, went to lie on my bed and fell into a peaceful sleep.

Chapter Fourteen

The next morning after I got up and took a much-needed shower, I made my way downstairs. My mom was in the kitchen making breakfast. When I went in, my entire family, including Hunter, Hailey, Jaylinn, and Mrs. McCormick were sitting at the table.

"Well, look who decided to finally grace us with her presence," my dad said as he got up from the table to wrap his arms around me.

"Morning, guess I was more tired than I thought I was. I feel a lot better today. So Chloe, are you ready for this weekend? How's my nephew been treating you?"

"Girl he never stops moving. I am so uncomfortable. I cannot wait for this to be over. I have to wake Jackson up all the time because I keep getting bad back cramps and I can't get up out of bed."

"Aww, leave my nephew alone. He's getting tough before he comes into this family. He's gonna need his muscles with all his uncles around," I said smiling at her.

"I just can't wait until I get to finally hold him in my arms."

"I bet. So what's the plans today mom?" I went to sit at the only open seat at the table, which happened to be next to Hunter. He leaned over and whispered good morning in my ear. I replied by reaching for his hand under the table and giving it a squeeze. I cast a quick glance in Mason's direction and saw him glaring at me.

"Well, you and I need to get all the decorations for the shower and stop by the hall and check it out real quick. Then we're going to come back and pick up all the girls and go get pedicures."

That sounded relaxing, and was just what I needed. "Ok sounds good. Hails, you going too?"

"No, I'm good. I have to spend some time with my mom," she told me, looking displeased.

The rest of breakfast consisted of small talk made by everyone. Hunter and I eyed each other the whole time and he found small ways to touch me. I could not explain the feelings I was developing for Hunter, but I knew for sure that every time I was with him, I felt safe and at ease. I guess my heart had finally started to heal.

After cleaning up from breakfast, mom and I headed out to the party store to pick up decorations, balloons, party favors and everything else we needed for Chloe's shower. After stopping by the hall, which was beautiful and perfect for the baby shower, we went to the grocery store to pick up last minute things for Thanksgiving dinner. About an hour later, we were finally on our way home, but when we pulled into the driveway, Jackson was outside, pacing back and forth.

"Hey Jackson, what's going on?" I asked, walking towards the trunk to grab some of the bags.

"Chloe is having back cramps again and she keeps crying because they are causing her so much pain. She just kicked me out and told me to go take a walk."

Mom walked over to him and grabbed his arm, pulling him to the trunk of the car to help with the bags. "Jackson, you need to calm down. You are making this worse for her. Help me and your sister get these bags in the house and then I'll go talk to her and see if she wants to go to the hospital."

"Mom, I'm not ready for this yet." Jackson was a nervous wreck. It was kind of cute seeing him like that because normally, he was the big tough guy. "We don't have anything set up at the apartment; we haven't even had the shower yet."

"Jackson, just relax. We are all here, and we will help you and Chloe with everything." Mom reassured him.

We got all the bags into the house. Jaylinn, Mrs. McCormick and I put all the food away while mom and Jackson went upstairs to check on Chloe. Thirty minutes later, mom and Chloe came downstairs and asked if I was ready to go get our pedicures.

"Chloe, are you sure you are up to going?" She still did not look as if she felt very well. Her flushed cheeks and pinched eyes let me know her pain had not gone away.

"Yeah, I need to get out and get my mind off this pain. The doctor said if I still have these pains by tomorrow morning to head over to the hospital. I was just at the doctor on Monday. With my being only two centimeters dilated, I am probably experiencing painful Braxton Hicks contractions. They aren't coming close together or anything, so he isn't too worried."

What the hell is a Braxton Hicks? "I have no idea what the hell that means, but if you still want to go, let's go." I told her laughing.

By the time we finished our pedicures, and had stopped for ice cream, Chloe said that she was feeling much better. We got home and convinced Jackson that Chloe really was fine, so they headed home for the night.

Heading up the stairs to my room, I thought I heard Hailey's giggle. I stopped and waited for it again. I needed to make sure it was Hailey before I walked in on Mason or Cooper with some girl. I heard it again and knew that it was definitely Hailey's giggle. I knocked on Mason and Cooper's door. Cooper opened it and I saw

Hails and Mason on his bed. Cooper and his friend Amy were sitting on his bed. Hunter and some blonde I did not know were sitting on the floor.

"Hey Hails, I thought I heard you. What are you up to?" I made sure not to look in Hunter's direction.

What the hell was he doing?

"Just hanging out. I came over to see you, thinking you would have been back by now, but Mason said you were still out with your mom and Chloe."

I glanced over at Hunter, then the girl next to him and then back to Hailey again. I said, "Ok, well, I don't want to interrupt you guys. I'll see you later." I turned around, shut the door and walked towards my room.

What the hell was Hunter doing with that girl? So fucking much for him waiting for me.

Just as I was about to open my door, Hunter called my name. I turned to him and said, "Hunter, whatever you are about to say, don't. Just go back in there, and I'll see you later." I walked into my room, locked the door and grabbed my iPod. I cranked the music on full blast and started to clean my room. If he tried to knock, I did not hear him. Around midnight, I fell into an exhausted sleep.

The next morning I woke up early and went downstairs to help my mom start cooking for Thanksgiving. I needed to stay busy so I would not think about Hunter. I needed to focus on me. I would not survive my heart being broken again.

"Good morning baby girl, how did you sleep?" Mom asked from the sink where she was washing the turkey out.

"I slept just fine. What do you need help with?"

"Start with making the stuffing."

The rest of the morning and early afternoon, I stayed busy helping my mom in the kitchen getting everything ready. A few hours before dinner, I went upstairs to take a shower and get myself ready before everyone came over. As I was going back downstairs, I ran into Hunter on the stairs.

"Hey."

"Hey, got a second to talk?"

"No, I need to get back downstairs and help mom get everything out for dinner...maybe later."

"CC, please don't do this. I don't want you pissed off at me. I'm not interested in that girl; I was just talking to her. She came with Amy. I couldn't just ignore her." I knew she did not mean anything to him. How could she? We have not even been here for months, but still, it bothered me.

"Hunter we aren't together. It doesn't matter who you talk to or don't. Now please excuse me; I need to go help mom." I refused to give in to my emotions. I wanted to hug him and tell him I believed him. I just could not take a chance with my still-mending heart.

"We're talking about this later CC," he stated.

Nodding my head, I passed him on the stairs and went to the kitchen to help mom set the table for dinner. I loved Thanksgiving dinner; we always got together, ate way too much food and watched football. I was setting the table when mom walked in with the turkey; once everything was on the table, we all sat down to eat. Everything was going great. Jackson and Chloe were there, but you could tell she was not feeling well and it looked like Jackson had not slept in days.

I kept feeling Hunters eyes on me throughout dinner. I caught Cooper looking at me and then at Hunter and shaking his head. I was not giving off any kind of signals so I do not know what he was thinking.

I think Mason caught on to the tension that was coming off Hunter and me because he spoke up. "Kenzie, what's wrong with you? You are really quiet today?"

"Nothing, I'm fine, just a lot going on lately. I'm good though, nothing I can't handle."

"Is Dominic still harassing you at school?" he asked.

"He is leaving me alone for the most part. How are things going with you and Hailey?" I already knew the answer; I just did not want to talk about Dominic.

"Good." Mason looked over at Hunter and asked, "Are you seeing anyone?"

"No, I'm hoping this girl from school will give me a chance, but lately she has been really distant, so we will see what happens."

Mason just glared at him when he said that. I was curious enough to ask, "Have I met this girl? I don't remember seeing anyone hanging around."

"Guess you're not paying attention then." Hunter's cell phone chirped. He reached in his pocket, read the message then cursed under his breath and stood up.

"I have to go. Thanks for dinner Mr. and Mrs. Cahill. Mom, Jay, I'll see you guys a little later. I'll be back before dessert and then I'll take you home."

"Dude, what's going on?" Cooper asked, standing up to follow Hunter into the kitchen with his plate. I could not hear what he said but when Cooper came back in, he looked at Mason and nodded his head.

"What the hell is going on?" I asked, with panic in my voice. The last time something like this happened, I found out my boyfriend was having a baby with another girl. I could not handle anything else.

"Nothing, everything is good. Hunter just had to go take care of something." Cooper said.

"Quit the bullshit Cooper, what's wrong?" I said glaring at him.

"Relax, it's nothing; he'll be back. If he wants you to know, he can tell you when he comes back."

"Whatever!" I yelled. I got up, took my plate to the kitchen and then went to the living room to watch the football game. I heard my mom and dad ask everyone what was going on, but Cooper and Mason just told them everything was fine. I must have fallen asleep on the couch because I woke to Hunter rubbing my arm.

I sat up as soon as I saw his split lip and the welt on his cheek; obliviously he got into some kind of fight. "Oh my God Hunter, what happened? Are you ok?"

"Yeah I'm fine, just had to go take care of something."

I reached out to touch his lip and he winced at first then kissed my finger. I stood up and pushed Hunter to sit on the couch. "I'll be right back." I disappeared into the kitchen to grab some ice. Mom looked over at me and asked if I was ok. I nodded my head to her and left the kitchen quickly.

"Here put this on your lip and cheek." I told him. His cheek was already turning black and blue.

"CC I'm fine really. Can we talk now?" Hunter asked, grabbing the ice from me and placing it on his lip.

"Yeah but not in here with everyone; let's go outside."

"It's raining."

"I need to get out of here." I told him. I really did not want to talk to him about us with the possibility of someone over hearing.

"Ok, let's go."

Hunter grabbed my hand, led me outside into the pouring rain and to his truck parked at the end of the driveway. He stopped walking when we reached his truck, looked from the ground to my lips and then he took a step closer to me, pushing me until my back was up against the cold wet truck. He reached up and cupped my face. "I'm done trying to stay away," he sighed then continued. "I can't do it anymore. I need you like my life depends on it." The rain was streaming down on us but right now, I did not care. "I just need you." He gently pulled my head to him and whispered, "I am going to kiss you now."

That is exactly what he did. I was tired of fighting my feelings for him, tired of being upset, just tired. That kiss was amazing; it had all the passion and longing we had been holding onto for so long. That is when the dam finally broke for me and I started crying. I knew right then that Hunter was the only one I wanted. He was my happily ever after.

Chapter Fifteen

All I could think about was Hunter's lips on mine. There was a tingly feeling that spread from my lips, down my chest and right between my legs. A deep growl came from Hunter; I knew he was feeling this too. He deepened the kiss; his tongue slipped in and found mine. I reached up and tangled my hands in his hair. I did not ever want this kiss to end. I was not sure what would happen when we broke apart. I would not be able to stop my heart from shattering if he said this was a mistake again. I did not care if our family was sitting in the house or not. I needed this kiss as if my life depended on it.

Hunter started to pull away but I tightened my hands in his hair, holding his head to me. I was so scared to pull away from him. He reached up, removed my hands and positioned them between us. He pulled back ever so slightly and caught my lower lip between his teeth. I whimpered. He rested his forehead against mine; we were both panting.

"You know," he said, chuckling, "We have a thing with kissing in the rain."

We were both soaked and I truly did not care, but then I remembered the cut on his lip.

"Oh god, I didn't hurt you did I?" I asked him, reaching up to run my thumb over his cut. God, what an idiot I am. That is why he was pulling away.

"It was worth it." He bent down and kissed me again. "I guess I'm forgiven for talking to that girl yesterday?"

"Yeah, I think you are, but just don't let it happen again." I said. "What happened to you?"

He pushed my bangs out of my face. "I got a text from Hailey telling me that she ran into a very drunk Dominic. He said he was on his way to talk to you. So, I had to stop him before he came over. Let's just say that he isn't going to be going anywhere for a while."

"Hunter, you shouldn't have done that." I was thankful that he handled Dominic but I did not want to see him like this.

"Yes, I should have. I couldn't have him come over here and throw himself at you, I can't handle that shit."

"KENZIE!" Mason yelled from the front door.

"Shit." Hunter said, stepping back from me.

"Get your ass in here. Mom wants you." Mason was glaring at us; I knew this was not going to go over well. I just hoped he would not make a scene with everyone here.

"Coming." I yelled back to him. "I guess we better get back inside." He reached in and grabbed his keys from his pocket. "I'll be back later; I'm going to run home and change. Tell my mom and Jay that I'll be back."

"Ok. See you in a little bit." I did not know what to do. Did I kiss him goodbye or just walk inside?

I did not have to wait long as Hunter grabbed both of my hands, entwined our fingers, pulled me closer to him and kissed me goodbye.

"You know, you can drag my ass out in the rain and kiss me anytime you want." I told him when we broke apart from our kiss.

Smirking at me, he said, "I'll have to remember that."

"Alright, see you in a little bit." I turned and walked back towards the house.

I ran up to my room and quickly changed and dried my hair.

Someone knocked on my door. I went over to it and opened it. Jaylinn was standing there with her hand on her hip and her eyebrows raised, frowning at me.

"Where did you run my brother off to?"

"He went home to change. He said to tell you he would be right back." I was trying not to smile at her.

"And why did he have to change?"

"Because we..."

She cut me off before I could answer her. "Wait, don't answer that. I don't even want to know."

I busted out laughing, I could not help it; I was on cloud nine from my kiss with Hunter. Jaylinn just shook her head at me.

"Well, I'm glad to finally see you laughing again and I'm glad it was Hunter that did it." Hailey said leaning against my doorframe.

"Well let's not get a head of ourselves. I still have to go downstairs and deal with my brothers." I pulled my hair up in a ponytail. "Alright, let's go face the music."

Everyone was in the living room hanging out and relaxing when we went downstairs. Hailey went over to Mason to try and run inference against the ass chewing I was about to get, and Jaylinn went over to Cooper.

I took a seat in the recliner next to Jackson and Chloe. "So Chloe, how are you feeling today? Any better?"

"No, not at all, I'm so uncomfortable." She said groaning. Poor girl, she was so ready to have this baby.

"Well with your shower on Saturday, hopefully it will take your mind off of it for a little while." I tried to shine some kind of light on the situation.

"I sure hope so."

Hunter walked in looking hot, even dressed in sweat pants and a t-shirt. There were not any seats anywhere, so I jumped up. "Here, sit here." I told him.

He walked over and sat in the recliner. I was going to sit on the floor between his legs, but he pulled me onto his lap instead.

I quickly glanced over at Mason and he practically leaped off the couch, throwing Hailey to the floor. "Dude, that's my fucking sister. What are you doing?"

"Mason, watch your mouth." My dad spoke up.

I glanced around the room and everyone was staring at us. I looked at Hunter and thought it was better just to sit on the floor; we did not need a huge family fight.

I got up off Hunter's lap and I think that surprised him because he was looking at me as if I just did something wrong.

"Kenzie, what are you doing? You're not sitting on the floor." Cooper said.

"Coop, it's fine." I did not want this shit to happen, not here on Thanksgiving with our whole family here.

I decided to try to defuse the situation so I walked into the kitchen to start doing the dishes that did not make it into the dishwasher. Mason followed me into the kitchen, I assumed to finish our argument, but he was not alone. Hunter and Cooper came too.

"What the fuck is going on between you two?" Mason seethed through his teeth.

Cooper put his hand on Mason's shoulder and said, "Mase man, just let it go."

"No, I'm not just going to let it go. You're only sticking up for them because you're fucking his sister." Mason fired back at Cooper.

My mouth dropped opened.

"What the fuck Mase!" Cooper yelled.

"You're what, Coop? That's my fucking sister." Hunter yelled back.

I thought it was going to be a free for all, but thankfully, Jackson and my dad walked in before anyone could get too crazy. I guess Hunter did not know about Cooper and his sister. I had kind of put two and two together but I did not know for sure.

"What the hell is going on? Why is everyone yelling?" My dad asked.

I just shook my head at my dad. I was not about to get into this. I turned and continued to do the dishes.

"Your daughter wants Hunter." Mason told my dad.

"Wait, I thought you were with Dominic." my dad said to me.

"Nope, haven't been for a few weeks. But while we're talking about it, Mason wants Hailey." I fired right back towards Mason.

My dad reached up to rub his forehead, surely from the headache that we were all causing.

"And what about you?" my dad asked Cooper.

I started laughing at what a complete disaster this is.

Hunter spoke up and answered before Cooper could. "He wants Jay."

My dad threw his hands up and walked out. That made me laugh, and earned me a glare from everyone but Jackson, who also thought this was insane.

"This is a cluster fuck." Jackson stated and then he turned around and walked back into the living room.

Mason and Cooper stormed out leaving me alone with Hunter in the kitchen. He walked over to me and caged me in as I continued to wash the dishes at the sink.

"Well, that went over great." He pushed my hair back off my neck then kissed it and put his hand back on the counter. "Did you know about Jay and Coop?"

I pushed back on him, snuggling a little closer and shook my head no. Hunter groaned and whispered, "Stop that."

"Stop what?" I asked innocently.

"You know what." Hunter moaned softly in my ear.

A throat cleared behind us. "Hunter," Mrs. McCormick said.

Hunter pushed off from my back and said, "Yeah Mom?"

"Could you run me and Jaylinn home now? We have to get up early to go shopping with the girls, so we need to get some sleep."

"Yeah sure. Get Jay and I'll meet you in the truck."

Mrs. McCormick walked over to me, gave me a hug and a kiss on the cheek and said, "I'll see you tomorrow morning sweetie."

When she walked out of the kitchen, Hunter crushed his lips to mine. I moaned a little when his tongue brushed against my lips. He picked me up and I wrapped my legs around him. He walked me over to the door and pushed me against it. All my muscles started to tense, both from the kiss and from the fact that anyone who walked in would catch us.

"God, I don't think I could ever get sick of kissing you." Hunter said.

"Good, cause I don't either."

Hunter set me down on my feet and kissed me again before he said, "I better get out of here. I'll see you tomorrow?"

"Maybe, I'm going shopping with the girls then we have to get the favors and stuff ready for Chloe's shower on Saturday."

Hunter locked his eyes with mine, those panty dropping eyes that I could get lost in forever. "I'll see you tomorrow." He was telling me, not asking.

Chapter Sixteen

Four in the morning came way too early, but this was a family tradition so I dragged my ass from bed. It was my birthday in just a few days. My mom always let me pick out my presents while we were shopping. Hailey had slept over last night with Mason, so we just had to go by Hunter's house to pick up his Mom and sister.

We pulled up to Hunter's, I ran up to the door to let them know we were here. I went to knock on the door but it opened before I could. Hunter appeared in the door; he reached for my hand and pulled me inside. As soon as the door closed behind me, he cupped my face and kissed me.

"Wow." It was the only response I had at an ungodly hour like this.

"Good morning." Hunter said, as he drifted his hands from my cheeks to my hips. "Damn, you even make yoga pants looks sexy."

"I make anything look sexy." I said, winking at him.

He groaned and brought his lips to mine again. When our tongues collided, I lost all sense as to where we were until I heard a throat clearing. Hunter either did not hear it or was ignoring it because he was not stopping. The throat cleared again and that time it caught Hunter's attention.

Hunter shifted his shoulder back slightly so he could see who it was. Jaylinn was standing there with her hands on her hips. "Can you stop molesting her so we can go shopping? Or do you plan on keeping her tied up all day? I am sure Mason would love to..."

Hunter cut off her off, "Shut up."

Jaylinn laughed and walked away.

Feeling slightly embarrassed, I said, "So, I um, guess I better get going now."

He gave me another peck on my lips and said, "Yeah. I'll see you later."

I followed Jaylinn and Mrs. McCormick out of the house and down the steps. At the bottom, I turned back around to Hunter. "What are you doing up this damn early anyway?"

He gave me that smile that made me tingle and said, "Because, there was something I had to do." He turned and closed the door. I shook my head and continued to the car.

The morning of shopping went great. I got most all my gifts bought, but still needed to get a few things before Christmas. Mom bought me a new Coach purse for my birthday, which made up for having to wake up so early. Hailey picked up a few things along with Jaylinn and Mrs. McCormick.

We stopped for lunch before we went home, knowing we would have to start getting things ready for the baby shower tomorrow. All morning, Mrs. McCormick kept watching me. I was not sure what she was up to but something was up.

Around lunchtime, we made it back to the house. When we walked in the front door, Jackson was pacing back and forth in front of the fireplace. Mason was sitting next to Chloe, rubbing his hand up and down the right side of her back. Cooper was doing the same thing on the other side, and Hunter was holding a bucket up to her face.

"What's going on?" My mom asked, as soon as she set her bags down on the dining room table.

Hunter looked over at me and shook his head. Cooper said, "She's been throwing up since she woke up."

My mom walked over to Chloe and bent down in front of her. Hunter moved back and handed my Mom the bucket. My mom said to Chloe, "Sweetie what's going on? Are you in any kind of pain?"

Her whole body was shaking and she had goose bumps on her arms. Before she could answer, Jackson spoke up and said, "She's been throwing up since her feet hit the ground this morning. The doctor said to keep her hydrated, and if she's no better in a few hours to take her to the hospital."

"Ok sweetie, let's get you back up to bed." Cooper and Mason both grabbed an arm and helped Chloe back upstairs while Jackson went to go get her a couple bottles of water.

Hunter came over to me and said, "I never want to go through that bullshit. It was no wonder Jackson had not left her side since she got knocked up."

"Yeah, she hasn't had it easy."

Mrs. McCormick took the seat where Cooper had just been sitting. "Hey Mom, you buy me anything good?" Hunter asked.

"Now you know I didn't. I don't like you that much." She said laughing.

"But she bought me something, because she loves me." Jaylinn piped up from behind us.

"Whatever." Hunter draped his arm around my shoulder, "You want to go catch a movie?"

"Not now, maybe later. We need to get started on the gift bags for the shower." Hunter frowned at me, but we needed to get them done.

Eventually, my mom made it back downstairs, and we all got started on the baby shower stuff. My dad and the boys all went outside to put the Christmas decorations up. By the time everything was done, we ordered pizza, and I ran upstairs to take a quick shower. After showering, I went into my room, and Hunter was sitting there on my bed.

"What are you doing up here?" I was feeling a little uncomfortable with him being in my room. After all, we were in my parent's house.

"Don't worry. Hailey and Mason went out to a movie, Cooper took my Mom and Jay home and your parents are too worried about Chloe to realize I'm in here."

Well then, I guess he had everything covered.

He got up off the bed and went over to lock the door. He stalked over to me, stopped right in front of me and lifted my chin so that I was looking up at him.

"Am I making you nervous?" He must have felt me shivering, but it was not because I was cold.

"No." I whispered.

Hunter put his arms around me and started walking me backwards to my bed. The back of my legs hit the bed, and he gently laid me back. Once my head hit the pillow so did all of my emotions. I wanted him. I had wanted him forever and now here he was.

Hunter hovered above me, not touching me. I wanted him to touch me. I slid my hands down his back and grazed my fingers under his shirt. He tensed for a second, then sat up and pulled his shirt over his head.

Hunter was handsome with all that tanned toned skin and those damn tattoos of his. I reached up and ran my hands from his chest down to his abs. He came back down with a hand on each side of me, caging my body in with his.

"You're killing me with this towel. I shouldn't be in here but..." he placed a kiss on my lips, "But I can't stay away either."

As if to prove his point, he lowered his body right between my legs. I could feel him hard and thick through his jeans. I tried to move my hips to get him right where I wanted him, but he pushed his hips harder into mine stopping me.

"Don't," he took a breath and let it out slowly, "I only have so much self-control and you're not ready yet."

He kissed the corner of my lips, then my neck. He leaned onto his right elbow and reached down to pull my towel loose. Before he pulled, he looked up at me for permission. When he pulled the towel, the back of his hand brushed the swell of my breast and my nipples instantly went hard.

"Damn CC." He said, just before he took one of my nipples into his mouth. He sucked and swirled his tongue around it and did the same to the other side.

Before I could even think of what I was doing, I lifted my legs around his hips and started rocking. That earned me a moan from deep within Hunter's chest. I reached down and ran my fingers through his hair.

He dragged his lips back up my neck and then finally my lips. Our tongues collided and it was pure bliss.

Hunter rested his forehead on mine for a few minutes and then said, "I've got to go."

"What? Why? Don't go yet." I was starting to panic.

"Trust me, I don't want to go but I have to go." He placed a quick kiss on my lips and then started to get up. I reached up and linked my fingers behind his neck.

Sighing, he looked down at where my towel had fallen down a little more and he said, "CC I really have to go. This can't happen."

Now, I let go of him and let him crawl off me. Suddenly feeling shy around him, I quickly grabbed the blankets at the foot of the bed and pulled them up to cover myself.

"What are you doing?" He asked.

I just shook my head at him. I could not answer him. He just told me this could not happen. I was stupid for believing that he could want me this way. He could not even tell me he loved me, but he could tell my brothers that.

"CC, don't ok. Whatever you're thinking in that gorgeous head of yours don't." He bent down to pick up his shirt off the floor.

I just nodded my head. He came over, gave me a kiss and said, "I'll see you tomorrow."

"Ok."

He walked over to the door but turned around to look at me before he walked out and said "Don't think, just feel it. I know you do; I can see it on your face." He winked and walked out of the door.

I threw myself back on my pillow and a huge smile broke out on my face.

The next morning I woke up to a text from Hunter.

Hunter – 7:46 am: Missed you. Hope you slept well

Me – 9:05 am: Miss your face, I slept great

I got out of bed, and went to get ready for the baby shower that was happening this afternoon. As I walked downstairs, I heard Chloe yell Jackson's name. Jackson ran up the stairs and right into his old room.

"Shit! Umm ok, what do we do now?" Jackson sounded panicked.

I walked towards their room to see what was going on. When I walked in, Chloe was sitting on the bed and Jackson was standing next to her.

"Hey guys, what's going on?" I asked. Nothing looked wrong.

"Umm, can you get mom? Yeah, you get mom." Jackson said

"Kenzie, my water broke." Chloe told me.

"Umm, yeah, I'll get mom." I said and then bolted downstairs.

A few hours later, we were all sitting in the hospital waiting on Alex's arrival instead of being at the shower that we had planned.

Mason, Cooper and Hunter were at Jackson's house attempting to put up the crib and Hailey was at home with her sister who had just come in this morning. I was starting to get impatient, so I decided to go take a walk to the gift shop downstairs.

I was looking at the blue monkey, thinking about buying it for Alex when I heard Dominic's mom call my name.

"MacKenzie, I'm surprised to see you here." When she said my name, it was like it left a bad taste in my mouth.

"My brother's having his baby upstairs." What the hell was her problem? I did not do anything to her son; I am not the one pregnant.

"Oh well, tell them congratulations." She picked up a Reese's, one of Dominic's favorites, and then she said, "You should visit Dominic while you're here. I'm sure he would be glad to see you."

What? "Dominic's here?"

"Yeah, after that boyfriend of yours damn near killed him."

Boyfriend? Was she serious?

"I don't have a boyfriend anymore. I had one but he couldn't seem to keep his dick in his pants." I snapped at her, and then went to pay for the monkey for Alex.

I went back upstairs to see how things were coming along with Jackson and Chloe. Hunter, Mason and Cooper were there. I walked over to where they were whispering in the corner.

"Oh hey, Kenzie." Cooper said placing a kiss on my forehead.

"Any update yet?"

"Not yet, Jackson was just out here, and he said anytime now." Mason answered.

"Umm, Hunter, can I talk to you for a minute?"

We walked just outside of the waiting room and I asked him, "You put Dominic in the hospital?"

He did not look at me. Instead, he looked down at the ground and nodded his head.

"And you didn't think it was important enough to tell me?"

"No, he shouldn't have been talking shit. None of this would have happened in the first place."

"Well I ran into his mom downstairs. She wasn't too happy about seeing me. She told me I should stop by and see him. He's been asking about me."

"Yeah, like that's going to happen."

He was right. I was not going to see him, at least not while Hunter was around. I needed to give Dominic some kind of closure so he could move on. I have moved on, and it is about time he does too.

Jackson walked in about twenty minutes later with a huge smile on his face and his camera in his hand. He showed us all the pictures he had taken and then gave us Alex's information.

Alex Jackson Cahill

8lbs 9oz

21 ½" long

Alex was precious with chubby little cheeks and a head of dark hair just like his daddy. I could not wait to get my hands on my little nephew.

Chapter Seventeen

I peaked in on my nephew before I went home for the night. I was exhausted from everything going on. I knew Chloe and Jackson were too, and they needed some one on one time with Alex.

Everyone went back to our house where we decided to order some pizza and just hang out. Mason and Hailey had disappeared after the pizza arrived, and Cooper and Jay were sitting in the living room watching Duck Dynasty. Mom and Dad were upstairs trying to get some sleep because they were exhausted.

Hunter and I were still sitting at the table, my legs in between his, talking and laughing about the three of them trying to put the crib together. The first attempt had the railings upside down and then they couldn't figure out how the grate that held the mattress went. He said it took them at least two hours before they had it completely put together.

"Come away with me for New Year's?" Hunter asked.

I stared at him trying to gauge where this was going. We always celebrated at my house with everyone, so why would he want to go away? "Where?"

"I want to surprise you with something." He placed a kiss on my lips to keep me from arguing, because he knew I hated surprises.

Whining, I told him, "I hate surprises Hunter; you know this."

Smirking at me through his dark, thick eyelashes, he said, "I know but you're not going to hate this."

I smiled and kissed him. "And what are we going to tell everyone? We don't need another argument like Thursday."

"Let me take care of that. I know someone who can help us out." He winked at me.

"All right, as long as everyone is ok with it."

"Don't worry; they'll be fine with it."

Hunter left a little after that with Jaylinn. He told me he we would come over tomorrow to pick me up because we had to head out around lunchtime to go back to school. I really was not looking forward to going back to school.

The next morning, my mom woke me up early. I wanted to sneak over to the hospital before anyone else since I was leaving the earliest.

"So you and Hunter huh?" She asked, just as we pulled up to the hospital. I was surprised she had not asked before now.

I just smiled and got out of the car. I could not exactly answer her since Hunter and I actually have not made anything official. I did not want to jinx anything by talking about it too much before it actually became true.

"Well, are you at least going to tell me what happened with Dominic?" She asked, opening the hospital doors.

I looked down to the ground and then back up. It still hurt to talk about it. "He um...cheated on me...and got the girl pregnant. He kept telling me that he wasn't cheating on me and that I should trust him. I trusted him with all my heart, right up until the night of the party when everything fell apart.

"Oh umm." She looked at me and then looked away.

"It's ok, I'm fine. I was lucky enough to have everyone there with me when it all went down. It hurts, but that was just the hand I was dealt."

Mom gave me one of her big smiles, wrapped her arms around me to give me a hug and said, "I'm sorry baby girl. Just remember everything happens for a reason. We just have to pick ourselves up, and look on the bright side of life."

I shrugged my shoulders. While it still hurt, I was grateful Hunter was there to ease the pain away. If he hadn't been there, it would have been a lot worse.

Mom and I visited with Jackson, Chloe and Alex for a little while before the rest of the family started showing up. Chloe really hoped her parents would show, but Jackson didn't seem to think they would. Once she had told them she was pregnant, they had completely cut her off.

On our way back to the car, I asked mom if she would do something with me. She agreed of course, not even knowing what I was going to ask. We went back inside to the check-in counter and I asked for Dominic's room.

My mom had a shocked look on her face. "Why is Dominic in here?" she asked when we were walking towards the elevator.

"Umm, Hunter," I didn't know if I should tell my mom this or not, but I was sure she would have put two and two together anyway. "Hunter got into a disagreement with him on Thanksgiving. Dominic didn't end up so....well."

She nodded her head and asked, "Is that where he disappeared to while we were eating?"

"Yeah, I didn't know he was here until yesterday when I ran into his mom. She wasn't too happy to see me, but she said that Dominic keeps asking about me. I want to give him closure so he can get over this. He has a kid to think about now, you know?"

She smiled at me for a good long minute before she told me, "I'm so proud of the young lady that you're becoming. You make your dad and me so proud. I know your brothers can be a bit over the top, but they love you none the less and are proud of you too."

Smiling I said, "Thanks mom."

We made it to Dominic's room. While I went in, mom stayed in the waiting room. Dominic's mom was sitting in the chair at the foot of his bed. Dominic was laying there in bed with two black eyes, a broken arm and stitches on the bridge of his nose and above his eye. Wow, Hunter had really done a number on him.

Dominic's mom looked up from the book she was reading; she took off her glasses and excused herself from the room.

"Good luck." Dominic's mom said to me on the way out.

Dominic looked out the window, turned to look at me and then turned his head back to the window. Maybe I shouldn't have come.

I walked to the other side of Dominic's bed and pulled up the chair that was by the wall. He looked completely defeated.

We sat there for a few minutes. He stared out the window and I stared at him. I really had no idea what to say to him. He must have just been thinking of what he wanted to say because he spoke up.

He looked from the window to me. "I'm sorry MacKenzie. I didn't mean for this to happen to us. I never wanted to hurt you. You were my everything."

"I know." I said, barely above a whisper.

"When I left home, I was so excited to be on my own and with you in the same building every day. As the first few weeks passed, things changed. I started drinking almost every day, and going to parties with the guys. I didn't really think about anything other than that. Being a football player, the girls just kind of flocked to me. They threw themselves at me and would do anything to be with me. I got careless. Brittany started flirting with me one night at one of the parties, and I let things get out of hand. The night I was supposed to come to your brothers' party was the day I woke up with Brittany in my bed. I didn't even realize what I had done until the next morning. That's what took me so long to show up; I didn't know what to do. I knew I couldn't let you down again by not showing up so I made the drive anyway. I beat myself up the whole way home for what I had done, and then I got to the shore house and we couldn't even be alone. That just made me even madder. Then, you were finally on campus and in my room. I thought everything was going to be fine. When Brittany showed up, I knew it wouldn't take you long to figure it out."

I nodded my head, agreeing with him because that was when everything started falling apart for us.

"I told her it couldn't happen again. She was pissed and said I was only using her. She's the one that left the panties in my room. She caught Tommy on the way out and he let her in. She knew you had my car because I had seen her earlier that day and she had asked me to give her a ride somewhere."

Sneaky bitch.

"I freaked out on her that day and I hadn't talked to her since. When you said you needed your space, I knew I had to give it to you or I would lose you. During our time apart, I realized what I had and I wanted you...forever. That is when I realized I wanted to marry you. I figured if I could get you to agree to marry me, then we could get over what I did."

How could he think that? Did he think I would just look the other way?

He reached over to tilt my head up to look at him. "When I showed up at that party and she told me she was pregnant, I knew I had made the biggest mistake of my life. I didn't even care about my football career anymore; all I cared about was you. I knew I had hurt you and that was the last thing I had wanted. You were always there for me, cheering me on."

The tears started. As much as I had wanted to come in here and be strong, I couldn't help them anymore.

He grabbed my left hand and rubbed his thumb of my ring finger. "I still love you MacKenzie. I think I always will, but I know I need to let you go. I know you are in good hands. Just look what those hands did to me." He said with a chuckle.

I laughed; yeah, I was in good hands all right. I just hope they wanted me as much as I wanted them.

"I love you too Dominic. I hope everything works out for you." I stood up and placed a kiss on his forehead.

I walked to the waiting room and told mom I was ready to go. She looked up, smiled at me and said, "Let's go home."

When we got back to the house, Mason, Hailey and Hunter were there. We got his truck all packed up with our stuff and said goodbye to everyone. I was going to miss being here and miss Alex too; winter break was only few weeks away, so I would get to see everyone soon.

Arriving back at the dorms was gloomy; I didn't really want to be back here. It brought back too many memories.

Hailey sighed behind me; she must have been thinking the same thing. "Do we really have to stay here?"

Hunter looked at her through the rearview mirror and then back at me. "You guys can always stay with me. You know Bentley doesn't mind."

"You would be ok if we stayed the night?" I asked. I wanted to make sure this wasn't too much, too soon.

"Of course, or I wouldn't have offered." He leaned over and whispered, "I get you in my bed. I'd be a damn fool not to want you to stay with me."

Hailey groaned from the backseat, "Will you two please knock that shit off."

I laughed at her. She was just jealous that Mason wasn't here. "Ok, let's go to your house."

Later that night, Hunter got Hailey all set up in the spare room since no one was using it. I took a long hot bath. I had my iPad playing music, a candle Hunter had lit and a glass of wine next to me, just relaxing.

Hunter knocked on the door before coming in; he walked over to the tub and kneeled down beside it. He bent down and captured my lips. When our lips touched, the sparks were flying again.

I pulled back and he moaned. "Get in with me?" I should feel nervous since I was naked in front of him but I wasn't.

He didn't move at first. I was expecting him to fight me but then he stood up and started stripping out of his clothes. Hunter had no reason to be ashamed. His body was perfect, all the way from his perfectly messy hair, his defined chest, his abs to that v between his hips. He was watching me rake my eyes up and down his body. I felt the flush reaching my cheeks, but he was too sexy for his own damn good.

Smirking at me with those bright blue eyes of his he said, "See something you like?"

"What is there not to like Hunter? You are absolutely gorgeous."

When he stepped into the tub, I sat up slightly so that he could sit behind me. Oh God, maybe this was not such a good idea. Once

Hunter settled in, he reached for me and pulled me back against his chest. I moaned at the contact of our skin.

We sat there for a while, maybe a little unsure of what the other wanted. Hunter took the lead by helping me sit up. He reached behind him to grab the body wash, poured some in his hands and started washing my back. He rubbed circles from my neck all the way down my back to my ass. I whimpered a little when he stopped, but then he pulled me back against his chest again and started the same process again on my front. He caressed my shoulders, and paid special attention to my breasts, lightly pinching my nipples. When he did that, I arched my back at the sensation. Sliding his fingers up and down my stomach, I shifted my hips and tried to get him to go down further to the spot I wanted him the most.

When my hips shifted, I heard him take a quick breathe. He grabbed my hips to keep me in place. "CC, don't move baby."

I whined, "Please Hunter, I need you to touch me. This is killing me."

He shook his head and said, "Not tonight babe. You're not ready."

Not ready, is he kidding? I was more than ready.

He kissed my shoulders and neck for a few minutes before he reached down, let the water out of the tub and then turned the shower on. He helped me rinse the soap from my body and helped wash my hair. As much as I wanted Hunter to touch my middle, he never did.

I grabbed the body wash and started massaging Hunter's body. He had me so worked up, that if I couldn't get him to touch me, than I planned to make sure he was just as worked up as me. I started at his broad shoulders, moved down his pecs and then traced his well-defined abs with my fingers before following the V between his hips. I stopped and looked up, meeting his hooded eyes.

He looked so intense that I knew he would not stop me so I took my chances. I wrapped my hand around his length. His head fell back, and a hiss escaped through his teeth. I stroked him a few times before I continued down his legs and then back up and I washed his hair.

We dried each other off and Hunter gave me one of his shirts to sleep in. We climbed in bed and fell fast asleep, cuddled in each other's arms.

I could only hope that whatever was going on between us lasted, but for now, I would take anything he would give me.

Chapter Eighteen

Three weeks have passed since Hunter kissed me in the rain on Thanksgiving and things have been blissful, perfect really. Hunter and I have practically been joined at the hip. Christmas was a little less than a week away and I was looking forward to going home. I wanted to spend time with my family, especially baby Alex. Chloe, Jackson and my mom were always texting me cute little pictures of him.

More importantly, I couldn't wait to get away from school and spend some alone time with Hunter. We only saw each other when we are on our lunch together during the week and on Sundays. He worked nights at the bar every night except Sunday and I worked Monday thru Thursday night at the library. Hailey still hung out with Zeke, so he kept us entertained when Hunter could not.

On the Friday before we headed home, Hailey and I decided we were going to go out. We asked a couple of girls that we were friends with if they wanted to come along too. Hunter and Zeke both had to work that night and they expected wall-to-wall college kids at the bar because winter break had officially started.

Hailey and I headed out to grab a cab to take us to the bar. As the cab pulled up to the curb, I noticed a couple fighting in the parking lot. I thought it looked like Brittany and Logan, but I pushed that thought from my head.

The line to get into the bar wrapped around the side of the building, so Hailey asked the cab driver to drop us off at the door instead of the side where the line ended. The girls and I got out and made our way to the door where I was sure Hunter or Zeke would be. Hunter spotted me the second I was in his view, and a shit-eating grin spread across his face.

He motioned me over with his head. I looked at the girls. They all started giggling except for Hailey, who just rolled her eyes.

Hunter stood up from the stool he was sitting on and half hugged me. I don't think he was even supposed to do that. "CC, what are you doing here?"

I shrugged my shoulders. "The girls and I wanted a night out, so what better place to come then here?"

He looked behind me and said, "Hey girls, give me your hand and I'll stamp you in."

Gracie, Hailey, Zoey and I had our hands stamped and we made our way into the bar. As I walked past Hunter, I heard him radio someone that we were here and to keep an eye on us.

After dancing for a little while, we went to the bar for a drink. Hailey and I planned to order a soda since we were not old enough to drink, but the bartender shook her head and looked towards the door. She didn't ask us what we wanted; she just made the drinks and set them down in front of us. I started pulling money out of my clutch and again, she just shook her head at me again and, looked at the door.

I heard Hailey clear her throat from beside me, and then she nudged me with her elbow and tilted her head to the right. There at the end of the bar were Brittany and Logan. What in the hell was she doing here?

"Hails, isn't that Logan? What's he doing with Brittany?" Gracie asked.

"Yeah, and I have no idea and I don't really care." Hailey responded back to her.

"I thought Britt was pregnant? Why in the hell would she be here?" Zoey asked.

I just shrugged my shoulders. I was not here to worry about Brittany and Logan. I grabbed Hailey's hand and started back towards the dance floor. While Hailey and I danced around the floor with Gracie and Zoey, Hunter came in to stand near the bar. Having reached maximum capacity, they weren't letting anyone else in the bar tonight.

Hunter stood there and watched my every move, so I decided to tease him a little and give him a show. I grabbed the guy that had tried to dance with me all night and started grinding on him, throwing my head back, and crawling up and down his body with my own, while I looked straight at Hunter.

He had to work, so there was nothing he could do to stop me. The guy I danced with must have noticed me staring at Hunter because he asked, "Is that your boyfriend? He's been eye fucking you all night."

"Nope." I told him as I turned him and circled around his body until I could get Hunter back in my view.

"You sure?" He leaned in to ask me.

"Yeah." I answered, still watching Hunter from where he stood at the bar, scowling at me.

Before I realized what had happened, the guy I was dancing with disappeared, and I was in Hunter's arms.

Completely shocked at what happened, I looked up at Hunter. He just shook his head and led me to a back room that seemed to be some kind of locker room.

"What the fuck was that CC?" Hunter seethed.

"Nothing, I was dancing." *Shit! I didn't mean to piss him off.*

"You call that dancing? It looked like you were about ready to fuck him out there."

"Far from it, did you not notice I was looking at you the whole time?" This was not going how I planned it.

"Yeah I did, but that guy was enjoying himself too damn much. Did you even notice how close to kissing you he was? If I didn't shove him back, he would have."

Damn it! "No, I guess I didn't. He knew I was watching you, though." I said, and then looked down to the floor. "And that you were watching my every move."

Hunter took a deep breath before he walked over to me, put his fingers under my chin and made me look up at him. "You got me all hot and bothered, and there's not a damn thing I can do about it while I'm working."

Now that's what I'm looking for!

I smiled at him and stood up on my tiptoes to place a kiss on his lips. With his lips pressed to mine, Hunter started walking us backwards until he pushed me up against the lockers. He reached down and grabbed the back of my legs, pulling me up to him. I wrapped my legs around his waist. Hunter slid his hands up and down my ass. I needed more, so I pushed myself until I felt his length pressed hard against my middle. He stopped moving his hands and pushed back against me.

Hunter started kissing from my lips down to my neck before he started nipping on my shoulder. We continued like this for a few minutes before he started sliding me down his body.

"You're gonna kill me, you know that?" He placed another kiss on my shoulder.

"Well, that would be a shame to have that happen, now wouldn't it?" I said, grinning at him.

"Such a smart ass."

"Learned it from the best!"

"Alright, let's get back out there before someone comes looking for us. I'm sure Zeke just had to save my ass tonight."

"Sorry, I guess I wasn't thinking." I said bashfully.

"Just don't do that shit to anyone else unless it's me." He placed another kiss on my lips before he pulled the door open. I walked through the door and he smacked me on the ass.

I turned back to look at him and just shook my head.

I made my way out the find Hailey, Gracie and Zoey to make sure everything was ok.

"What the hell happened?" Hailey asked.

"Hunter didn't like me dancing with that guy." I shrugged and walked past her towards the bar.

"Well Zeke is done for the night; he said he'd drop us off at the dorms on his way home."

I downed the rest of my drink, hopped off the stool, grabbed her arm and started towards the door.

The next morning, the ringing of my phone woke me up. "Hello?" I said sleepily.

"Morning Sunshine, get your ass out of bed. I'm outside." Hunter said all chipper like.

I groaned. "What the hell are you so happy about? And what time is it anyway?"

"It's nine a.m. and I want to get home, so get your hot little ass out of bed and get down here."

I rubbed my eyes with the palms of my hands and hung up the phone, not caring that I did not say goodbye. I hated mornings, especially with happy people!

"Hails, get up; Hunter is here." I said, walking towards the bathroom.

Thirty minutes later, Hailey and I lugged all our stuff out to Hunter's truck to head home for Winter break.

I woke the next morning with a fever and an earache; this was not how I wanted my break from school to start. I went downstairs and asked my mom to get me a doctor's appointment.

I sat at the table when my mom picked up the phone to call Hunter's mom because she was a nurse at our doctor's office. Mom told her what was going on, and she asked that I come right over so that the doctor could see me before they closed up early because Christmas was the next day.

Two hours later, manned with antibiotics and fever reducer, I was laying on the couch when Hunter came by to see how I was doing.

He walked in with chicken noodle soup and a movie. My heart melted a little more for him.

I curled up on the couch and rested my head on Hunter's lap. Hailey, Mason, Cooper and Jaylinn walked in.

Mason sat on the end of the couch where my feet were and said to me, "Get up."

"Mase don't start; I don't feel good."

"I don't give a shit; lay your head on this end." *Really?* Is he kidding me?

"Just let her be man." Hunter spoke up.

Mason did not like that, not at all. Cooper just looked at Hunter as if he were crazy.

I tried to defuse the situation. I sat up and asked Hailey and Jaylinn, "Are you girls all ready for Christmas tomorrow? All your stuff wrapped?"

"Yeah, we just got back from the mall, getting our last minute things." Jaylinn said.

"I still have a few more things to wrap. Kenz, come help me with this last one I have." Hailey asked.

I moved the covers out of my way and made my way upstairs with Hailey and Jaylinn to my room.

I was waiting for her to go to Mason's room to grab the gift to wrap, but she just reached in her purse, pulled out a piece of paper and some kind of passes.

I looked at the passes; they were for skiing in the Poconos this coming weekend. New Year's Eve weekend, the weekend I was going away with Hunter.

She winked at me and said, "I have to keep him busy somehow. There's only so much I can handle of him before I can't walk."

"Oh my God Hailey! I don't want to hear about that shit!" I said, completely disgusted by the thoughts running through my head.

"No really, I told Hunter I would help him. I'm not sure this is going to work but it should, since he has no idea you are going away with him." Hailey said.

I looked over at Jaylinn, waiting for her to tell me what she was going to be doing to keep Cooper busy. They claimed nothing was going on between them but I knew different. Cooper was never one to settle but Jaylinn was just the right person to change that.

"I don't have any plans. Cooper said he was busy." Jaylinn said with an unsettled look on her face.

"Coop doesn't have shit planned Jaylinn. You guys are coming with us; just don't tell him I told you. It's supposed to be a surprise. And you," Hailey said pointing at me, "better make this time worth it."

I walked over to her and gave her a huge hug, "Love you Hails."

Jaylinn joined in on our hugging and said "Love you too Hails."

After we got our last minutes gifts wrapped up, we made our way back downstairs to the boys. We all hung out for a little while before calling it a night.

"So you, your mom and Jaylinn are coming over tomorrow for breakfast?" I asked Hunter, walking him towards the door and away from Mason and Cooper so I could steal a kiss.

"Yeah, we'll open our gifts then come here."

"Ok, then I'll see you in the morning."

Hunter pulled me close and looked over my shoulder before he kissed me. He pulled back and said, "I'll see you in the morning. Make sure you take your medicine. I need you better for this weekend," he whispered.

I smiled and nodded my head. After Hunter and Jaylinn left, I went upstairs to get some sleep before a long day tomorrow.

Chapter Nineteen

I woke up Christmas morning feeling slightly better, my fever gone at least. I was so excited; I loved Christmas and I got to spend it with my little nephew. I quickly got up, showered and made it downstairs just as Jackson, Chloe and Alex were walking in. I walked over to Jackson and grabbed the car seat from him; I couldn't wait to get my hands on Alex any longer.

"Merry Christmas to you too Kenzie." Jackson said sarcastically.

"Just wait, I need my nephew first." I unfastened Alex from the car seat and picked him up. He was so much bigger than the last time I saw him just a few weeks ago.

"Merry Christmas baby Alex." I cooed to him, and he grabbed a hold of my finger. He was so sweet and handsome. He looked so much like Jackson, with a little touch of Chloe.

I walked into the dining room where my mom, dad, Jackson, Chloe and Cooper were. As soon as I walked in, I lost Alex to Cooper. Now that my hands were free, I went over to Jackson, put my arms around him and wished him and Chloe a Merry Christmas.

There was a knock on the door. I figured it was Hunter, Jaylinn and Mrs. McCormick. I went to answer it but was in for a surprise when I saw Dominic standing there.

Shit!

"Merry Christmas." Dominic said.

"Um, Merry Christmas. What are you doing here?" I asked with a slight panic in my voice. I did not need there to be a fight on Christmas and I was sure there would be one.

"I just wanted to stop by and say thanks." He reached up and ran his hand over his jaw.

Huh? "What are you talking about? Is this something that can wait for another day? Hunter is going to be here any minute and I don't want there to be another fight."

Cooper came up behind me and said, "What the fuck are you doing here? Did you not learn your damn lesson over Thanksgiving?"

"I'm not here to start any shit Cooper; I just came by to let your sister know that Brittany isn't pregnant. She lied about the whole damn thing." Dominic said, looking over at me.

"That's good and it explains why she was at the bar the other night with Logan."

"She was at the bar with Logan? You sure?" Dominic asked.

Maybe I should have kept my mouth shut. "Yeah. Look, you really should leave before Hunter shows. I'm glad you got an extra Christmas present this year."

I stepped back into the house with Cooper, shut the door, turned towards Cooper and said, "Not a word that he was here, got it?"

"Yeah alright. It's my business anyway. I got my own damn problems," Cooper said, stalking off towards the kitchen.

Hailey, who must have come downstairs when I was out front with Dominic, was helping my Mom and Chloe make breakfast.

"Merry Christmas Hails." I went over and kissed her cheek.

"Get off my girl." Mason said, sneaking up on me.

"Your girl? I think she was mine first." I wrapped my arms around Mason. "Merry Christmas Mase."

"Merry Christmas Kenz. What are you doing for New Year's?"

Shit! "Umm, I don't have any plans just yet; maybe hang out here with mom, dad, Jackson, Chloe and baby Alex. What are your plans?"

"Probably the same thing. Maybe we should invite everyone over here and have a party. I don't really feel like going out anywhere."

I glanced over at Hailey who had her eyes on the pancake mix that she was mixing. "Yeah, ok, sounds good."

Just as everything was about finished cooking, Hunter, Mrs. McCormick and Jaylinn showed up, armed with gifts.

I walked into the pantry to grab a roll of paper towels when Hunter snuck up behind me and wrapped his arms around me. "Merry Christmas CC."

"Merry Christmas." Turning around in his arms, I stood on my tiptoes and kissed him. He grabbed the back of my head with one hand; he let his other hand slide down my sides and around my waist to caress my ass. His tongue brushed my lips, wanting access into my mouth.

"What the fuck!" Mason yelled.

Hunter and I broke apart but Hunter grabbed my hand, started pulling me back in the kitchen, towards Mason. Mason stopped us from passing.

"I told you to leave my sister alone dude." Mason gritted through his teeth.

Hailey came up behind Mason and tried to grab his hand, but he moved his hand away from hers. Looking at me with his jaw set, he was waiting for one of us to answer him.

No one was saying anything. It was Christmas. I did not want there to be a fight. Hailey walked away. Jackson came up behind Mason and put his hands on Mason's shoulders, pulling him backwards. Hunter and I walked out to the dining room, still hand in hand.

Mason walked out a few minutes later and took a seat next to me but didn't say a word. Hailey, who was sitting on the other side of him, gave me a sympathetic smile. Even with everyone seated around the table, you could still feel the tension in the air. Cooper was doing his best to make everyone laugh as he normally did, but not this time.

I couldn't finish my breakfast so I got up to clean my plate and put it in the dishwasher. I needed to get some air so I stepped out the back door. Chloe, who was in the kitchen feeding the baby, came out a few minutes later.

"You ok?" She asked, zipping up her jacket.

"Kind of. I just wish Mase didn't have such a problem with Hunter and me. I don't have a problem with him dating Hailey."

"He's just protecting you; you know how they are. Jackson told me he doesn't like the fact you're dating Hunter either but he would rather it be him than anyone else."

"See I don't get it. Am I supposed to just stay single the rest of my life?" I gripped the railing a little harder, trying to keep myself calm. This was why I didn't want to go to school with them; I needed to live my life, away from my brothers who always felt the need to interfere with everything I did.

"No you're not. They will just have to get over it. You are smart enough to make smart decisions; they just have to trust you and let you live a little. They love you," she tapped me with her elbow on my arm "sometimes I think a little too much."

I smiled at her and took a few deep breathes. "Well, it's freezing out here; we better head back in before they send the search team out for us."

Laughing at me, she linked her arm with mine and we walked back in. Mason, Hunter, Cooper and Jackson were all in hallway when we walked in, and from what it looked like it was a very heated conversation. I walked past them and went into the living room to start handing gifts out.

Mrs. McCormick walked over to me, gave me a hug, handed me a little square box and said "Merry Christmas Sweetie."

"Thank you but you really shouldn't have."

She winked, said, "I didn't," and walked away, I stood there for a few seconds trying to figure out what she meant, before I looked at the card and saw it was from Hunter. I guess he asked her to give it to me so my brothers wouldn't give him shit. I set it aside to open it later when no one was around.

Everybody opened their presents for the next few hours. Mason was excited when he opened Hailey's Poconos trip for next weekend and so was Jaylinn, even though she knew ahead of time that she was going. She played that gift up and I did everything in my power not to laugh at her. She definitely put it on thick. Hailey loved the necklace that Mason got her; Cooper loved the new baseball glove that Jaylinn bought him. Mom and Dad loved their weekend getaway that we all got for them. Jackson and Chloe received a weekend getaway from all of us. We figured they could use it with just having had Alex. Mrs. McCormick loved the Kindle that we all bought her. Hunter and I didn't exchange gifts in front of everyone. I had something special planned for him this weekend, and I had the gift his mom had given me that I would open up later when I was by myself.

Mason and Hailey left after everyone was done to go spend time at her house with her family. Now that they were gone, the tension seemed to be gone as well. I knew Cooper and Jackson didn't like me being with Hunter but they didn't seem to hate the idea of it as much as Mason did.

I sat in the living room, curled up on the couch, watching A Christmas Story. Hunter came and sat with me. He made sure not to stir the pot and sat in the recliner.

Looking over at me he asked "You didn't say whether you liked my gift or not."

Smiling, I told him "I didn't open it yet. I'll open it tonight when I'm alone or if you want, I can open it now."

"No, you can open it tonight. I just thought you didn't like it or something." Hunter said looking slightly embarrassed.

"Anything you give me I like. You know that bobble head turtle you bought for me when you went to the Bahamas' a few years ago?"

"Yeah."

"I loved that little thing. I even brought it with me to school."

Looking around to make sure no one was in earshot, he said, "Do you think Mason realized we aren't going with them this weekend?"

"No, and hopefully Hailey keeps him distracted enough. I'm staying out of his line of sight as much as possible, so we'll probably be staying at your house a lot this week if you want to see me."

He got up, walked over to me and whispered, "You in my bed is something I can't wait to see."

Groaning, I reached up, wrapped my hands around his neck and pulled him into a kiss. Just him saying those words had my skin on fire.

After dinner everybody slowly started to say their goodbyes and I just could not wait to get upstairs and open my gift from Hunter. Finally, around eight everyone was gone and I promised Hunter I would call him after I opened my gift.

I ran up to my room and as soon as the door closed behind me, I ripped the card open.

The front of the card was blank; the inside, filled with his handwriting.

CC~

Hope you like the gift. Open the gift and then finish reading this.

I quickly tore open the box and inside was a necklace with a locket. I picked back up the letter and finished reading.

Now that you have the necklace in your hands, I can tell you that this is my heart; no one has ever had a piece of it like you. I know I don't always tell you how I feel, but with this, I hope you now know. A key goes with it as well that I will give to you later when you are ready for it.

Love

Hunter

Wow, I had no idea he ever paid that much attention to me all these years. I picked up my phone and quickly sent him a text message.

Me – 10:48pm: Love the necklace, thank you

Hunter – 10:51pm: Glad you like it

Me – 10:53pm: Can't wait for this weekend so I can give you yours

Hunter – 10:56pm: I told you not to get me anything having you alone is enough

Me – 10:59pm: Goodnight Hunter xoxo

Hunter – 11:01pm: xoxo

He had no idea what my gift was; I just really hope he likes it. I fell asleep quickly that night thinking of all the things I had planned to do to him.

Chapter Twenty

Hunter and I spent a lot of time together over the week, mostly at his house. Mason and Cooper were pretty distracted with their upcoming Pocono trip and they still had not mentioned Hunter and I going with them, which was fine by me.

Friday morning, I was up early. I couldn't sleep. I was too excited for my surprise from Hunter. I was hanging around the house acting as if everything was normal when my mom cornered me in the sitting room. I hated this room. The only reason I was even in here was to look out the window to see if Hunter had pulled up.

"So since your brothers are heading to the Pocono's this weekend. What are your plans? I thought you would be going with them."

"Oh well, Hunter and I decided to do something else, you know, like give the couples their time together." I said like it was the right thing to do.

"For some reason, I think you're up to something." She walked over to the couch, picked up the pillow and then put it down again. "I know you and Hunter have been spending a lot of time together. Are you guys seeing each other?"

I never lied to my mom and I wasn't going to start now. "No, we aren't seeing each other." It's the truth; we never made anything official. "But we are seeing where things could go. It's kind of hard to have any kind of relationship with the boys always involving themselves in what I do."

Sighing she said, "Come sit with me." I walked over, sat at the end of the couch and placed a pillow on my lap. "Your brothers love you; they feel like they have to protect you from everything and anything. This may be your dad's and my fault for always telling them they had to look out for you all the time. I wouldn't change that for anything baby girl. I know you don't understand now, but when you have a girl of your own, you will understand."

"I understand mom, but I feel like I can't breathe sometimes around them. I need to learn from my mistakes, but I don't ever have the chance to do that with them breathing down my neck all the time. I know they don't like me and Hunter being together, but I want to see where it goes, even if it breaks my heart in the end."

"I know you do baby girl; just try seeing it from their point of view. You're going to be dating their best friend, the same person who they talk to about all the girls they have been with, and all the stupid stuff guys talk about. They aren't going to want to talk about that stuff with Hunter anymore."

Well, if that is the case, then I should be just as upset as they are about Mason dating Hailey. She is my best friend and I don't want to hear about the stuff that the two of them do but I don't go all crazy on them. I try to embrace the fact that they are both happy with each other.

"I get it mom, I really do but you can't help who you like. It just happens. You know how long I have liked Hunter, and now that I could finally have the chance to be with him, I'm going for it. I don't care if it pisses them off."

"Oh MacKenzie, you are my daughter." Mom chuckled. Mom had three brothers growing up as well, so I knew she could relate to me.

"Good, now can you help me get out of here without them throwing a fit when Hunter shows up?" I got up off the couch and walked over to my mom.

She stood up and I hugged her. "Yes, but first you have to tell me where you are going. I don't like the fact you are going away with him by yourself."

"Well that's going to be a problem; I don't know where we are going."

Sighing, she said, "Well, that's a good thing." She winked at me. "Because you're going to love it, and I trust you and Hunter enough to let you go by yourself."

"Wait, you know where I'm going?" How did she know and I could not get Hunter to even give me a clue.

"Yes, now go get your bags before your brothers wake up."

I started towards the stairs before I stopped and looked back at my mom. "Love you mom; thanks for understanding."

She smiled and went to fix the pillow I had just thrown back on the couch. I ran upstairs and grabbed my bags. Just as I came back downstairs, Hunter walked in the door with his mom and Jaylinn.

"Hi Mrs. McCormick." I said when I walked over to her to kiss her cheek.

"Hi sweetie, have fun this weekend." I smiled at her and walked over to Hunter.

My mom spoke up just as we were getting ready to walk away. "Hunter," Hunter turned towards her, "Be careful with her."

"I will," is all he said and those words caused goose bumps to rise on my arms.

When we got all settled in Hunter's truck, I had to start digging for answers as to where we were going. "So are you going to tell me yet where we are going?" I asked, practically jumping up and down in my seat.

"Nope, but get comfortable for a long drive." Hunter said, smiling over at me.

I settled into my seat and pulled out my phone to see if Hailey had sent me a text. I slid it open and saw that I had five texts from Mason wanting to know where I was and why I wasn't at the house when he got up. I decided not to answer him since I was on my own little get away and did not want to deal with his drama. I pulled out my iPad and started reading for a while. I knew we were heading south due to the state signs I saw. We stopped for gas and food after about 5 hours of driving. Once we got back on the road, I fell asleep.

"CC, get up; we're here." Hunter said, running his hand up my leg that stretched out on the seat.

I yawned and wiped my eyes. When I opened them, I was in shock of where we were. All around us were trees, mountains and nothing else. The house was a huge two-story log cabin with a wraparound porch and green roof; it was gorgeous.

Hunter came over, opened my door and held his hand out to me. I grabbed his hand and slid out of the truck.

"Wow, this house is beautiful." I was in heaven; there wasn't anyone around for miles, just Hunter and me for the next three days.

"Glad you like it; wait till you see the inside." He walked around to the bed of the truck to grab our bags.

"How did you find this place?" I asked, grabbing one of the bags from him.

"I know some people." He said with a shrug of shoulder.

When we walked in, it astounded me. The house had hardwood floors in every room, exposed beams and cathedral ceilings. The kitchen was all stainless steel appliances and granite counters; the dining room had a table that sat eight people. When you first walked in, there was a fireplace directly in front of you with a TV mounted above it, a couch and a loveseat. To the right of that was a sliding glass door that led out to the back deck where there was a hot tub nestled in the corner.

On the second floor, there were two bedrooms. The master suite had a king size bed, two dressers, a closet and in the corner a fireplace with a TV above it. The carpet was so plush that I had to take my shoes off to run my feet over it. Off the bedroom was a master bath that had a whirlpool big enough to fit four people. Next to that was a shower with a one-way window overlooking the mountains. Behind a closed door in the master bathroom was a toilet in its own little room. There were even a his-and-her sink in there as well.

The second bedroom was just like the master except it didn't have a whirlpool or fireplace. It had a sliding glass door that led out to a little private deck.

In the basement, there was a pool table, a bar and a huge movie screen with two rows of couches lined up in front of it. The back wall was all ceiling to floor windows with a view of the mountains.

"Oh Hunter, this house is just unbelievable and it must have cost a fortune. You really didn't have to do all this." I said, wrapping my arms around his side.

"Don't worry about how much it cost; just enjoy it." He placed a kiss on the top of my head. "Well, let's get our bags upstairs."

We walked back up to the main floor to grab our bags. After we unpacked, Hunter asked me, "Are you hungry? I could go downstairs and make us something to eat."

"No I'm still full from earlier but I would love to try out the whirlpool." I told him. The minute I had seen it, I wanted to get in it to relax after that ten-hour drive.

"Ok, you go get in; I'll be there in a few minutes. I'm going to go grab something to eat."

While Hunter was downstairs, I walked into the bathroom, turned on the water and stripped out of my clothes. I was alone in the tub for a while before Hunter finally came in. For a little bit I did not think he was going to come in.

"Hey, what took you so long?" I asked. He started stripping out of his jeans and that black t-shirt that I loved so much that stretched over his broad chest.

"I told you I was hungry, plus what's the rush? We have all weekend to ourselves." He stepped in the whirlpool settling in between my legs, facing me.

I felt a little exposed this way; I moved my legs up to my chest and hugged my arms around them. Hunter frowned when I did that. He grabbed my hand and pulled me to him so we were chest to chest. The second our skin made contact, I shivered; he really had no idea what he did to me.

"This feels nice after that long drive." Hunter moaned laying his head back on the edge.

I started placing kisses on his neck while running my right hand up his chest down his stomach and back again. He grabbed my hand, held it over his chest and then looked at me, so intently.

"Do you feel it?" He asked.

"It's beating so fast." I said. I broke our eye contact, laid my head on his chest and listened to his heartbeat.

"Every time you're near me this happens." He said and turned his head to kiss my forehead.

He started rubbing his hand up and down my back, causing me to shiver again. I started running my hand up and down his chest and stomach, causing him to shiver this time too.

"Hunter," I said as he kissed my shoulder. "Make love to me." Hunter stopped kissing me and sucked in a breath, slowly letting it out as he closed his eyes.

"CC..."

"Please Hunter," I said. "I want to be with you; I'm ready. I've waited this long to share this with you; I don't want to wait any longer."

"Are you sure?"

Nodding at him, I said, "It just feels right; we need this, and I need this."

Hunter did not respond. Neither of us needed words anymore. He helped me from the whirlpool. He helped dry me off and then I did the same to him, both of us taking our time, kissing every part of each other's body from our heads to our legs.

Looking down at me, he slowly ran his hands down my sides to my hips. A whimper escaped from me at what was to come next. He picked me up and walked me over to the bed; he carefully laid me on my back while he climbed on top of me. His knees nestled inside of mine.

"If you change your mind at any time, just tell me," Hunter said while placing kisses on my neck. I shifted my hips so that he was at my entrance. "Let me do this for you ok? Tonight is all about you."

Pulling back from me slightly, he rubbed his hands against my breasts. My eyes closed as he brought a nipple to his mouth and sucked lightly on it, causing my back to arch.

I sucked in a quick breath with realization settling in. Was I really about to do this with him? I have dreamt about this day for so many years that my first would be with Hunter. I wanted it, but was so nervous at the same time.

"CC we can stop now..."

Cutting him off, I said, "Hunter, I don't want to stop; I'm just a little anxious but I want to do this."

"I'm going to be as gentle as I can with you." Reaching up to him, I put my hand over his heart and felt it thumping hard. He was nervous too. Tilting my neck, Hunter bent down and started placing kisses on it. "I'll go slowly; if it hurts just tell me, and we'll stop."

He started pushing through my entrance. "This might hurt some." As he said that, I reached up and dug my fingernails into his back at the first sting of pain. Once Hunter was through the barrier, he stilled inside me, giving me a chance to adjust to him. Then he started moving slowly again and the pain started subsiding. We felt like two puzzle pieces fitting together so perfectly.

As I started moaning louder, Hunter grabbed my hands, laced our fingers together and put them above our heads. As Hunter continued to thrust in and out of me, I hitched my legs up around his hips so he would thrust deeper. I felt like I could not get him close enough. Snuggling into his neck, I started nipping as I felt the tension starting to grow between my legs.

"Come with me CC, I want to feel it." He moaned softly in my ear. After a few more thrusts, I was falling over the ledge. Hunter thrust in two more times and then stilled as his own release hit. After a few minutes, Hunter rolled over and he pulled me against him to snuggle. Laying there, I placed my hand over his heart, feeling it beat wildly still, just like mine.

"Are you ok? I didn't hurt you did I?" Hunter asked after his breathing went back to normal.

Speaking for the first time since we started, I lifted my head and looked into his bright blue eyes. "I couldn't have asked for it to be better than it was." Smiling at him, I reached up and ran my hand through his hair. "Thank you." I wanted to tell him I loved him. After that, there was no doubt in my mind that he loved me and he would tell me when he was ready.

He kissed me and then said. "Good night CC."

"Sweet dreams Hunter."

Chapter Twenty-One

A few hours later, I woke to Hunter holding a warm compress between my legs. God that felt good; I was sore but not too sore.

"Sorry, I didn't mean to wake you up. I just wanted to make sure you were ok." When he pulled the towel up, I noticed the blood on it.

How embarrassing, I did not even think of this part. I started flushing while reaching for the towel. "It's ok; I'll take care of it." I started to move my legs off the bed but he stopped me.

"Don't be embarrassed CC." He reached over on the end table and handed me a glass of water and some pain reliever.

Looking at him, I had to smile. Leave it to Hunter to think of everything. "You're going to spoil me, you know that right?" I took the pain reliever and water from him. "Thank you." I handed him the empty glass back. "I think I'm going to take a quick shower."

I walked into the bathroom and quickly took a shower, wanting to get back to Hunter. I dried my hair as best I could with the towel and put it up in a ponytail. When I walked back into the room, he had changed the sheets. Now, he laid on his back, his arm over his eyes with the sheets pulled up just enough to cover his hips. Walking over to the dresser, I reached in and pulled out a t-shirt.

"What are you doing?" Hunter asked me.

I turned around to face him and shrugged my shoulder at him, "Just putting something to sleep in on."

"Don't do that." He pulled the covers back. "Come here."

I threw the shirt on top of the dresser, walked over to the bed and cuddled up next to him.

Hunter ran his fingers lightly up and down my back. He sighed and spoke so low I barely heard him, "You've wrecked me for anyone else."

I didn't respond; I don't think I was meant me to hear that. I've wrecked him; he has wrecked me just as much if not more. He has my heart in his hands and I just hoped he doesn't break it.

The next morning when I woke up, I knew before I even opened my eyes that he was not in bed. I reached over to his side of the bed and it was cold, so I knew he had been up for a while. I threw on some clothes and went to go find him.

When I walked downstairs, it was so silent that you could hear a pin drop. Where was he? I walked downstairs to the rec room, thinking maybe he was watching a movie and didn't want to wake me up, but he wasn't there either. I walked back upstairs to our room, grabbed my cell phone and tried to call him. As I was dialing his number, I heard the door shut downstairs. I quickly turned around and went back downstairs.

He was all sweaty and flushed; he must have gone for a run. His shirt was wet from his sweat and clung to his chest, and his shorts rode low on his hips. "Morning handsome."

"Morning CC, did I wake you?" He asked, walking towards the fridge. He took out a bottle of water and drank the whole thing.

"No but I didn't like waking up and you not being there. Why didn't you wake me up?" I asked as I perched myself on the barstool next to the breakfast nook.

He shook his head and ran his hands through his hair. "I needed to clear my head." My heart sped up, thinking he regretted last night. "Stop it; it's not what you think."

"Then what is it?" I asked.

Sighing, he walked over to me and turned my chair to face him. He looked like he was going to have a panic attack. "What is it? Just tell me."

"We um," He closed his eyes, took a deep breath, then opened them and looked at me. "We didn't use a condom last night; I was so caught up in you that I didn't even think about it. I'm so sorry."

So, this was what had him acting strange. I smiled and said, "Don't worry about it. I'm on the pill. I should have mentioned it last night. I figured since you knew I didn't sleep with anyone, and you know everything else about me, that you knew this too."

He stared at me for a minute before he responded. "Doesn't matter, CC. I still should have used one, and I'm sorry."

"Stop it, I'm not sorry." I put my hands on his shoulders and said, "Let's go get a shower. You need one." I pushed him away and ran up the stairs laughing.

Moaning, he ran up the stairs behind me. We forgot all about that conversation as we helped each other out of our clothes. We stepped into the shower, washed each other and spent time memorizing each other's bodies.

I wanted him and I knew he wanted me by the way he was groaning as my hand was running up and down the length of him. Hunter spun me around and lifted me against the wall; I wrapped my arms around his neck and my legs around his hips.

He was right at my entrance, but before he entered, he asked, "You're not too sore are you?"

"No." I answered, and then sunk down on him.

He buried himself deep inside me and whispered, "God, you are so tight." He groaned. "This is going to be hard and fast."

I buried my face in his neck, kissed him and lightly bit him. He thrust so hard and so fast, bringing me closer to my orgasm. Everything started to tingle and the back of my head hit the shower wall.

Hunter threw his head back and moaned, "Let go CC" and we both fell over the edge at the same time.

As we started to come down from our high, Hunter rested his forehead on mine and said, "I'll never get enough of this." Then he slowly kissed me a few more times before he lowered my legs.

We cleaned up again, and he walked out of the bathroom in just a towel. When he walked back in, he had put on a pair of boxer briefs. In his hand was a blow dryer. He plugged it in, pulled me in front of him and started drying my hair.

No one had ever done this for me, no one except for my mom when I was little. I hated when someone dried my hair all wrong, but when Hunter did it, I didn't care if he did it right or not. When my hair was all dried, I turned around, and looked up at him to tell him thank you. All I could see was love in his eyes and him smiling down at me.

Hunter picked me up, carried me over to the bed and gently laid me down. "Now, stay here while I go make us breakfast." He walked out of the door, and a second later, he stuck his head back in the doorway. "And don't put any clothes on. Actually, don't put clothes on at all this weekend." Then he walked away again.

I laughed, threw myself back on the pillows and reached over to grab my phone. There was a text message from Hailey.

Hailey – 9:37am: How's the v-card

Laughing and shaking my head I sent her a text back.

Me – 11:02am: What v-card? Xoxo

Then I scrolled to my mom's text.

Mom – 10:48am: Hope you're enjoying your time with Hunter.

Me – 11:05am: I am love u

A few minutes later I got a text back from Hailey, or at least that's who it said it was from.

Hailey – 11:11am: WHAT! Hope your fucking kidding?

A few seconds later, I heard Hunter's phone ringing downstairs. *Fuck!* I guess Mason saw the text. I didn't hear Hunter answer, so I guess he let it go to voicemail. He walked up a few minutes later with pancakes, eggs, orange juice and a stargazer, my favorite flower. Leave it to Hunter to remember this stuff, when I never thought through the years that he had cared or even paid attention.

"So, um," I started, but I did not want to ruin the mood. I had to make sure he knew what had happened so if he answered his phone, he would be prepared. "I think Mason knows about us."

Looking confused, he said, "What do you mean he knows about us? He's seen us kissing and shit."

Shaking my head, I said, "No, I mean he knows we slept together." I looked down to my hands and back up at him. "Hailey and I were texting. I think he saw the text where I said "what v-card" when she asked how it was going."

He didn't say anything for a while. I didn't want to ruin our time alone together but he had needed to know.

He surprised me when he spoke up and said, "We'll deal with it when we get back."

"Alright." We ate our breakfast in bed, while we watched TV, not really talking at all.

When we finished, Hunter asked if I wanted to learn how to play pool. Little did he know, I already knew but I didn't tell him that little secret. I quickly threw on a pair of yoga pants and a tank top. We went downstairs to the rec room and Hunter set up the balls and then explained to me how to break. The first time I missed, and he showed me again. The second time, I nailed it, exactly as I always did.

Hunter eyed me but did not say anything. I sunk two solids so it was still my turn. All the shots for me to take were hard and I wasn't ready for Hunter to catch on to the fact that I knew how to play. I looked over at him and asked, "You going to stand there or help me?"

Smirking, he walked over and stood flush with my body, then pointed to the one he wanted me to hit. He slightly bent me over and positioned me to hit the ball. As he pulled back, I wiggled my ass and he completely missed.

He thrust his hips into me as I started laughing. "You think this is funny do you?"

"No, not at all." I said still laughing and wiggling my ass again.

He turned me around to face him then picked me up and placed me on the table. He slowly drew my tank up and off me. "I love these." He whispered, as he took the back of one of his fingers and trailed it from my cheek, down my neck and then circled my nipple. He placed a kiss over it and then did the same to the other one. He replaced his lips with his tongue and circled my hard nipple.

He was driving me crazy doing this, taking his time with my body.

"Hunter." I whimpered his name and arched my back when he lightly bit my nipples.

Thankfully, he didn't tease me for too long before he started placing open mouth kisses from the valley between my breasts. He traveled down my stomach, twirling his tongue in my belly button and then placed a kiss on each of my hips before he looked up at me.

"You ok if I do this?" Hunter asked. Thank God, Hailey and I went and had our waxes done this week.

I could not even form words, so I just smiled and nodded my head. He placed each of my feet on the table, slid my ass forward and spread my legs, giving him access. I was so nervous, no one has ever done this to me before, yeah Dominic and I have messed around but I never let him go down on me.

As he bent down and placed his hand on my knees, he said, "CC, you're shaking baby." He kissed the inside of my knee before resting it on his shoulder. "Don't be nervous." He kissed the inside of my other knee before he placed it on his other shoulder.

He looked at me with such intensity in his eyes. "So pretty," he whispered, before he placed a kiss on my sex. As soon as his lips touched me, I bucked my hips off the table. Hunter chuckled and then did it again and again.

Hunter reached around my right leg and separated my folds with his fingers, then placed an open mouth kiss there. He replaced his kisses with his tongue, and my hips again bucked right off the table.

This was too much and too intense.

"I got you CC." Hunter groaned. "Let me taste you, all of you."

I wanted to tell him to stop but I couldn't even think of forming words as his tongue started torturing me. Sucking and twirling his tongue was almost my undoing. I was panting and whimpering so hard, it was almost embarrassing.

Hunter pulled his mouth from me, looked up, smirked and put a finger inside me. Then he started lapping his tongue all over me again. I was so close; my legs started squeezing his head; my fingers locked in his hair, trying to ease the intensity.

Pulling back he whispered, "Let go CC."

Oh God, did I. I came so hard, and so fast I was seeing stars.

After I came back down from my high, Hunter was right there waiting for me. He looked at me with this expression on his face that I could not explain. He picked me up and carried me back upstairs to the bedroom where we both snuggled up and fell asleep.

Chapter Twenty-Two

When I woke up a few hours later, Hunter just laid there watching me sleep. "Do you ever sleep?"

"Yeah, but not this weekend; I want to spend every minute with you," he said, before he kissed me. "I had plans to take you hiking, but I don't even want to share you with the trees and mountains."

I smiled and said, "Good, cause I don't want to share you with anyone either."

We laid around the house for the rest of the night. We went downstairs and curled up on the couch together to watch a movie. We relaxed in front of the fireplace in the living room, talking about all the crazy stuff we did growing up together. We wrapped up in blankets, ordered a pizza for dinner and ate in front of the fire.

After Hunter finished off the last of the pizza, we went outside to get into the hot tub. I slipped off the robe that I was wearing, since Hunter refused to let me get dressed, followed him outside and climbed into the hot water.

When he stepped into the hot tub, I stopped him when he tried to sit down between my legs. I sat up on my knees, and feeling completely brave, I ran my hands from his ankles all the way up to his legs to his hips. I looked up at him watching me with hooded eyes. Still working off my bravery, I grabbed the base of his cock and his head fell back. I stuck my tongue out and licked his cock from the base to the tip, memorizing every inch of him. Then I took him in my mouth. Hunter's head fell forward to look down at what I was doing; he didn't say anything, he just watched everything.

Adjusting to the size of him, I started bobbing my head up and down, twirling my tongue around his head. He was still watching me with an intense aroused look on his face. As I started to pick up speed, he wrapped his hands in my hair. That was all the approval I needed from him. I took my right hand that was holding onto his leg, and grabbed the base of him. I started working his base with my hand and sucked as much as I could of him in my mouth, working on a good rhythm. It only took a couple of minutes before he started to tense and I knew he was close.

"Damn CC, you have to stop or I'm going to come in your mouth." He said breathing heavy.

I moaned when he said that. It sent that tingling feeling straight to my middle, and the vibrations of my moan nearly pushed him over the edge.

"Fuck, don't do that," he said panting.

I picked up my speed, stroking and sucking, harder and faster. Hunter stopped moving my head, his legs locked and he cried out his release. Now I've done this to Dominic before, but this with Hunter was something completely different. I never liked the taste of Dominic but I would never get enough of Hunter.

Reaching his hand down, he slowly pulled me up his body. When I was finally within reach, he placed opened mouth kisses on my shoulders up to my neck and then to my lips.

He rested his forehead on mine and said, "Now it's my turn to return the favor."

Smiling I said, "Next time, I'll take an IOU for now." I winked at him.

Hunter and I relaxed in the hot tub until we started turning all wrinkly. We ran back inside and up to our room. Hunter started the fireplace while I went to dry my hair.

After my hair was dry, I climbed into bed and cuddled up next to Hunter. We laid there, not talking to each other, just being content to be in the same room together. We watched the fireworks go off out through the bedroom window, nestled with each other and when midnight fell upon us, Hunter kissed me with those amazing lips of his until we were both breathless. We stayed up until the fire died out and then both of us fell asleep peacefully, wrapped in each other's arms.

A nightmare woke me in the middle of the night; it took me a few minutes to realize whom I was with, and where I was. The nightmare had me shaken a bit; I didn't want my time here with Hunter to end when morning came.

I felt the sting of tears hit my eyes when I looked at Hunter sleeping. I tried to hold the sob back, but I just couldn't. I knew deep in my heart that when we went back home, things were going to change.

Hunter stirred and opened his eyes. He raised his hand to wipe the tears away. "CC don't cry baby."

Each kiss and touch from Hunter was filled with so much passion. He climbed on top of me and stared into my eyes. He pushed himself in and stilled. I tried to move under him but he just shook his head.

"Please Hunter, I need this. I need you." I said, begging.

"CC," he said with a hushed voice, "I love you so much baby."

I sucked in a breath; those words were not words I was expecting him to say. "I love you too Hunter."

I now understood why he never told me those words before. He was waiting until I was ready for them, until I needed them the most.

We made love, so slow, with so much adoration for what seemed like hours. We were worshipping each other's bodies, begging the other to understand without the words.

After we were done, we fell back asleep, wrapped in each other's arms.

When we woke up the next morning, there was apprehension in the air as to what would come when we made it home in the next ten hours. Hunter and I took a shower together, made love one last time and told each other how much we loved each other again and again. The rest of the morning was very quiet between the both of us. We got everything packed up and started our dreadful ride home.

It was around dinnertime when we arrived home on Sunday. When we were home from school, everyone hung out at our house. This would work in our favor, because with our whole family around, I would not have to worry about anything getting out of control.

Hunter turned off the truck but didn't make a move to get out; he reached over and grabbed my hand. "No matter what happens when we step foot out of this truck, just know I love you and nothing will ever change that, nothing."

A few tears fell from my eyes; I knew with those words that there were going to be problems. I wiped my eyes with the back of my hands and smiled over at him while saying. "I love you too." I took one deep breath and let it out slowly. "Ok let's go face the music."

We walked into the house hand in hand; everyone had gathered at the table, just about ready to eat. I did not look anyone in the eye when we walked in. I went directly into the kitchen, still holding Hunter's hand. I was thankful he had not dropped it yet. I knew he would and when he did, a little piece of my heart would stop.

Mason, Cooper and Jackson were standing by the stove quietly talking. When they noticed we had walked in, they stopped and all three scowled at us. I expected the least amount of problems with Cooper because he and Jaylinn were together.

"We need to talk." Jackson spoke up first.

Hunter and I nodded in agreement. Mason looked from Hunter to me and then back to Hunter before he shook his head and walked out. Great!

The four of us walked outside to the garage. No one said anything for a few minutes, no one wanting to address the elephant in the room.

I decided I needed to speak up first and at least address Cooper, who had no valid argument. "Look I know you guys don't like the idea of me and Hunter. You have your own reasons and I don't completely understand but whatever. Coop, you can't even put up a fight since Hunter knows you're with Jaylinn. He knows you will take care of her even with your track record." This conversation had me worked up. "From the day he found out about you and her in the kitchen, he hasn't said shit to you about it. And now, you're going to start shit because he and I are together?"

Cooper looked over at Jackson and then back at me. "I know and I don't really have a problem with it. I know he'll treat you right, but I know he broke your heart once before too and that's what I don't like." He looked at Hunter and continued. "You're like a brother to me; you are a brother to me. Don't break my sister's heart, and we won't have a problem."

Hunter nodded and said, "Same goes to you; just because I'm not giving you shit for going after my sister doesn't mean I don't give a shit if she gets hurt. You know she has shitty taste in guys. I'm pretty sure you beat the shit out of a few of them."

I looked at Jackson, waiting for his reasoning. He looked in Hunter's direction and said, "Look, I don't have a problem with this. Yeah, it bothers me a little because she's my sister, but you're already family. I don't have to worry about someone looking after her and protecting her." He looked at me and said, "We aren't your problem, Mason is. He hates this. We tried to talk to him, but he's not hearing us. Maybe if you talked to him one on one he might listen."

"Yeah alright, I'll try." I walked over to Cooper and Jackson, and gave them both a huge hug and a kiss on the cheek.

I grabbed Hunter's hand and whispered, "Two down, one to go."

He scratched his head and said, "Um, make that two to go. Your dad still hasn't said a word to either of us."

Jackson chuckled, slapped Hunter on the shoulder and said, "He's easy. Just have Kenzie bat her eyelashes. It's always works."

Laughing, I told him, "Shut up, you're just jealous."

The four of us walked back in the kitchen, grabbed something to eat and sat at the table with everyone else. Mason was still missing but Hailey was there and mouthed, "Sorry." I shrugged my shoulder and gave her a small smile, because there was nothing she could do. She gave me my weekend alone with Hunter, and I could not ask for anything more than that.

After dinner was all done, the girls and I were cleaning up and doing the dishes. I heard the front door open and slam shut. I snapped my head over to Hailey, knowing who it was. She shook her head, dried her hands and went after Mason. I gave her a few minutes before following her out.

When I walked into the sitting room, it was chaos. Mason and Hunter were nose to nose. Jackson and Cooper both had a hold of them so no one would take a swing. Both were yelling at each other. My dad walked up behind me and broke them up.

"Mason walk away now!" He yelled at Mason.

"This is my fucking house. I'm not going anywhere. He can fucking leave," Mason yelled back at my dad.

I looked over at Hunter. He looked at me and shoved Jackson's arm off him. "Fine, I'll fucking go." Then he stormed past me towards the front door.

"Wait, Hunter, don't go." He was not stopping, so I ran after him. "Wait, I'll go with you. Just let me grab my shoes."

I ran into the dining room where I left my Uggs and quickly put them on. When I stepped back in the hallway, my dad was there talking to Hunter while Mason was yelling something at someone.

"Daddy," I started to say, but he cut me off.

"Baby girl, just go upstairs." He said angrily.

Well he was still calling me Baby girl, so he wasn't pissed at me. Not wanting to push him any further, I walked off towards my room. Before I walked out, I turned to look at Hunter who was looking at me. I mouthed, "I love you," trying to remind him of what he said in the truck to me.

Hailey came into my room a few minutes after me; I was lying on my bed staring up at the ceiling.

She laid down next to me and sighed. "I'm sorry he's being such an asshole about this. He ruined the whole weekend for all of us once he figured out that you and Hunter were doing your own thing. When he saw the text, he just lost it." She turned on her side to face me. "The message popped up in the screen, so it's not like he was snooping or anything."

"It's ok, I shouldn't have responded." I turned to look at her. "Thanks for helping me though."

She sat up and had a huge smile on her face. "So, tell me everything!"

"Oh my God Hails, it was perfect; he was perfect." I sat up and stretched my legs out in front of me. "I'm so glad I waited for him. I can't even explain to you how I feel about him now after this weekend."

"Aww, I wish the asshole didn't ruin my weekend though. I had plans for us."

Groaning, I said, "Please don't, I don't want to hear it."

She laughed at me and said, "See we can get along, why the hell can't they?"

Shaking my head, I say, "I don't know Hails. I knew this was going to mess shit up with Hunter and me though. I just hope he doesn't choose them over me."

"Don't even think like that Kenz, seriously. If he wasn't serious about you, he wouldn't have gone away with you, and I am pretty damn sure he would have left by now."

"Yeah, I guess you're right." I really hope she is right.

Hailey and I talked about everything we did during the weekend for a while before my dad appeared in my doorway. *Damn!* I wonder how long he has been standing there. I hoped not that long, or he would now know that Hunter and I slept together and that I was no longer a virgin.

Hailey climbed off the bed and excused herself. When she passed my dad, he walked in, sat on the end of my bed and patted the spot next to him.

"You know I love you baby girl." I nodded. "I talked to Hunter and Mason. I don't know what good it did, but I tried. I don't like all this fighting. Are you sure that this is what you want? Mason seems to think you're going to get hurt for some reason."

"Dad I'm sure, even if it doesn't work out between me and Hunter, and I get my heart broken." I looked down to the floor. "I love him Dad."

My Dad sighed loudly and shook his head. "I thought so. You always did have a crush on him."

I looked over at him and he was smiling at me. "Just protect your heart baby girl. You know I already think of Hunter as a son and he has always looked out for you, so I'm leaving this to you two to figure out."

"Thanks Daddy, I love you." I threw my arms around his neck and hugged him.

"Love you too."

Hunter knocked on the open door and I waved him in. I let go of my dad and went to stand next to Hunter. "You ok?"

He looked at me, contemplating his answer. "Yeah."

My dad excused himself and left. I sat on the bed, pulled Hunter between my legs and I started massaging his shoulders.

"So what did Mase say?"

He tensed a little bit under my hands, "He told me I'm not good enough for you."

Sighing, I told him, "He's wrong Hunter. You are." I kissed the back of his neck and continued to rub his shoulders.

"I think I'm going to get out of here and let shit cool off." He stood up and pulled me up to wrap his arms around me. "I love you CC."

I reached up with both my hands and grabbed his face. "I love you too." I kissed him and then told him, "You give me the chills when you say that."

He looked at my arms to see the goose bumps, and then kissed me again. "Let me run downstairs to grab your bags."

"Oh right, I almost forgot."

We walked out to Hunter's truck to grab my bags, and passed Mason on the porch with Hailey on his lap. We stood behind Hunter's truck out of Mason's view. I kissed Hunter goodbye and asked him, "When are we leaving to head back school?"

"I'll be over around ten. I got class on Tuesday or I would stay for a few more days." He kissed me one last time and said, "Plus, I'm pretty sure Mason is ready to get rid of me."

"Stop it, he'll come around. I'm his sister; he can't stay mad forever." He grunted, climbed up into his truck and took off.

I grabbed my bag off the driveway, made my way back up to the porch and stopped in front of Mason and Hailey. "Mase, can we talk?"

Hailey tried to get up off his lap but he pulled her back so she couldn't move. Hailey looked down at him, and he looked up at her. She said, "You need to talk to her. Knock this shit off, Mase."

He looked at me and then back to her, and asked, "Talk to who?"

I stood there, stunned that he would say something like that to me. Hailey pushed his shoulder back, got up, and walked in the house. A second later, she came out with her purse and keys and told Mason, "I'm leaving. When you decide to grow up call me." Then she looked at me and said, "Love you Kenzie. I'll see you in the morning."

I didn't answer her, and she kept walking towards her car, I wasn't sure if I was going to cry or scream. Mason got up and pulled the door open with such force it banged against the house, and then I heard him say "Bitch."

After standing there for a few more minutes, I walked inside and threw myself into doing my laundry and cleaning up my room, before finally falling asleep.

Chapter Twenty-Three

The last two months had flown by in a haze. All my classes were going great; I was getting mostly A's and B's. Hailey and I had moved out of the dorms and moved in with Hunter and Bentley. We only stayed at the dorms once a week to make our presence known. I had offered Bentley money for Hailey and me staying there all the time but he told me as long as we cooked dinner 3 times a week that was payment enough. Otherwise, they would still be eating pizza every night.

Mason still wasn't talking to me, Hunter or Hailey. Hailey always said she was fine and that she wasn't worried about Mason. I knew it was eating her up inside. There were a few times I caught her crying late at night. She said they talked a few times but never for long, because baseball was taking up a lot of his time. I talked to Cooper and he said that Mason was still being a dick about all this shit. He was snapping at him and Jaylinn all the time and Cooper was fed up with it. I asked about what he was doing all the time that he claimed he was busy. Coop said that he was at baseball most of the time but when he wasn't he was out partying and getting trashed.

Hunter was not himself since that night at the house when he and Mason got into it. It was eating at him. I think when he caught Hailey crying a few days ago, that it caught up to him, because he started to take it out on me. He would pick a fight for no reason. I was late getting home from work last night and he flipped out and asked me a million times where I was.

I was starting to get sick from all of the tension around Hunter and me; my stomach never could handle that. Just the other day, as soon as I opened my eyes, I had to run to the bathroom to get sick.

I woke up this morning and as soon as my eyes opened, I ran off towards the bathroom to throw up. Hunter came in as he has the last few times and held my hair back for me. When I was done, he would help me in the shower. He apologized for taking things out on me and I would always forgive him. How could I not, when he looked at me with those eyes of his that had my stomach doing flip-flops. After we showered, he carried me back to bed and made love to me. He always made sure to take his time with me after I got sick or after fighting.

I must have fallen asleep after we were done because Hunter's side of the bed was empty and cold. After getting dressed, I went downstairs to get something to eat because I started to feel sick again. Hailey was sitting on the bar stool, eating a sandwich and reading a book.

"Hey Hails."

"Hey sleeping beauty. Hunter keeping you up all hours of the night?" she said laughing.

I shook my head. Only Hailey would bring that up. "No, actually he isn't keeping me up at all lately."

"You sure have been sleeping a lot. You feeling ok?" She asked.

"Not really, all this tension with Mason and all of us is really starting to wear me down. I wish he would just get over it so we can all move on. It's been two months since that fight, and enough is enough." I said, turning to grab a bowl from the cabinet.

"I know, I keep trying but as soon as I bring it up, he makes some kind of excuse to get off the phone." She closed the book in her hand and put it on the table.

"Hails, work on your relationship with Mase. Don't worry about us; I'm his sister. He has to get over this eventually. Once we go home for the summer, Mom will put a stop to this bullshit."

"I know..." A raging Hunter, who had just walked in and slammed the door, cut her off.

"What the fuck, CC?"

"Hunter, what the hell is going on?"

"You tell me, what else are you hiding from me?" He walked over and stood inches away from me.

"I have no idea what you're talking about." My stomach started turning. "What's going on?"

"Dominic showed up on Christmas morning and you never told me?"

I grabbed my stomach, trying not to think about getting sick again. "It wasn't a big deal. Cooper was there with me. He just stopped by to tell me that Brittany lied about being pregnant. That's it; he wasn't there more than 5 minutes before I told him he had to go."

Oh my God, I was going to lose it. I took off running towards the bathroom to throw up again.

Someone knocked on the door. "Come in." I said moaning from the bathroom floor. The tiles were cooling my face off.

"Oh sweetie, are you ok?" Hailey said lifting my head on to her lap.

"Hailey, you have to get me out of here. I can't do this shit anymore." My stomach was turning again; I held it tight trying to make it stop. "I can't be around him. Every time I am, my stomach knots up and I get sick."

I started crying. I didn't want this to happen. I tried to ignore it but it just wasn't going away. He was pissed off about something that happened two months ago, something that was no big deal at all.

"Alright look, you go grab your stuff and meet me back downstairs. I'll get us back to the dorms. I think you just need a little space." Hailey said while she was running her fingers through my hair.

I got up off the floor, threw some water on my face and went upstairs to grab my things. I quickly put everything in a bag. I didn't want to have another fight with Hunter; I just needed to get out of here. I was walking down the stairs and I could hear Hailey and Hunter's voices. I couldn't hear what they were saying so I walked out the front door quietly to wait for Hailey. She was taking forever in there with him. Bentley had pulled up in the driveway. I ran over to him before he got out.

"Bentley, could you give me a ride back to the dorms please?" I didn't wait for an answer. I just climbed in his car.

"Yeah sure, everything ok?"

"No, but it will be."

He dropped me off and I said, "Don't tell Hunter. If he asks if you saw me, just say no."

"Kenzie, you know I can't do that." I knew that I shouldn't ask him to lie for me but I just didn't want him coming after me.

"It's fine. Don't worry about it. Thanks for the ride Bentley." I opened the car door just as Hunter and Hailey pulled up behind us. "Shit!"

Hunter came stalking over to me. "Don't ever take off like that again. I am not fucking around CC. I don't give a shit if we are fighting or not." Then he stalked back to his car and Hailey got out.

"Come on sweetie; let's get you up to our room." Hailey grabbed my hand and we walked into the building. I turned one last time to look over at Hunter but someone blocked my view. Once my focus came to the person in front of me, I was surprised to see Dominic with Brittany off in the distance.

Great fucking timing, I thought. I haven't seen him since he showed up on Christmas morning, here I had just had a fight with Hunter over him and now he is standing in front of me all within an hour of Hunter mentioning his name.

"You ok, MacKenzie? You don't look so good." I looked past him to see Hunter speed out of the parking lot.

"Dom, today's not a good day ok. I really need to get her upstairs." Hailey opened the door, and we walked in.

Dominic followed us the whole way up, but didn't say anything more. I walked into our room, went right over to my bed and pulled the covers over my head, begging sleep to come.

♡♡♡

I had not heard from Hunter for two weeks, not one word. I saw him a few times around campus while walking to class. He always had his head down, so I knew he never saw me. I was still throwing up every day from the stress of losing Hunter. I had hoped nothing like this would happen to us but when Mason refused to come around, I knew that it would eventually lead to Hunter and me splitting apart.

I was at work one day, sitting behind the counter scanning ID badges, when Logan came in with a cheeseburger in his hand. The smell of it made me immediately sick; I could not even make it to the bathroom. I got sick in the trashcan right next to where I was sitting.

After I was done, I looked up to Logan, who had his jaw dropped open slightly. "I'm sorry; I haven't been feeling well lately. Whatever that is," I said, pointing at his cheese burger, "made my stomach turn."

Logan closed his mouth, nodded his head and walked off towards the back office. I went to find him, because I wanted to apologize again for getting sick in front of him while he was eating. I heard him talking on the phone and waited a minute before I walked in.

"Dude I think she's pregnant." I shook my head, guessing he got someone pregnant. "You have to get her to take a test." I wondered why he couldn't just get her to take the test. He got her pregnant. "Because, when I was home over Christmas break, my sister was the exact same way." Forget it; I will talk to him about it later since it didn't sound like he was getting off anytime soon.

When he came back out about ten minutes later, he said, "Go home."

"What?" Shit, I shouldn't have waited to talk to him. "I don't get off for another two hours. If you're worried about me getting sick again, I won't."

"I'm not worried about that; just go home. I'll cover you." Logan grabbed my hand and helped me off the stool I was sitting on.

"Are you sure? I really don't mind staying. I already feel better."

"I'm sure." He said with a stern look on his face.

I reached down to grab my purse from under the counter and put the strap on my shoulder. Logan asked, "Are you leaving Friday for spring break?"

"Yeah, Hailey and I are heading home. Why what's up?"

"I got your shift covered tomorrow; I'll see you after you get back." Logan said while he grabbed a student's ID to scan.

"If you're sure? I know Hailey wanted to go home early so this would be great."

"I'm sure; see you when you get back."

"Thanks."

"Hey, Kenzie?" Logan called out. I stopped walking and turned around to look at him. "Take care of yourself."

"I will."

As soon as I walked out of the library, I sent Hailey a text to see where she was. I was walking and texting when Dominic snuck up behind me.

"Damn it, Dominic." I said.

"Sorry, thought you heard me coming up." I finished my text and slid my phone back in my purse. "Are you heading back to the dorms?"

"Yeah, I was just texting Hailey to find out where she was. Logan is covering for me, so we can get out of here sooner for break."

"You talking to Hunter yet?" Dominic asked, kicking a rock that was lying on the sidewalk.

"No." I watched as the rock bounced in the street and saw Brittany standing at the ending of the sidewalk watching us. I had seen Dominic and her talking a few times but I wasn't sure what the story was with them.

"How are you getting home then?"

"I asked Jackson to come pick us up."

"Well I can take you; I was actually getting ready to leave tonight anyway. I got a nap in earlier and I'm not tired now, so I thought I would head out tonight."

"Um, let me call Hailey." I reached in my purse and dialed Hailey's number.

She must have been out with Zeke or Bentley because I heard the radio volume lower before she said, "Hello."

"Hey, where are you?"

"Oh I'm out with Zeke; he's taking me back to the dorms right now. Why what's up?"

"So Logan sent me home because I got sick at work and gave me tomorrow off. Dominic offered to take us home tonight. You want to go?"

"Hell yeah! I'll be there in ten minutes. Love you, bye." Then she hung up on me. I guess she was in a hurry to get home.

"I guess we're heading home tonight. Thanks Dominic."

"Sure no problem. I have a few last minute things to pack and take care of so I'll come meet you in about an hour?"

"Yeah sure."

I walked off towards the dorms and Dominic took off the other way towards Brittany. Hailey and I got everything ready to go and put all our bags by the door, waiting for Dominic to come. He finally showed up right on time. We got all the bags loaded in his car and left to head home.

Chapter Twenty-Four

We were finally back in town late at night but Dominic claimed he had to pick up something from the drug store before he dropped us off. He ran in quickly, got what he needed and then we pulled up to Hailey's house first. It didn't make any sense to me since he lived closer to her.

"So I'll see you in the morning, I guess. Cooper said they were coming home tomorrow at some point." I said to Hailey as she was pulling her last bag out of the trunk.

"Yeah, I'm just going to unpack and then I'll be over."

"Ok see you later."

"Thanks again Dom." Hailey said.

"Sure no problem."

We got into the car but pulled over right up the street from Hailey's house.

I looked over at Dominic, "What are you doing?"

"I need to talk to you and if I have you in my car, it's a lot easier. Besides, now there isn't anyone else around."

"Dominic, please just take me home. I can't do this with you right now ok."

"Just listen to me ok."

I crossed my arms over my chest and stared straight ahead.

He cleared his throat. "I know this isn't any of my business but did you sleep with Hunter?"

Groaning, I dropped my head to the back on the seat. "I'm not talking to you about this Dominic. It's none of your business. I don't ask what's going on with you and Brittany; don't ask about me and Hunter."

"I know but just answer the question, it's important."

"It's not important and it's none of your business." I spat back at him.

"Damn it Kenzie, just answer the question!" He raised his voice to me.

I was fuming but I knew him well enough to know if I didn't answer him, I would be here all night and I really just wanted to go home. Huffing I said, "Yes."

He ran his left hand through his hair and then reached in the center console with his right, grabbed the drug store bag and handed it to me. "You need to take this."

I opened the bag that he handed to me and I shot my eyes up to him, "Are you fucking kidding me? I'm not pregnant asshole. You know how I am when I get upset over shit." I closed the bag back up and stuck it back in the console then crossed my arms over my chest again. *Was he crazy?*

"I can't be pregnant, I'm on the pill and you know this." I told him after a few minutes.

He looked over at me and said, "Please just take it when you get home, just to make sure. I know how you get when you get upset over something but this, what you have, is different. You're different."

"Fine, I'll take the damn test but I already know the answer. Now can you please take me home?" I huffed still looking straight ahead.

Dominic put the car in drive and took me home. I got out of the car and went to grab my bags. He came around his side with the drug store bag and handed it to me. I took it and shoved it in my purse.

"Thanks for the ride; I'll see you back at school I guess."

"Yeah sure, let me know if you need a ride back."

I nodded and grabbed my last bag that he had in his hand and went into the house. "Kenzie," Dominic called out.

"Yeah?"

"If you need to talk or anything, call me." He didn't wait for me to answer; he got back in his car and backed out of the driveway.

My mom was pacing the floor when I walked in; I knew something was wrong when I saw her. "Mom? What's wrong?"

"Oh thank God." She ran towards me and squeezed me.

"Mom?"

"Hunter has been calling nonstop looking for you. He said your phone is turned off and he couldn't get a hold of you."

Nice, why is he calling now? "Well Hunter shouldn't worry about me; he hasn't for the last two weeks. Hailey and I got a ride home from Dominic."

"What do you mean he hasn't worried for the last two weeks? Are you guys fighting?"

"Yeah, because of Mason's bullshit."

"Oh baby girl, I'm so sorry." She started rocking me back and forth slowly as she did every time she comforted me. The swaying was doing nothing for my stomach.

"Look, I'm really tired and I just want to go to sleep. We'll catch up later." I kissed her cheek and started for the stairs.

"What do you want me to tell Hunter when he calls back?" she asked.

"Tell him whatever you want." I don't care if he gets pissed off because I took off again or because Dominic took us home.

"Alright."

I went upstairs, dropped my bags, slipped off my shoes and curled up in bed. I fell asleep for a little while but that drug store bag was taunting me. It was after three in the morning when I finally had enough and got up to take the test just to prove to Dominic that I was not pregnant. Ok, maybe to myself too.

I grabbed the bag and walked towards the bathroom. Hailey was standing in the hallway talking to Mason. What the hell was Mason doing here this late at night with Hailey?

I tried to walk past them, but Mason grabbed my arm stopping me. He pulled me into his chest and hugged me. "I'm sorry I've been such an asshole lately."

I pushed off him a little. "If you don't mean it, then don't apologize to me Mase. I know you're only saying it because I'm not with Hunter anymore."

Taken back a little by my remark, he frowned and said, "I am sorry. I just don't want to see you hurt and from what Hailey's told me you are hurting." He pulled me back to his chest and kissed my forehead. "I'm sorry. I'll talk to Hunter tomorrow."

Shaking my head and trying to hold in the tears, I said, "Don't worry about it. It's over between us."

"I'll fix it; it's my fault. I just don't think he's good enough for my little sister, but I don't want to see you like this every day."

Tears were streaming down my face and soaking his shirt, "Please don't; just let it be, for me."

Sighing he said, "Ok," he grabbed my face and wiped the tears away. "Just because you asked I won't say anything."

"Thanks Mase." I turned towards Hailey and said, "Can I talk to you for a minute."

"Yeah, sure."

I grabbed her hand and pulled her into the bathroom with me. I turned on the faucet so Mason couldn't hear us. I pulled out the test from the bag, and her eyes flew open wide. "You have to be shitting me!"

"Shh, Hailey." I flipped the box over and read the directions, then opened the box and set the test on the sink. "Turn around. When I'm done, I need you to look at this and tell me its negative, ok?"

She turned around and nodded. I pulled my pants down, sat on the toilet, peed on the stick and quickly put the cap on. I cleaned myself up, all the while not looking at the godforsaken test.

"Ok, look at the test and tell me it's negative."

Hailey slowly turned around, gasped and put her hand over her mouth. That was not the reaction I wanted. "Hailey, it's negative right?"

She just looked at me but didn't say anything.

Fine, I guess I had to do this on my own. "Fuck!" I yelled and then put my hand over my mouth. Five, ten, twenty minutes went by and we both just stared at the test both in disbelief.

Mason must have been worrying because he came banging on the door, making us both jump. "Kenzie, Hailey you guys ok? You've been in there forever."

Startled and worried he would pick the lock, I picked up the test, threw it back in the bag and shoved it under my shirt. I looked over at Hailey, "Don't say a word to anyone Hails."

I opened the door and walked straight into my room; I took the test out from under my shirt and shoved it in the back of my underwear drawer. I paced the floor for the rest of the night. The test had to be wrong. I always took my pill at the same time every day, and I never missed. There had to be a mistake.

Around eight the next morning, I still could not even think about going to sleep. I need to talk to someone. I couldn't talk to my mom; Hailey had no idea about being pregnant. Chloe! I went over to my purse, grabbed my cell and dialed Chloe.

"Kenzie, what in the hell are you doing up so early?" She yawned and I heard Alex crying in the background.

"Um, can I come over? I need to talk to you." I was already walking downstairs to grab my keys.

"Yeah sure but stop and grab us coffee first. Alex has been up most of the night and it was my turn to stay up with him."

"Yeah sure, I'll grab you a coffee. Should I get one for Jackson?" I started the car.

"Better pick him up one so when he gets up, he doesn't bitch about it."

"Ok see you in a few."

Fifteen minutes later, I pulled up to Jackson and Chloe's little house that they just recently bought. I grabbed the coffee and made my way inside, Alex was lying on his back on his little play mat and Chloe, who looked like she hasn't slept in hours, was in the kitchen making bacon. As soon as I smelled it, I ran into the kitchen, dropped the coffee down on the table, spilling some in the process and darted to the bathroom to throw up.

I heard mumbling outside of the bathroom door and then someone knocked.

"Kenz let me in." Chloe said.

"Hold on a second." I quickly got up and rinsed my mouth out before I opened the door. "Sorry, I just had to pee."

Shaking her head at me, Chloe said, "Not buying it. You're pregnant aren't you?"

"Shh, I don't know. That's why I'm here." I grabbed her hand, pulled her into the bathroom, turned the water back on and said, "I took a test, but it can't be right Chloe. I take my pills every day. What the hell am I going to do? I need you to fix this."

She raised her eyebrows at me. "You didn't use protection?" I shook my head. It was a huge mistake on my part for telling Hunter it was ok. "You're smarter than that Kenz. I'm not going to lecture you though. Have you taken another test since last night?"

"No, that was the only one. I didn't even think about any of this shit until Dominic mentioned it to me. He gave me the test to take."

"He what? How did he know?" She asked confused.

"I don't really know, I never asked." I sat down on the edge of the tub. "What do I do? I'm freaking out."

"Freaking out isn't going to help you at all. Let me go throw on a pair of shoes and I'll tell Jackson I forgot to grab eggs. We will run to the store and grab another test. Although I'm pretty sure that one is right. I took twenty tests in three days because I refused to believe I was pregnant."

"Alright, let's go."

We walked out of the bathroom. Chloe went into the living room to grab Alex and take him to Jackson who was still in bed. I covered my nose with my shirt to keep from smelling the bacon that she was still cooking.

"You're pregnant." She said when she saw me holding my nose. "I was the same way; everything smells nasty and turns your stomach."

"Alright Dr. Oz, can we go please?" She laughed at me, clearly amused by my panic.

We ran into town to the nearest drug store, picked up a test and made it back to the house within fifteen minutes.

"Go take the test, and I'll go distract Jackson." Chloe said when we pulled into the driveway.

I walked in and went right in to the bathroom to take the test. Five minutes later, I still had the same damn results.

PREGNANT.

Chapter Twenty-Five

What was I going to do? Neither one of us was ready to have a baby, neither one could afford to provide for a baby. Hunter was graduating this year and then would be enrolling into a police academy; I wasn't even sure where he was planning on living. I still had 3 years to finish so that I could become a teacher, something I have always wanted to do since I was little. Yes, Hunter and I both had jobs to help pay for things we needed but not enough to take care of a baby. Would he even want our baby? Would I be a single mom? There was no way I was aborting my baby or giving him or her up for adoption. I could not even think about it. It just wasn't an option for me.

Mom and dad are going to be so disappointed in me, Hunter's mom too. All they want is to see us graduate and make something of ourselves, and I messed it all up. I dread telling them that I made a mistake, but I would live up to it. It was my fault that I got Hunter and me into this mess.

My brothers are going to kill Hunter. Yes, Cooper and Jackson were ok with us dating, but now to have to tell them about this? Oh God. Mason really was going to murder Hunter. There is no way I can let them find out.

I needed to get out of here; I needed to figure out what I was going to do. I put the test back in the box and shoved it in my purse. I opened the door and the smell of bacon and eggs immediately hit me again. I quickly shut the door and took a couple of deep breaths, trying to think of anything but getting sick.

My stomach settled. I took a few more deep breaths in and out of my mouth. I could do this. I would walk out there and say I have to go do something with mom and pray I don't get sick.

I opened the door and took a few more breaths. I can do this. I walked into the living room and lay down next to Alex on the floor. "Hey baby, Aunt Kenzie has to go. Grandma needs me to go with her to the store. I'll see you later, ok." I kissed the little peach fuzz on his head.

I went over to Jackson, reached up, placed a kiss on his cheek and told him, "I'll talk to you later. Mom wants me to run some errands with her."

"You're not going to stay for breakfast?" The second he even mentioned it, my stomach clenched.

"No, I'm not really hungry anyway."

I went over to Chloe and kissed her cheek. She whispered in my ear, "Call me later."

"I'll talk to you guys later. Chloe, maybe we could grab lunch or dinner this week since I'm home on break."

"Yeah sure sounds good, we have to talk about the wedding anyway, get some ideas for bridesmaids dresses." Chloe said as she walked and put her arms around Jackson.

Oh my God, there is no way I can be in that wedding looking like a whale. "Um yeah sure sounds good."

I was walking down the driveway when I heard footsteps behind me. Damn it, I thought I was in the clear. I acted as if I didn't hear anything, quickly made it into the car and started it up but Jackson was at the window knocking on it.

I pressed the button and the window rolled down. "You sure everything is ok? You hate waking up before noon Kenzie."

"Yeah, I just couldn't sleep. I haven't been sleeping well since Hunter and I broke up. No big deal." I shrugged my shoulder, praying he would buy it.

"I'll talk to Mason and Hunter this week and get this shit worked out. I don't want there to be any problems at my wedding."

"No!" I yelled a little too loud. "No, its fine. Mason said he was going to talk to Hunter, so just let them work it out, ok?"

Huffing he said, "Fine but if by the end of the week those assholes aren't talking, I'm going to make them."

"Fine, do whatever you want, but just let them work it out themselves first." My phone beeped from inside my purse. I dug it out. It was Chloe, saving me. "Look I have to go. That was mom looking for me."

"Yeah alright, love ya, see ya later." Jackson stepped away from the car and I put it in reverse and made my way home.

When I got home, Hunter's truck was in the driveway. I didn't want to go in, but I didn't have anywhere else to go since Hailey was here. My other friends were gone for spring break or still at school. I parked next to Hunter's truck, and decided to try to sneak in the back door and right up the steps.

I wasn't so lucky, because Hunter, Mason and Hailey were sitting at the kitchen table. I turned, shut the door, kept my head down and walked right out of the kitchen. I heard the legs of the chair scrape the floor and Hunter saying, "Wait."

I didn't wait though; as soon as my feet hit the steps, I took off, ran into my room and locked it. I rested my back against the door just as Hunter banged on it.

"CC, we need to talk. Let me in." He yelled through the door.

I dropped my head back against the door. Why now? I can't do this. I can't worry about him. I needed to worry about me. I needed to ignore him until I can figure this out.

"CC, please open the door." He tried to wiggle the door handle.

"Hunter, just go away. I don't have anything to say to you." My voice started to crack. I just wanted him to come in here and tell me everything would be ok. He wouldn't though because he didn't know. If he did he would be running the other way.

"Fine, for right now, I'll leave you alone, but this isn't over." he said, sounding frustrated.

I kicked off my shoes, laid in my bed and started sobbing. I thought of how I really messed everything up. Once Hunter found out about me being pregnant, he would leave me, probably for good. How could I be so stupid? I put my headphones in, and eventually, cried myself to sleep.

When I finally woke up, it was dark in my room. I pulled my headphones out, reached over and turned the lamp next to my bed on. Hunter sat on the chest at the end of the bed with his head in his hands.

I sat up and asked, "What are you doing in here?"

He turned around to look at me. "Mason picked the lock since you weren't answering anyone. Once we came in, we realized you had your headphones in." He shook his head and continued. "I thought you did something stupid."

"Well, now that you know I didn't, you can go." I didn't want him in here; I didn't want anyone in here.

He sighed. "Is this how things are going to be with us now? Can we not even be in the same room together? I love you CC. I'm sorry for the way shit went down between us; I didn't know how to handle it."

"Hunter, it's a little too late for apologies now." *Do not cry. Hold it together.* "You told me you wouldn't break my heart again, and you did. You said you picked me this time, but you didn't." The tears started flowing. "Please just leave." I begged.

"No, I'm not leaving. I did pick you. I do pick you." He walked over and sat next to me on the bed, and I moved away. He frowned, "I know I acted like an asshole. I am an asshole. I shouldn't have been taking that shit out on you. You don't need that. Mason and I talked, and I think he finally gets that I am not going to hurt you. Look..."

I cut him off, "But you did exactly what he said you would do. You hurt me Hunter. I can't..."

He slammed his lips down on mine. He tried to deepen the kiss but I wasn't having it. I couldn't with this secret between us. Hunter's fingertips reached the bottom of my shirt, lying on my stomach.

I pushed him back; I couldn't let him touch me, especially not my stomach. "Stop, you can't make everything better by doing that."

"CC, I love you. I need you." Hunter said, breathing heavy.

I turned my head towards the window and whispered, "I don't need you."

He sucked in sharp breath, "You don't mean that; I know you don't. Your flushed body and goose bumps tell me you don't mean that. CC, baby, please talk to me. We have to fix this. I'm screwed up without you."

I had to get him out of here. He was killing me, and I knew I had to say something that would hurt him. "There isn't anything left for you to fix. Dominic took care of me when you wouldn't." I sobbed the last part out. I could not believe that had come out of my mouth.

Hunter sat up, and ran his hand threw his hair. I wanted to run my hands through the same hair. God, why could he not just leave? It was killing me to hurt him like this. He stared at me. I could see the storm in his eyes, the rage pulsing through his body. This was what I needed him to feel to keep him away from me. I needed to figure out this pregnancy on my own. I couldn't burden him with this.

"Are you fucking serious?" he finally asked.

I nodded. He got up and stormed out of my room. A few minutes later, I heard his truck start. I quickly scrambled over to my purse called Dominic.

"Kenzie, hang on." He must be at some kind of party, because the music was blasting. "Hey, everything ok?"

Twisting my fingers, I said, "Um, not really. Where are you?"

"At Jason's party with Brittany, what's going on?"

"I kind of just told Hunter that you've been taking care of me. I'm sorry; I didn't know what else to tell him. He wouldn't leave me alone." I said nervously.

"Don't worry about it. So, I guess you took the test?" I heard keys jiggling in the background.

"Yeah and I'm sure you already know the answer." I said, trying not to cry again for the hundredth time.

"Yeah, I'm going to swing by. Is that ok?" He asked as I heard his car start up.

"What about Brittany? I don't think it's such a good idea. Hunter might come back. And then world war three might start." That was the last thing that needed to happen right now.

"Don't worry about Brittany. She'll understand. Why don't you meet me at the park around the corner? I'll pick you up there and we'll talk."

I looked over at the clock. It was only nine, and I had slept for so long that I wasn't even tired. "Yeah ok, ten minutes and I'll meet you there."

"Yeah, I'll be waiting," Then he hung up.

I put my shoes back on, threw my hair up in a ponytail and pulled on one of Hunter's hoodies that I stole from his home. It still smelled exactly like him. It gave me a little comfort knowing his smell wrapped around me. The pain in my chest was not any less but I would deal with that one day at a time.

No one seemed to be home, so walking out of the house was easy. I made it to the park in no time. Dominic was there waiting for me on one of the park benches, with some crackers and a ginger ale.

I looked at Dominic and smiled. This was my old Dominic: sweet, caring and loving. "This always helps when I get sick." He shrugged his shoulders.

I smiled, a real smile. "Thank you, but I think it's better if I don't eat for now since my stomach is settled."

"Yeah, ok. So, you are pregnant huh?" He could not look me in the eyes when he asked.

"Yes, but you already knew that." I grabbed his hand and he looked at me. "How did you know?"

Dominic chuckled. "Well actually I didn't. Logan did."

What? "Logan knew?" I'm confused. I didn't even know until now. "How?"

Dominic moved his hand back into his lap. "He called me Thursday while you were working and said he knew you were. His sister was the exact same way when he was home on Christmas break."

"Oh." Logan was talking about *me*. He did not get anyone pregnant. Now it made sense. Maybe Logan was a good guy after all. He could have just looked the other way and I still wouldn't know I was pregnant.

"So," He looked nervous, like he wasn't sure we should be talking about this or not. "What are you going to do?"

"Honestly," I looked over at him and met his stare. "I have no idea. I'm so scared; I'm not ready to be a mom yet, but...," I took a deep breath. "I don't really have a choice now. It's not weird or anything for me to be talking to you about this is it?"

"No, I think I always knew deep down that you would wind up with Hunter, but I kept hoping it would be me." he said, giving me a wink.

Dominic and I talked for two hours before I realized how late it was. I didn't take my phone with me, so I knew that my brothers would come looking for me. Dominic walked me home, even though I insisted that I was fine. Everyone was home when we made it to the house and Hunter's truck was back in the driveway.

"So, it's probably a good idea if I walk up alone." I wrapped my arms around myself.

"Yeah, I guess you're right. I've had Hunter beat my ass enough this year." He said laughing. "Plus, Brittany is waiting for me."

"Funny." I said sarcastically. "How are things with Brittany anyway?"

"Well, not so good right now. She came all the way up here to confront me about knocking you up."

"What! How does she know?"

"She doesn't. I denied everything. She just thought she knew."

"Well thanks for everything Dominic. I'll talk to you later, I'm sure."

He tucked his hands in his pocket and nodded. "I think you should tell him Kenzie. He may be pissed off at first. Shit, he may not even believe you, but he needs to know. Figure things out together you know. He is just as much a part as this as you are."

A few tears fell. He was being so sweet. "Thanks, we'll see what happens." I gave him a kiss on the cheek, and went home.

Chapter Twenty-Six

When I made it home that night, everyone was in the living room watching movies. I peeked in to see if Hunter was in there, and thankfully, he wasn't. I sat on the arm of the couch near Mason. "Hey guys."

"Hey, where were you?" Hailey asked.

"Oh, I just went for a walk, trying to clear my head." I grabbed the hem of my shirt, messing with it, trying not to make eye contact.

"Kenzie, can I talk to you for a minute outside?" Jaylinn asked, standing up from Coopers lap.

"Um, yeah sure." I put my hands in my pockets, and looked down to the ground, then made my way outside with her.

"So I know shit is all screwed up with you and Hunter, but what you said to him was fucked up Kenz. You know how much he hates Dom for what he did to you. What do you do? You go and throw that shit in his face that Dom was there for you and Hunter wasn't. That's low Kenz."

I didn't think she would understand and I didn't expect her to. I just hoped after I figured everything out, that she would understand. "You don't understand what's been going on and I don't expect you to. But I stay out of your relationship with Coop, and you need to stay out of mine."

Looking apologetic, she said, "I know and I am trying. I just want you to know that it is killing him Kenz. He's a mess. Coop and I had to go pick him up from the bar just a little bit ago. He never drinks like this Kenz." A shadow passed by the light from the deck, but she kept talking. "Please, at least talk to him."

"Stay out of it Jay!" Hunter's voice boomed through the silent night. He came down the stairs to where we were on the patio. "Mind your own fucking business." He was furious, livid.

Jaylinn looked at Hunter and then back at me, closed her eyes and shook her head. "I'm just trying to help, but you two seem to be doing such a fucking good job yourselves that I will let you be." She stomped off towards the house.

I did not want to wait around to see if I was the one who got yelled at next, so I followed her in and went up to my room. In a small way, I hoped Hunter would have asked me to talk, but I knew it was for the best that he didn't.

I grabbed a pair of shorts and a tank top and decided to relax in a nice hot bath. I had to deal with this one way or another; this wasn't something that would just go away with time. Realizing I didn't have the first clue where to start, I figured I would talk to my mom. She had handled Jackson and Chloe telling her she was pregnant pretty well. I could only hope she would handle this that well too.

After I turned all wrinkly, and the water had run cold, I got out and went to put my clothes on, but realized I left them on my dresser. I opened the door to make sure no one was in the hallway, and quickly ran into my room.

I had dropped my towel, and was pulling on my tank top when the door to my room flew open. I yelped in surprise. "What the hell Hunter, get out."

He froze in place, staring at my bare ass. "Hunter!" I yelled again.

Shaking his head, he looked at me and then moved towards me. "Why didn't you lock the door?"

I quickly grabbed my shorts and pulled them on. "I shouldn't have to. Normal people knock first, asshole."

He reached up, tucked a piece of my hair behind my ear and took a deep breath. I stood completely still, waiting for his next move. "God CC, you're killing me. You need to talk to me, tell me what's going on with us. I know I screwed up and took shit out on you, but we can work it out. Just stop running from me." He started swaying where he stood.

"Hunter, you're drunk. I'm not talking to you about anything. Now get out." I pushed his shoulders back a little, letting him know I was serious but I didn't let go of him for fear he would fall over.

"I'm not drunk." He was slightly slurring his words. He may not be drunk but he was feeling pretty good. "I want you so fucking bad it hurts, CC."

His words were squeezing my heart so tight I felt like I couldn't breathe. I wanted him too, but not like this, not until he knew my secret. "I can't Hunter. It hurts me too, but I just can't do it."

I needed him to wrap me in his arms and tell me everything would be ok, that we would figure things out together. I gripped his shirt where my hands were still on his shoulders and pulled him so we were close but not quite touching. I closed my eyes and took a deep breath; he smelled manly and clean, with a hint of his cologne that I loved so much. His smell settled me. He lifted my chin with his fingers. He was shaking, or maybe that was me.

"CC please, even if it's for tonight. I just need to hold you."

I took a deep breath. I could do this. We didn't need to do anything and I doubt he would even remember come morning. I know this is a bad idea, but I need him too. I'll slip out before he wakes and hope he doesn't remember this.

"Fine, but nothing is happening Hunter. It can't." I let go of him, went to pull down the covers from my bed and crawled in. I heard Hunter wrestling with something behind me. Please let it only be his shoes. I cannot have him cuddled up to me skin to skin. Luck wasn't on my side tonight. When he got in bed, he was in nothing except his boxers.

"Hunter, you need to put your clothes back on. I don't need my parents walking in here, and seeing you practically naked, lying in my bed." My parents wouldn't come in here but he didn't need to know that. I just needed his clothes back on.

"It's fine CC, just lay here with me." Hunter said, with his eyes half closed.

Huffing, I reached under my head, took one of my pillows and shoved it between us; Hunter looked down at the pillow, reached for it and threw it on the floor, then pulled my body so my back was against his chest. "Stop fighting me." He whispered.

His arm snaked around my waist and his hand spread out over my stomach. I tensed. "Stop pushing it." I moved his hand down my body so it rested on my hip. I was self-conscience about my stomach, knowing I was pregnant now.

After a few minutes of complete stillness, I heard Hunter whisper, "I love you," and then a second later he was lightly snoring. I was finally able to relax and fall asleep. I snuggled up to him a little closer, wanting to take advantage of this time.

The next morning, I woke up before Hunter even stirred. As soon as I opened my eyes, I ran to the bathroom to throw up. After that, I went back into my room as quietly as I could, grabbed some clothes and went back into the bathroom to get ready for what could be the worst day of my life.

Mom was leaning against the kitchen island reading the paper and drinking her coffee. I could not see anyone else around, and thankfully, she wasn't cooking anything. "Morning, Mom."

She took off her glasses and set them down on the island. "Morning baby girl, you want something for breakfast?"

I took a deep breath, trying hard not to think of food. "No thanks, I was going to go for a walk. You want to come with me?"

"Oh, um, sure." She finished her coffee, sat the cup in the sink and we left for our walk.

"So," She crossed her arms over her chest. We were walking down the sidewalk towards the park I met Dominic at last night. "You want to tell me what's going on with you and Hunter?"

Here goes nothing I guess. It is probably better to start at the beginning. "Well, it was Mason that we were fighting over; things were pretty tense for a while. We were fighting off and on and I was constantly panicking that at any minute he would tell me he couldn't work things out with me. I kept getting sick, worrying about it all the time. He found out that Dominic came over to the house on Christmas, and was pissed off because I hadn't told him. I told Hailey I needed some space from him, so I took off one night from his house while waiting for Hailey; I guess that pissed him off even more. He didn't talk to me for two weeks after that. A guy from school covered my shift yesterday so I could leave early and come home." We stopped at the stop sign, looked to make sure there were no cars coming then crossed the street. "I ran into Dominic on my way home from work that night, and he asked if we needed a ride home. I guess Hunter came looking for me and when I wasn't there he panicked and called you."

"He told me he had a feeling you were with Dominic. He went to Dominic's dorm room and he wasn't there either but Hunter wasn't sure. Sweetie, I know this isn't any of my business but he really does love you and your brothers. He was torn between you guys."

"I know mom, I just wish things didn't end the way they did. Mason, I think, finally got his head out of his ass about us, but it's a little too late now."

"It's not too late if you don't let it be. I know you love him." Mom said smiling at me.

I started crying, and sat on a bench that we were passing. "Mom, he's going to hate me for what I did. He is going to think I'm trapping him. I don't know how I am going to be able to tell him. I'm so scarred he's going to leave me for good."

She sat down next to me, and hugged me into her side. "Tell me what's going on baby girl."

I took a deep breath. Here goes nothing. I wiped the tears from my eyes and looked her direction, "I'm so sorry mom. I didn't mean for this to happen but I'm pregnant."

Mom blinked a few times, letting the words sink in. Disappointment crossed over her face, and then realization as to what I just said hit her. She didn't say anything for a while; I started shaking from my nerves. Was she upset, mad? I needed her to say something, anything.

She reached over and grabbed my hand, I sighed with relief. Maybe things would be ok. I could deal with her being upset with me because I was upset with myself.

"MacKenzie," She squeezed my hand. "I can see how upset this is making you and it should. You have such a bright future ahead of you. I'm not saying you can't have that now, but it's going to be a struggle." A few tears fell from her eyes. "I didn't want this to happen to you. I am disappointed, but it has happened and now we have to deal with it. We, sweetie, not just you. Your whole family is here for you."

The tears flow freely now, and my mom wraps me in her arms and shushes me.

"I take it you haven't told anyone yet?" She asks, running her hands through my hair.

"Not really, only Chloe, Hailey and Dominic." I said through the sobs.

"Dominic?" I knew she would be surprised. After all, she knows I don't talk to him anymore.

"Yeah, he's actually the one that bought me the test. Logan, the guy I work with, figured it out pretty quickly. He told Dominic that I was acting the same way his sister did over winter break. I think that's why Dominic took us home. Any other reason and I don't think he would have chanced it with Hunter and the boys."

Nodding at me, she said, "You need to tell Hunter sweetie. This isn't something you can hide from him. If he doesn't want any part of this, then it is what it is but I don't think that will happen. Your family is here for you, and before you even ask, yes, they are going to be upset over this, but no one will turn their backs on you or my little grandchild in there." She said as she rubbed my stomach.

Calming down a little, I wiped the final tears out of my eyes, and hugged my mom as tight as I could. "I love you mom."

"Aww, I love you too baby girl." She said hugging me back. "Have you called the doctors or anything yet?"

"No. I have no idea what I need to do, which is another reason I decided to talk to you first."

She took my hand in hers. "Well, first thing we need to do is call and make an appointment to see the ob-gyn. They will have you take a test in the office and will also do some blood work." She stood up, and pulled me up with her. "Let's get back to the house," she pulled her sleeve up to look at her watch. "and make an appointment. Someone should be in the office until noon."

Smiling my first real smile in a few days, I said, "Let's do it."

Mom stopped walking and gave me another apologetic smile. "You are going to have to tell your brothers and your father, but I'll be there with you."

"Well, Mason was pissed at me already, so I might as well add this to his list of reasons now; I just hope he doesn't murder Hunter. I know Coop and Jackson will be upset with me. And dad, ugh I don't even want to think about it."

"We will get through it as a family sweetie."

Chapter Twenty-Seven

Mom was able to pull some strings and got me an appointment for Monday morning to see the ob-gyn. They confirmed that I was indeed pregnant, and they did some blood work to confirm how far along I was and give me a better due date. They told me I would have the results back in a day or so. Until I got the results back, I was staying clear of everyone.

Wednesday night Mom and I decided to get some ice cream and sneak off to the bookstore to get me some books on my pregnancy. Chloe surprised us back at the house with a few things for me as well, and we went into the sitting room to talk about the wedding.

"Chloe, I'm going to look like a whale in your wedding. I really would just rather do something else special for you." I begged her.

Glaring at me, she said "Oh no, I need you there with me. You are my maid of honor and you cannot back out on me. It's not an option."

"Come on Chloe, you really want to take pictures with Shamu standing next to you? I'll probably be waddling like a duck, walking down the aisle." I started laughing picturing it.

Mom joined in on laughing at me too, and Chloe was still glaring at me. "Just because you went and got knocked up doesn't mean..."

I heard someone clear there throat behind me. *Oh, please be Hailey, please!*

Chloe and Mom turned their head, but I knew who it was, felt who it was. Once they saw who it was, they looked right at me and confirmed what I already knew.

"Hello Hunter, the boys aren't here. I think they went to the movies or something." Mom told him.

"Yeah I know. Can I uh, talk to CC alone?" Hunter asked them.

"You ok?" Chloe asked, looking at me apologetically.

I could feel my cheeks starting to burn red, and I didn't trust my voice to speak just yet, so I just nodded my head. I folded my hands in my lap, and curled my legs Indian style on the couch. Chloe and mom got up, but mom stopped, kissed the side of my head and whispered, "Tell him sweetie. I think he may just surprise you." I just nodded.

They walked out, and Hunter came to sit across from me. He didn't say anything. He just looked at me. I started biting my lip, nervous about this conversation. This could be the end of us, the end of us all being a family. No more holidays, Sunday dinners, birthdays, graduations, no nothing if this didn't go over well. I looked away from him and glanced down at the table that was between us where the baby books and magazines were sitting.

Hunter cleared his throat again, and looked down at the table where I was looking. If he didn't have an idea what we were talking about before, he sure did now. I watched his face closely as he was putting two and two together. "So um..." He scratched the scuff that was on his face. He looked at the books and back up at me. "Are they yours?"

My hands were sweating; I was shaking, "Yeah."

His eyes went wide, "You're pregnant?"

I nodded.

"Why didn't you tell me?" he asked, looking a little hurt.

"Hunter, just listen to me for a minute, okay? You are twenty-two, and ready to graduate from college in a few months. I don't want this to stop you from making something of yourself. Just because this baby is ours doesn't mean you have to be with us." I stood up from the couch and started pacing. "I want to be with you, Christ knows I do. Don't get me wrong. I can raise this baby on my own. You didn't ask for this and I don't want you to think I trapped you."

"Are you done?" He asked with a smirk on his face.

"Yes."

"CC, I love you more than you will ever know. I never stopped. I understand why you haven't told me, why you didn't come to me first. I've been an asshole." He stood up, and came over to me, grabbed both of my hands with his, and pulled them between us. "I'm sorry; I didn't know what to do. Our families are so close, and I felt like I was ruining it. I broke my promise to you that I wouldn't break your heart. I need to make that up to you."

I interrupted him. "You don't need to make anything up to me. Hunter, I ruined us. I told you I was protected. I thought I was. Remember when I was sick over Christmas break, and the doctor put me on antibiotics?"

"Yeah, when you had your ear infection."

"Well, it cancelled out my birth control. I'm so sorry." The tears were pooling in my eyes. "I wasn't thinking. I don't want you to hate me; I swear I wouldn't do something like this to trap you."

I started sobbing; now he's going to tell me he hates and he's done with me.

"I know you wouldn't do anything like that CC and I love you for that. I want this with you, with our baby. I want to be a family. I want to take care of you and our baby. I know you didn't trap me, and I want you to stop thinking that. You know everything happens for a reason, right? Please stop crying."

I took a shuddering breath. "Yes, but I feel like I'm holding you back now, trapping you. I don't want you to regret doing this with me."

He reached up, cupped my face in his strong hands and used his thumbs to brush the tears away. "CC I could never regret anything about you, ever." Hunter dropped his hands, moved them on my hips and pulled me towards him. "You know I'm going to marry you one day, right?"

"Are you going to marry me just because I'm pregnant?" He could not be serious. Just because I was having our baby didn't mean I was expecting him to propose.

He kissed me, "No. Because I'm never letting you go again. You are it for me. I don't give a shit if your brothers don't like it or not. I'm done trying to make everyone happy. I should have been done a long time ago. I'm going to make it up to you, I promise." He kissed me again, lingering a little longer this time.

I reached up, and entwined my fingers behind his neck. "I love you Hunter."

"Hmmm, I love you too CC. I guess I need to talk to them and do some explaining. First, I need to show you something. I should wait until it's finished, but this is for you now too." He led me out to his truck. It was just starting to rain, but the sun was shining bright, and a rainbow was out over the field across the street.

He stopped and kissed me before opening the door to his truck for me to get in. "You know I love kissing you in the rain. I just couldn't help myself." He winked at me, then opened the door and helped me in.

We drove for about twenty minutes, and pulled up to a cute little neighborhood. The houses were beautiful, mostly two stories with nicely manicured lawns. Hunter turned into the driveway of one that was towards the end of the street.

"Who do you know who lives here?" I looked at him suspiciously.

The house was two stories with tan siding, white trim and white shutters. It had a two-car garage and with a little work, nice landscaping. The bushes needed to be trimmed and there were a few bare spots in the lawn.

"Come on, I'll tell you when we go inside." He came around the truck, and opened the door for me.

He laced our fingers together, and we walked up the walkway to the house. He reached in his pocket, pulled out his keys and unlocked the door. I gave him a funny look.

He pulled on my hand and ushered me inside. Once he closed the door, he put his hands around my waist and rested them over my stomach. I tensed, but then soon relaxed when he started rubbing his hands over it.

"Welcome home CC." He said softly to me.

"What? This is yours?"

Shaking his head at me, he says, "No, this is ours."

Was I missing something? How could this be his?

"I don't understand. How can you buy a house like this, and when did you have the time to even look for a house?"

Chuckling at me, clearly amused by my confusion he says, "Well, when I turned twenty-one, my trust fund kicked in. I knew I was coming back to Jersey to live, so Mom has been on the lookout for me. She found this around Christmas; I just signed the papers on Friday when I got back. It needs a lot of work but it's not too bad. Come on, I'll show you."

In front of us was a staircase that led to the second floor. Off to the right, there was a living room with a fireplace and a bay window. When we walked past the stairs, there was the dining room with floor to ceiling windows and off the dining room was the kitchen. The kitchen was beautiful. It had dark granite counter tops, black appliances, plenty of counter space and tons of cabinets. Next to the kitchen was a full bathroom with a stand up shower. It needed some fixing up and a good cleaning but was not too bad. There was a huge family room with sliding glass doors leading to a nice sized back yard with an in-ground swimming pool.

"That door leads to the basement, but it's a mess down there. I don't want you getting hurt on the steps since there are a few broken ones." Hunter pointed at a door in the family room. "Come on, I'll show you the upstairs."

He led me up the stairs to the first bedroom on the right. Bright yellow paint and stained carpet greeted me. "Don't worry; this is getting new paint and hardwood floors. Actually, all the other rooms are too. The only room that is already finished is our room." He lifted my hand and kissed it.

He took me into the second room and the mint green paint and dark green carpet was hideous. Yes, this has to go too.

The bathroom was at the end of the hallway. It was very out dated but it was huge. With a few upgrades, it would be great.

"Ok, now I'm going to close your eyes. This is our room." He stood behind me, and covered my eyes with his hands.

"Use your left hand and reach straight ahead for the door knob." I complied and opened the door.

Hunter walked us into the room and lowered his hands. The room was gorgeous; I fell in love with it. It was enormous compared to the other two. Chestnut hardwood covered the floors, and there was a king-size canopy bed positioned between two wide windows. There was a dresser and a bureau, both black. Behind the only door in the room was a walk in closet with all the shelves and racks you could ever use and in the center, there was a tall square table with drawers.

We walked out of the closet, and I turned to Hunter, who was observing me in complete awe of this room, this whole house. "So what do you think? Could you live here with me?"

I wrapped my arms around him and he tucked me under his chin and of course, I started crying when I said, "Hunter, it's perfect. Are you positive this is what you want, and it's not just because of the baby?"

He reached down and lifted my chin so I was looking at him. "Yes, I'm positive. I was going to ask you to move in with me once we worked everything out, so yes, this is what I really want."

He wiped my tears again and I laughed. "It's just these stupid hormones."

He laughed with me, "Guess I better get used to that, huh?"

"Yeah, that seems to be all I do, well that plus throwing up every day, all day."

Hunter finally figured out that I was not getting sick because of the stress and all the fighting we were doing. He said, "Hm, I guess that explains why you kept getting sick?"

"Yeah, the doctor said it should only last my first trimester, but sometimes longer. The mornings are the worst it seems, and anything greasy sets me off." I got the chills just thinking about it.

"I'll have to remember that." He brushed his hands down my arms, cause me to get more goosebumps.

He pulled me to the bed, grabbed the bottom of my shirt and lifted it above my head, and tossed it behind him. Then he unclasped my bra and pushed me back so I was sitting on the bed. He kneeled in front on me, placed a single kiss on my stomach, then looked up at me and placed a few more kisses. He worked his way up to one of my nipples and sucked it into his mouth. I cried out in ecstasy at the sensation because it was so sensitive.

I sat up and he leaned up with me. I reached down to the bottom of his shirt, pulled it off him and threw it behind us. Then I reached for the button and zipper on his jeans, but he stopped me before I could start to pull them down.

Frowning he asked, "Can you do this?"

Laughing at him, I said, "I'm pregnant not broken Hunter." I wrapped my arms around his neck and pulled him towards me.

Hunter and I spent the next hour memorizing each other bodies, whispering how much we loved each other and through our lovemaking, apologizing for all the hurt that we had caused each other. After we were completely spent, I wrapped myself on his right side and placed my hand over his heart and he placed his hand over mine and whispered, "You are my heart, always and forever."

Chapter Twenty-Eight

I woke the next morning, still wrapped contently around Hunter, my hand still pressed to his heart and his hand still on mine. I didn't want to move but I knew I would be getting sick any minute now. I tried not to think about it. I tried to focus on Hunter lying here with me, our lovemaking from last night.

"Mm..." Hunter lifted his hand, lightly ran his fingers up my arm and his right arm squeezed me to him a little tighter. "I love waking up with you wrapped in my arms."

I lifted my head up to look at him but regretted it as soon as I did. My stomach rolled. I closed my eyes and took a deep breath, begging for my stomach to calm down. It didn't work and I was sprinting to the bathroom.

After my stomach was empty, I noticed Hunter sitting on the edge of the tub with a glass of water in his hand. "Does this happen every day?"

Nodding my head, I say, "Yeah, sometimes a few times a day. The doctor said to try and eat something before I even got out of bed but the second I move even to just turn over I lose it." I realized I was kneeling on the bathroom floor and I was naked. I tried to stand up to go back to the room to grab my clothes but Hunter put his hand on my shoulder and stopped me from moving.

"Take a shower with me?" He asked when my eyes made contact with his.

I reached up and grabbed the hand that was on my shoulder and he helped me up. "Where are the towels?" Hunter reached around me and opened a cabinet in the wall. I didn't realize it was there last night. He pulled two out, and then turned to turn the water on. After adjusting it a few times, he reached for my hand and helped me in the shower with him.

Hunter pressed his lips to my neck and pushed back on me until the shower tiles pressed up against me. He hands slowly lowered down my back, passed my ass and stopped on the backs of my thighs and he picked me up. I wrapped my legs around him and he pressed himself into me.

Groaning into my neck and thrusting slow and hard, he again started apologizing for choosing my brothers over me. "I'll never forgive myself for pushing you away CC, I was so fucking stupid."

Adjusting my hips slightly so that he could go deeper, I told him, "Everything is fine now; we worked it out."

"I know but you'll never know what that did to me. I didn't think I would ever get this with you," He said panting in my ear.

Moaning his name aloud as my body started tightening, my head hit the tiles with a thud and everything started going out of focus with my release. Hunter thrust a few more time and then spilled his release into me.

After we both caught our breath, Hunter slowly lowered me to my feet but still held me against the wall. I was thankful for that considering my legs felt like Jell-O. He helped me wash my hair and body, spending extra time on my belly. I loved watching him in complete awe of my tiny baby pouch, of how my body was changing daily.

After we got out of the shower, he wrapped me in one of his over-sized navy blue fluffy towels and we went back to his room. I went to go grab my clothes but Hunter handed me a pair of my yoga pants and one of his t-shirts to wear. "You left them at my place and I was going to return them to you but hadn't had the chance yet." He must have noticed the quizzical look on my face.

"Well I'm glad you didn't. But I really need a toothbrush more than I do my pants now." I told him, still feeling disgusting since throwing up.

"Yeah, sorry, there is an extra in the drawer in the bathroom."

I quickly made my way to the bathroom to grab the toothbrush and brush my teeth. Hunter came in behind me, wrapped his arms around my waist and rested his hands on my stomach. "I can't believe there's a little piece of me in here." He kissed the side of my neck.

I spit the toothpaste out and rinsed my mouth. "I know, I was really scared at first but it's kind of growing on me now." I twisted in his arms and reached up on my tip toes to kiss him. He lifted me and sat me on the bathroom sink and I pulled him between my legs. I giggled when I felt how hard he was again.

He pulled back from the kiss, smirking at me as he said, "I can't help it." He kissed me again harder this time, but I pushed him back before things could get crazy.

Sighing, he said, "I know, I know." He kissed me a few times before he helped me down off the sink. "We should probably head back to your parents' house and tell everyone what's going on."

I knew he was right, but I didn't want to ruin what we had going on. "I guess you are right. Mason and Cooper will probably just wind up here anyway."

"Just trust me ok? I know I don't deserve it, but I want to tell everyone. There is going to be a bunch of bullshit that goes down, but it is you and me CC. I will not let anyone come between us."

I hoped he was right this time. "Ok let's get going."

On the drive back to my parents' house, I told Hunter that I was going to finish out the semester at ODU. I would transfer my credits back to a college in New Jersey close to the house. That way, I could still figure out how to get my teaching degree and be close to him where we would have help with the baby. Mom and Dad were in the kitchen eating lunch when we arrived. Mom smiled at us and Dad frowned.

"Hey Mom," I went over and kissed her cheek then went over to my dad and kissed his as well. "Hey Dad."

"Mr. and Mrs. Cahill, we, um, need to talk to you guys." Hunter, who never gets nervous, was standing before me, sweating.

"Well, I'm glad you two are back to speaking again." My dad spoke up and said. "I didn't like seeing you guys fighting. It was worse than you fighting with Mason."

"Um, dad, things might not be so well between us and Mason once he finds out what is going on." I reached over and grabbed Hunter's hand; I needed the connection with him.

Hunter squeezed my hand and cleared his throat, "CC and I are going to move in together when I graduate college in a few months."

Looking puzzled he asked, "Kenzie still has 3 years left of school." He looked at me for answers, "You want to transfer back home just to be closer to Hunter? That's not like you."

I looked from my Dad to Hunter then to mom, who gave me a small smile and nodded her head, and back to dad, "I'm pregnant Dad."

He had the same reaction as my mom disappointment, hurt. "I don't know what to say really.

"I'm sorry Dad, I know you're disappointed in me, and I'm more disappointed in myself." I started crying and he turned his head away from me, got up from his chair and went to stand by my mom who was at the sink. Hunter wrapped me in his arms and pulled me close to him.

Dad was rubbing his forehead with his thumb and index finger, something he always did when he was upset with one of his kids. "You know about this?" Dad asked mom. She nodded. "What are you going to do about school? You need to finish MacKenzie; you need a college education now a days."

"She'll finish, I'll make sure of it. We will do whatever we have to do to make sure she gets her degree. I have a job lined up when I graduate and I still have some money saved up from my inheritance. She will be taken care of Mr. Cahill, you have my word." Hunter told him. I was proud of him for standing up to dad and it made me fall a little more in love with him that he was so eager to take care of me. If you would have asked me this when I first got home on Thursday night I would have laughed.

Dad looked over at my mom and she grabbed my dad's hand. He looked at her. They were having their own private conversation. My parents were the perfect example of what I wanted to have. Mom and dad didn't always have to talk to each other. They had a connection so strong that words weren't needed to know what the other thought. There love was unbreakable, having four children was trying at times, always putting us first, making sure we never wanted for anything. Always involved in what we were doing, always being our biggest fans but at the end of the day they always made time for themselves even if it was only ten minutes. That is what I wanted with my future husband, Hunter.

"This isn't going to be easy Mackenzie; you are basically giving up your life, you understand that right? You are sure this is something you want? You are ready for such a huge responsibility?"

I looked up at Hunter and gave him a half smile then returned to my dad, "Yes this is what I want. I want to raise," I squeezed Hunter harder, "our child together Dad. I know things are going to be tough and I'll have to work extra hard but I have to do this."

"We'll do it together, always and forever, remember?" Hunter said softly mainly for me to hear.

"Hunter, you are in this for good now, right? You are going to take care of my little girl, protect her and my grandchild." Dad said sternly.

"Yes Sir. No one comes between us ever again."

"You know I already think of you as a son, but I'm glad it's you that this happened with and not some other asshole. I'm not happy with it at all but as long as you give me your word I'll accept it."

Hunter cleared his throat and said, "You have it sir, she's it for it." He looked at me and winked.

"I take it your brothers don't know yet?" Dad asked me, and then asked Hunter. "And your Mom and sister don't know?

"No not yet." We said at the same time. "I'm actually going to run over there now since we wanted to talk to you guys first."

"I want to go with you. Um mom do you think you can invite everyone over for dinner so we can tell everyone together?"

"Yeah, I'll call your brothers and have them over for dinner tonight." Mom came over, hugged Hunter and kissed his cheek. "Thank you for stepping up and taking care of her. I knew you would turn out to be a great man."

"Thanks, that means a lot."

Hunter and I left shortly after that and went to talk to his mom, his sister was out somewhere with Cooper so she would find out later tonight when we told my brothers. His mom took it pretty well. She was disappointed, but that was to be expected, but was proud of her son for standing up and taking responsibility. She rode with us back to my parents for dinner.

Cooper, Jaylinn, Chloe, Jackson and Alex were at the house already when we got back but Mason was out picking up Hailey. Mom had dad grill so that the smell wouldn't turn my stomach, she was already helping me already so much with my pregnancy.

Mason finally showed up with Hailey looking a little flushed when she noticed I was staring at her she raised her eyebrows at me and shrugged her shoulders. I was being stupid I knew what she was up too. She already knew what was going on since I had been talking and texting her about it all along but she didn't know I would be telling everyone tonight. She didn't even know I talked to Hunter since I hadn't had time to call her a head of time.

As we served dinner, we all gathered around the dining table. I was sweating profusely and shaking. I decided to wait until everyone was mostly done with dinner before making our announcement. Everyone was talking about what was going on with their lives; Cooper and Mason were in the full swing of baseball. Jackson and Chloe were working on last minute details of their wedding that would happen in just a few months. Alex captured the attention of Mrs. McCormick, mom and dad.

I took my last bite of food set down my fork, Hunter grabbed my left hand Chloe, who I had told what I was doing while setting the table, grabbed my right. I looked at Hunter and cleared my throat, everyone quieted down. "So, I, um..." Hunter squeezed my hand giving me the courage to finish my sentence. I squeezed my eyes shut, "I'm pregnant." I whispered.

Everything stopped; Mason was in mid bite, frozen in place. Cooper set his fork down. Jackson set his cup down on the table. Hailey and Jaylinn stared at me with wide eyes. Dad sighed. Chloe squeezed my hand that she was still holding. Mrs. McCormick and my mom shared a look and Alex was the only one making noise with his little rattle.

"You're kidding right?" Mason asked.

I shook my head.

Jackson looked from me to Chloe and then to where our hands were together. "You know? And you didn't tell me?" He glared at her. "That's why she was at the house so early Saturday morning." He said putting the pieces together.

I nodded confirming what he already figured out, "Yes that is why; I was scared and didn't know who else to talk to. If I wasn't pregnant and it was just a misread I didn't want to have to tell anyone."

I looked at Cooper; he was looking at me but not meeting my eyes. He didn't say anything, I am not sure if this is a good thing or a bad thing.

Mason and Cooper both looked at each other, got up from the table and a few minutes later I heard their car start out front. I pulled my hands away from Hunter and Chloe and pinched the bridge of my nose and rested my elbow on the table, Hunter ran his hand up and down my back, trying to comfort me. I was hoping they would be supportive and not freak out but that was just wishful thinking.

Jackson didn't say anything more about the pregnancy; I didn't really expect him too. Chloe said she would catch up with me later in the week and then the three of them left. Jaylinn and Hailey were both happy for us. Mom and I were in the kitchen cleaning up dinner when Hunter came walking in with Mason and Cooper.

They both had their hands in their pockets, no one was shooting daggers at each other, all good signs except for Hunter's busted up lip. Hunter came over, took the dishrag from my hand and motioned with his head to go to them. I did and they led the way to the sitting room since everyone was in the living room watching TV.

"Before you guys say...." I started to say but Cooper cut me off. "We talked to Hunter, we're all good."

"I'm not good with it but I'll deal. He gave us his word and that's all I need to deal with it." Mason said.

"What happened with Hunter's lip then?"

"Nothing." Cooper said, as always. This was his answer when they got into a fight over me.

"Didn't look like nothing."

"Kenz, drop it." Mason said stretching out his hand; at least I knew who hit him.

I didn't like that they hit him but it was over with now. Now that everyone knew, the weight I had felt on my shoulders was gone. I had everyone behind me and I actually for once wanted protection for anything that would be thrown my way.

Hunter and I went to our house later that night and I went straight to bed, I was completely exhausted from the stress over the last few days. Hunter helped me strip out of all my clothes, I wasn't use to sleeping like this but he insisted and who was I to fight him.

"So tell me more about these doctors' appointment and stuff. I have no clue about any of this shit." He fluffed up his pillow and laid back. I curled up in the nook of his arm and rested my hand on over his heart, something I loved to do.

"Well since I am still pretty early on in my pregnancy I go to the doctors every four weeks, around eighteen weeks or so we can find out what we are having." I lifted my head to look at him. "Do you want to know what we are having?"

"Do you? I don't really care as long has he is happy."

I smiled at his slip, "You just said he. You want a son?"

Smirking at me he said, "Yeah I would like a son."

"Well I'll let you decide if you want to find out or not, we have a little while before we have to think about that. I only have one small problem though; I really want to keep my doctors up here so we will have to make two trips back here over the next two months so I can get my checkups."

"That's cool; I could check in on the house renovations and shit while we are here too. I meant to ask you earlier how you figured out that you were pregnant."

Shit! I could lie to him and tell him my mom figured it by seeing me getting sick but I didn't want to start our relationship off with a lie. "I need you to promise me you will not get pissed off." He nodded. "It was actually Logan."

He glared at me and then I explained to him everything that had happened up until the day he found out. He hated that Logan figured it out and that Dominic was involved at all.

My eyes were growing heavy listening to Hunter's heart beating, "I love you."

"I love you too CC." Hunter whispered and that was the last thing I remembered that night.

Chapter Twenty-Nine

Hunter, Hailey, and I returned to school that weekend, on the way back I told Hailey what my plans were for next year. I explained about going to school in Jersey so that I was closer to home and the baby and I could be with Hunter. She agreed with me that, that would be for the best. She said she would be transferring too since there was nothing left there for her. I was staying in Jersey and Mason would be moving back to Jersey as well.

Hailey and I made an appointment to speak with our councilors that week to explain to them the situation and started the process of transferring our credits to our local community college.

Hunter had refused to let me stay at the dorms after the first night that we were back. He said he didn't like the fact that he couldn't take care of me the way he wanted. He spoke with Bentley, and they both agreed to have Hailey and I move in with them. I felt bad for not giving Bentley a choice but he assured me that he was perfectly ok with us and he even joked around with Hailey and me about cooking to earn our keep. I stuck my nose in the air at the mention of food while Hailey and Hunter laughed at me. They had to explain that cooking food made me sick but Hailey said she had it covered. I was really going to miss seeing Bentley when we moved back home; he turned out to be a great guy even when he threw some crazy parties.

Hunter and I had our first little argument since getting back together about me keeping my part time job at the library.

He had his hands on his hips, scowling at me he said, "I don't want you working, you don't have any reason to."

"Yes I do, I'm not just going to quit when I am perfectly capable of working."

"I don't like it Kenzie. You need your rest."

"Hunter, I'm fine. If I feel it becoming too much I'll give them my two weeks' notice."

I eventually won since he had no valid point that I couldn't. My first day back, I pulled Logan aside and thanked him for talking to Dominic about him figuring out that I was expecting. Hailey stopped by one evening to check up on me, Hunter's part of the agreement that I could work, and she and Logan talked about what happened earlier in the year. It came down to a huge misunderstanding about Brittany. Dominic was also stopping by a few times as well to check in and see how I was going, Hunter didn't like that but he was dealing with it. Dominic told me how he and Brittany were fighting once again because she refused to believe that the baby wasn't his.

"I don't mind telling her myself that this baby is Hunter's, Dominic. Just say the word." I told him one night as he was walking out to Hunter's truck.

"No I don't want you anywhere near that crazy bitch. I told her if she kept this up that we were done." Dominic shifted his weight from one foot to the other while standing next to the passenger side of the truck.

"Ok well the offer still stands." I reached up to open the door and Dominic helped me in.

"No, I'll take care of it." Dominic and Hunter mumbled hellos and then Hunter took me home.

"So what was all that about?" Hunter asked as he reached over to rest his hand on my thigh.

"Brittany is giving him problems. She is convinced that this is Dominic's baby. I offered to set her straight but he refused my offer."

"Good, stay away from that nasty whore CC."

I didn't even attempt to argue back, I just let it go.

I was still doing well in my classes despite missing a few because of headaches and morning sickness. April rolled around, and Hunter and I drove back home for a doctor's appointment and to meet with a contractor my dad found to help with the house. We had our first ultrasound scheduled for this appointment. It was the ugliest thing and most beautiful thing I had ever seen. Hunter said it looked like a gummy bear with his heart on the outside; we were also able to hear his or her heartbeat for the first time that day too. Mrs. McCormick, Mom and Dad met us at the house along with the contractor after our appointment was over. We showed off all the pictures the nurse gave us to our parents who were excited about becoming grandparents again. The contractor arrived while we were showing the pictures off so my Dad and Hunter told them what we were looking for and told them we would get the contract back to them as soon as we reviewed there proposal. Later that night we made our journey back to school.

Hailey, Hunter and I were in full swing of finals and were busy studying every night. Chloe had been calling me a lot lately since their wedding was fast approaching. I promised that we would go dress shopping as soon as I moved back in a little over a week. I didn't want to go too soon, because my baby bump was getting bigger and bigger. I wanted to make sure the dress still fit by the time the wedding came.

We all took our finals in the middle of May, and Hunter graduated the following week. We had a full house the week of graduation. Mrs. McCormick and Jaylinn stayed with us so that they could attend Hunter's graduation and help us pack up all of our belongings. Mom and Dad were going to see Cooper and Mason graduate in Boston, so we said we would plan a party for them once everyone was back home.

When we arrived home, it looked like a completely different place. With the renovations finished, it finally felt like home. Hunter told me the baby's room was off limits since he wanted to work on it himself.

We had another ultrasound scheduled so we could find out the sex of the baby. Sitting in the waiting room, Hunter and I discussed whether we wanted to find out or not, but we still did not have an answer when the nurse called us back.

"Hunter, we are going to have you wait right out here while we get some measurements of the baby. Then, we will have you come in, and show you everything as well." The nurse explained all this while leading us back to the Ultrasound room.

"Sure, that's no problem." Hunter kissed my forehead before I disappeared behind the curtains.

After the nurse finished all of her measurements, she stepped out of the room and asked Hunter to join us.

"So, I will let you guys listen to the heartbeat for a few minutes while l work on getting you two some pictures."

Hunter stood next to my head, reached for my hand and gave it a little squeeze. The baby's heartbeat was nice and strong. It was like music to our ears. I wished we could bottle the sound up and take it home with us.

"So would you like to know the sex of the baby?" The nurse asked us.

Hunter looked down at me and I smiled. I was letting him make this call. He knew I really didn't want to know.

"No we're going to let it be a surprise."

"Very well then, Ms. Cahill, you are all done here."

I cleaned up and we went to Baby's R Us to look around at all the different stuff that we were going to need. We knew we needed to stick with natural colors that would work for either a girl or a boy.

Two weeks later, we threw the boys a graduation party at the shore house and had the wedding rehearsal for Jackson and Chloe, all on the same weekend. We tried to fit everything in, and we took up everyone's weekend.

After the rehearsal was over, I was feeding Alex his bottle while Chloe took a nap. Jackson walked in and did a double take when he saw me sitting on his couch.

"Getting your practice in?" He asked, after he kicked off his running shoes.

"I guess you can call it that." I looked down at Alex and gave him little kisses on his little chunky cheeks. "Or you can call it spending time with my awesome little nephew."

"Did you burp him yet?" Jackson asked, taking a seat next to me.

"Not yet, he just started drinking it." I took the bottle out of Alex's mouth and checked the ounces. It still had one ounce left, so I gave it back to him.

"I know what you're thinking Kenzie. Trust me; it's harder than it looks. You are up all hours of the night, leaving the house takes forever and you have to pack half the house just to go around the damn block." He reached over, grabbed Alex's little hand and Alex grabbed hold of his pinky. "Don't get me wrong. I wouldn't trade it for the world, but it is hard work."

I blinked away the tears, "I know." I sniffled.

"Everything will work out." He looked down at Alex's bottle and took it from me. "Now give me my son. Hunter is looking for you out back."

"Thanks Jackson." I kissed Alex's head since Jackson was already burping him, then I kissed Jackson on his cheek and left to go find Hunter.

I went out the sliding glass doors expecting Hunter to be outside on the deck but he was nowhere to be found. I walked out towards the ocean, thinking that maybe he was down there. When I made it past the sand dunes, there he was, standing there in khaki shorts with a black button down shirt and his black hat. I looked down at his feet and saw he was standing in the middle of a heart made out of candles and seashells.

As I approached, I scanned up and down the beach and we were the only ones out here. *How did he do that in the peak of the season?* He reached for my hand and pulled me to him; he smiled that panty-dropping smile and kissed me.

"What's going on?" I asked.

He looked over my shoulder, and lifted his chin in the direction that I had just come from. I turned around and saw all of our friends and family standing there, and then it hit me. He was proposing. My free hand came up to cover my mouth. As I turned back to Hunter, he dropped to one knee.

I was a complete blubbering mess. Hunter pulled out the hand that was still behind his back, and held out a Tiffany's little blue box that held a princess cut diamond ring, with little diamonds wrapped around the band. He looked up at me with glassy eyes. "CC, you're my world, you're my light in the darkness, my safe haven. I love you more than anything. I want to spend the rest of my life with you. Will you marry me?"

I was sobbing so hard, all I could do was nod. He took the gorgeous ring out of the box and placed it on my finger. He put both of his hands on my stomach and said, "You hear that little man," He looked at me, winked and then continued, "Your mama is gonna marry me." He leaned forward and placed a kiss on my stomach. At that exact same moment, the baby kicked for the first time, right where Hunter's lips were.

His eyes shot up to me all wide and asked, "Was that the baby kicking?"

I just laughed through the tears and winked at him. "Yeah, I guess our little peanut likes that we're gonna get married."

Hunter stood up and wrapped his arms around me and all our family came rushing towards us congratulating us. Everyone was so happy for us including Mason, which made this day a little extra special. We had a lot to celebrate that weekend.

The following week was extremely busy. I had my final fitting for my maid of honor dress, we were throwing a bachelorette at Chloe's house Friday night and the wedding was Saturday afternoon.

Chloe and Jackson's beach wedding was stunning. All the girls wore coral color dresses; Jackson and the guys wore khakis pants with white shirts and coral ties. Chloe looked breathtaking in her dress; she decided to go with a destination dress, with an empire waist, all white with clear and pink crystals spread over the train. Her hair was curled and pulled up off her neck. Her parents didn't show up for the wedding, so my dad walked her down the aisle. Hailey was holding Alex in his little white tuxedo. He looked so handsome.

Chloe and Jackson were going on a cruise for their honeymoon, and I was watching Alex while they were gone. Jackson volunteered me, saying it was good practice; I didn't have a problem with it since Hunter was going to be starting his new job that week. He was working with the local police department in the investigation unit. He was excited that he was able to land this job.

Mom, Mrs. McCormick, Hailey, and Chloe threw me a surprise baby shower two weeks after Chloe got back from her honeymoon. Hunter and I got everything we needed for the baby, plus more. Hunter still refused to let me see the baby's room until it was not finished. I began having some swelling issues around my thirty-third week, was put on bed rest and had to go to the doctors twice a week for monitoring.

Chapter Thirty

Today I was thirty-seven weeks. I had a doctor's appointment and another ultrasound set up. This would be the last one before we would finally get to meet our little chunky monkey. Hunter had to work today, so he was going to meet me at the doctor's office on his lunch break.

I got out of bed and started getting ready for the appointment when my cell phone started ringing.

"Hello?"

"Hey Kenzie, how's my little man doing?" Hailey was always asking how little man was doing, never how I am feeling and she refused to entertain the idea that I might be having a girl.

"You know, I think you love the baby more than you love me." I laughed, "The baby's doing well, me not so much. My feet are really swollen and I'm waddling more and more like a duck."

"Put the phone up to your belly. I want to talk to him."

Laughing, I did as she asked. After a good minute, I put the phone back up to my ear and told her, "I have a doctor's appointment around lunch time today so I will have more pictures to show you. Do you want me to stop over when I'm done?"

"Yeah, that would be good. Mason is supposed to come over and take me to dinner tonight."

"Oh, really?" Hailey and Mason's relationship was rocky right now. Something was going on, but they both refused to talk about it. Any time I mentioned anything about it, they told me it was really nothing for me to worry myself. I tried talking to Hunter about it, but he just told me everything would be ok between them. He explained they weren't really fighting themselves. They were fighting about something else that was going on.

"Nothing special just dinner."

"Ok. I really wish you would talk to me, and tell me what is going on Hails. I hate seeing you guys like this."

Hailey let out a big sigh. "You don't need the added stress; remember what the doctor said? You need to stay nice and relaxed. Everyone is taking care of everything. Stop worrying that pretty little head of yours."

I was getting a little irritated because everyone was treating me as if I was made of glass. "It's stressing me out that you will not talk to me about it Hails. You talk to me about everything; why not this?"

She huffed, "Because I just can't. Now stop worrying and go get ready."

"Fine, but this isn't over. I'll call you when I'm on my way."

"OK, love you and little man."

I laughed and said, "It's Princess and I love you too."

I was standing in my closet trying to find something to wear when I heard a crack of thunder that made me jump. I was rubbing my belly as the baby moved around. "Oh boy, chunky monkey, it's raining. We better hurry up and get out of here so we aren't late."

After I changed, I walked to the front door, slipped on my flip-flops and grabbed the umbrella. It was pouring outside; even with the umbrella, I was still getting wet. I noticed there was a car parked at the end of the driveway, which was unusual for our neighborhood. I started the car and backed out. I thought it looked like Brittany in the car, but it couldn't have been. She and Dominic broke up right after school was over. I brushed it off, and left our development, heading towards the highway.

Merging onto the highway, the rain was coming down harder. It was making it very hard to see, even with the wipers on full speed. I looked in my rearview mirror and noticed the car that had parked at the end of my driveway was now following behind me. I only needed to go about two exits up on Route 295. I figured I would be ok as long as I took it nice and slow and did not panic.

About a half mile before my exit, I saw the car directly in front of me start to hydroplane. The driver must have panicked, because the car started swerving into the lane next to it. Just as the driver jerked the steering wheel, he collided with another car. I tried to slam on my breaks to avoid the accident, but the person that was following me slammed into me. I slid off the highway, down an embankment.

Screaming, I braced myself for the collision I knew was coming. It didn't happen right away. I flipped upside down three times before I finally felt the car stop. Everything was fuzzy, I couldn't see straight and my body felt numb.

I don't know how long I had laid there before I heard someone approaching. I tried to yell for help but nothing came out. I saw a shadow of a person look in through the side of the passenger side door.

Why are they not helping me? I thought.

I heard a girl speak, "If I can't have him, neither can you bitch."

I got a razor sharp stab of pain in my stomach. It was so strong; I was seeing stars, and then nothing after that.

When I woke up, my whole body hurt. It was almost unbearable but something was pulling me from my sleep. I tried to open my eyes but they were just too heavy. I tried to concentrate and figure out what was going on, where I was. I felt like there was something gagging me; there was pain in my stomach, chest and right leg, lots of pain. I remember driving; it was really raining hard. There was a bad crash, my car flipping. Someone was there looking into my car and then there was darkness.

I felt something warm run down my face. I tried to reach up and wipe it away but my arms were too heavy. I heard humming and knew Hunter was here with me, wherever I am.

"Sweetheart, why don't you go home for a few hours? You could shower, grab some food and try to get some sleep? I will stay here with MacKenzie and the baby. They both need you to be strong for them." I knew that voice; it was my mom's, but what was she talking about a baby for?

A violent stab of a pain hit my head. I was trying desperately not to give back into the darkness.

The humming stopped and Hunter's voice spoke, "I'm not leaving them, I can't."

I heard little whimpers of a cry, and then he went back to humming.

I felt so confused. I tried opening my eyes again but they were still too heavy. I felt someone grab my hand. I tried to squeeze it but I didn't have the strength.

"Oh baby girl." mom said, rubbing circles on the back on my hand with her thumb. "You have to wake up your boys need you."

My boys, does she mean my brothers? Another flashback came back to me. I was on my way to meet Hunter somewhere. Why was I meeting him?

The pain was increasing and the pull into the darkness was becoming too much to fight.

The noise in the room started phasing out except for a beeping noise.

"Baby girl, if you can hear me squeeze my hand." Mom said.

Beep.

I tried to squeeze but I just couldn't.

Beep.

I felt a warm fingers touch my face and gently rub from my temple to my jaw and back again. "CC, please open your bright blue eyes for me baby."

Beep.

"I need you; I can't do this on my own." I heard him sniffle. "He looks just like you. Same little nose, head full of dark curly hair." He sniffled again. "I love you baby."

Then there was a long beep and the blackness finally took over.

Look for part two of their story

in the fall of 2013

Easy

TO

LOVE YOU

Book Two in the Love Series

Acknowledgements

To my husband ~ Thank you for always being by my side. I know I drove you crazy but I could not have done it without you. I love you!

Monkey ~ Thank you for always making me laugh and making me the proudest mommy EVER! I love you to the moon and back.

Dad, Mom and my sisters ~ Thank you for helping me with everything and believing in me. Love you!

MaKayla (Cody), Holly M., Wendy R. and Chrissy S. (BFF from another state) ~ You are the best beta readers EVER. Thank you so much for all your help and listening to me rants and rave!

Heidi (my personal cheerleader) ~ Thank you for giving me all your feedback, you have no idea how much it really did help me. Also thank you SO much for allowing me to use your photos (Thank you Luke and Jada). Can't wait to get started on the next one!

Tammy Crawford my #1 fan (Even though you're my Aunt and don't have a choice) ~ I love you and thank you so much for believing in me, pushing me and encouraging me.

Shey ~ Thanks for taking a chance on me with doing beta reading for you. You opened my eyes to the author world. I would have never done this with you!

Katie Mac ~ Thank you for being such a damn good editor. My book would be a wreck without you. I cannot thank you enough for everything you did for me!

Robin ~ Thank you for designing my awesome cover and for helping me with my last minute changes.

My author friends ~ Your support makes me feel like I can make anything happen. Thanks for taking the time to always help!

Kim Person and all the other bloggers who help spread the word and support indie authors, THANK YOU!

36167543R00160

Made in the USA
Lexington, KY
09 October 2014